Praise for

The Last Days of Ptolemy Grey

"A tour de force. Narrated in an intimate whisper, the story draws us deep into the mind of an old man wandering through the remnants of his memories, searching for the key to an old mystery."

—*The New York Times Book Review*

"With his thirtieth novel, *The Last Days of Ptolemy Grey*, Walter Mosley not only returns to top form but also moves again past the boundaries of the hard-boiled suspense genre in which his best work has always been rooted . . . a beautifully wrought story . . . an unexpectedly profound novel of the subtle links between memory and identity."

—*Los Angeles Times*

"*The Last Days of Ptolemy Grey* is a rich and profound exploration of generosity, greed, love, loss; the indignities of old age; the value of memory; and the true meaning of family."

—The Associated Press

"The plot, the pure sweetness and believability of this story, comes from the romance that springs up between the seventeen-year-old girl and the ninety-one-year-old man, as together they create a world where nothing can be stolen, only given, with the limitless generosity of love."

—*The Washington Post*

"[An] eloquent and elegant study of a decent man grown old in a brutal world."

—*The Newark Star-Ledger*

"Unforgettable."

— *Boston Herald*

"*The Last Days of Ptolemy Grey* is a beautiful meditation on love, frailty, and old age. Filled with Walter Mosley's signature humor and narrative mastery, it is as much a page-turner as it is a heart-tugger. It is a novel that stays with you long after you read the last word and immediately urges you to read it again."

—Edwidge Danticat

"[A] remarkable, beautifully written novel . . . rich and profound."

—*The Indiana Gazette*

"*The Last Days of Ptolemy Grey* . . . finds Mosley at the height of his imaginative faculties, focusing his restless intelligence on the quandaries of growing old, and creating an unflinching portrait of a man who, even as his mind betrays him, keeps a firm grip on his dignity."

—*AARP Magazine*

Also by Walter Mosley

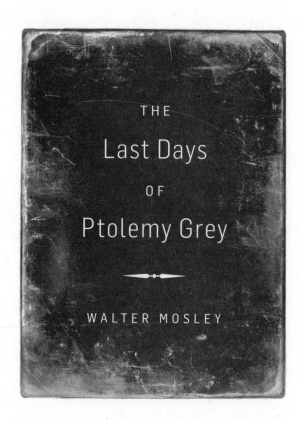

THE

Last Days

OF

Ptolemy Grey

WALTER MOSLEY

RIVERHEAD BOOKS

New York

RIVERHEAD BOOKS
Published by the Penguin Group
Penguin Group (USA) Inc.
375 Hudson Street, New York, New York 10014, USA
Penguin Group (Canada), 90 Eglinton Avenue East, Suite 700, Toronto, Ontario M4P 2Y3, Canada
(a division of Pearson Penguin Canada Inc.)
Penguin Books Ltd., 80 Strand, London WC2R 0RL, England
Penguin Group Ireland, 25 St. Stephen's Green, Dublin 2, Ireland (a division of Penguin Books Ltd.)
Penguin Group (Australia), 250 Camberwell Road, Camberwell, Victoria 3124, Australia
(a division of Pearson Australia Group Pty. Ltd.)
Penguin Books India Pvt. Ltd., 11 Community Centre, Panchsheel Park, New Delhi—110 017, India
Penguin Group (NZ), 67 Apollo Drive, Rosedale, Auckland 0632, New Zealand
(a division of Pearson New Zealand Ltd.)
Penguin Books (South Africa) (Pty.) Ltd., 24 Sturdee Avenue, Rosebank, Johannesburg 2196,
South Africa

Penguin Books Ltd., Registered Offices: 80 Strand, London WC2R 0RL, England

This is a work of fiction. Names, characters, places, and incidents either are the product of the author's imagination or are used fictitiously, and any resemblance to actual persons, living or dead, business establishments, events, or locales is entirely coincidental. The publisher does not have any control over and does not assume any responsibility for author or third-party websites or their content.

First Riverhead hardcover edition: November 2010
First Riverhead trade paperback edition: November 2011
Riverhead trade paperback ISBN: 978-1-59448-550-3

The Library of Congress has catalogued the Riverhead hardcover edition as follows:

Mosley, Walter.
    The Last Days of Ptolemy Grey / Walter Mosley.
        p. cm.
        ISBN 978-1-59448-772-9
    1. Older African Americans—Fiction. 2. African American families—Fiction.
3. Old age—Fiction. 4. Memory—Fiction. 5. Domestic fiction.
6. Psychological fiction. I. Title.
PS3563.O88456L37 2010   2010012317
813'.54—dc22

PRINTED IN THE UNITED STATES OF AMERICA

8th Printing

For the man who gave everything—Leroy Mosley

AFTERWARD

Dear Robyn,

You are away for two days with Beckford and I'm sitting here in this apartment waiting to finally be a man. I have the Devil's medicine burning in my veins and Coydog McCann whispering in my left ear. I have you in my life. That was something I never suspected, expected, or even dreamed about. I love you and I couldn't be here right now if it wasn't for you taking care of me. And if you were twenty years older and I fifty years less I'd ask you to be my wife and not a soul on this earth would have ever had better.

I want you to know that everybody in my family is counting on you. They might not like you. They might be mad that I made you my heir. But in the end they will all be better for your strength, my guidance, and Coy's righteous crime so many years ago.

*I'm sitting here waiting on the man with two names
to come and tell me the truth. That's all I ask for. I
need to know what happened and why. Because even
though I can remember as far back as I have years,
ninety-one years, I still don't know what happened.
And a man has to know the truth and act
accordingly—that's only right.*

*So if something should happen and I don't make it
past this afternoon I want you to know how much I
love you and I am in love with you. You deserve the
best I can offer up and that's why I'm sitting here with
a pistol under the cushion and a gold doubloon on the
coffee table. You might not understand. You might
think that it don't have a thing to do with you and you
don't want me acting a fool like this. You might say
why live a whole life being careful and then throw it
all away at the last minute?*

*But baby girl I should have run into that tarpaper
fire when I was a boy. I should have run down with a
rock or stick when Coy was dancing on flames. I
should have walked out on Sensia and stayed away
even though it would have killed me.*

*I have to do this baby girl because you gave me
the heart and the chance and because when I saw you
I knew.*

I love you always,

Ptolemy Usher Grey

Hello?" the very, very old black man said into the receiver.

The phone had not rung for more than a week and a half by his reckoning but really it had only been a little more than three days. Somebody had called, a woman. She seemed sad. He remembered that she'd called more than once.

Classical piano played softly from a radio in the background. A console television prattled away, set on a twenty-four-hour news station.

"Is somebody there?" the old man asked before his caller could speak.

"Papa Grey?" a male voice said. It was a young man's voice, free from the strain and gravel of age.

"Is that you, Reggie? Where you been, boy? I been waitin' for you to come by for a week. No, no, two weeks. I don't know exactly but it's been a long time."

"No, Papa Grey, no, it's me, Hilly."

"Who? Where's Reggie?"

Hilly went silent for two seconds and the old man said, "Is anybody there?"

"I'm here, Papa Grey," the voice assured. "I'm here."

He was certainly there, on the other end of the line, but who was it? the old man wondered. He looked around the room for a clue to his caller's identity but all he saw were piles of newspapers, boxes of every size and shape, and furniture. There were at least a dozen chairs and a big bureau that was tilted over on a broken leg; two dining tables were flush up against the south and east walls. His tattered mattress under its thin army blanket lay beneath the southern table.

"That was Etude no. 2 in A-flat Major by Chopin," the radio announcer was saying. "Now we're going to hear from . . ."

"Papa Grey?" a voice said.

". . . half a dozen bombs went off in and around Baghdad today. Sixty-four people were killed . . ."

Was the voice coming from the radio or the TV? No. It was in his ear. The telephone—

"Who is this?" Ptolemy Grey asked, remembering that he was having a phone conversation.

"It's Hilly, Papa. Your great-nephew. June's daughter's son."

"Who?"

"Hilly," the young man said, raising his voice slightly. "Your nephew."

"Where's Reggie?" Ptolemy asked. "Where's my son?"

"He can't come today, Uncle," Hilly said. "Mama asked me to call you to see if you needed anything."

"Heck yeah," Ptolemy said, wondering what *anything* the call and the caller meant.

"Do you?"

"Do I what?"

"Do you need anything?"

"Sure I do. I need all kinds of things. Reggie haven't called me in, in a week, maybe, maybe it's only three days. I still got four cans of sardines and he always buy me a box of fourteen. I eat one every day for lunch. But he haven't called and I don't know what I'm gonna eat when the fish an', an', an' cornflakes run out."

A piano sonata began.

"What do you want me to get you?" Hilly asked.

"Get me? Yeah, yeah. Come get me and we can go shoppin'. I mean me and Reggie."

"I can go with you, I guess, Uncle," Hilly said unenthusiastically.

"Do you know where the store is?" his great-uncle asked.

"Sure I do."

"I don't know. I never seen you there."

"But I do know."

"Is Reggie coming?"

"Not today."

"Why? No . . . no, don't tell me why. Don't do that. Are you comin', um, uh, Hilly?" Ptolemy smiled that he could remember the name.

"Yes, Papa Grey."

"When?"

"One hour."

Ptolemy peered at the clock on top of his staggering bureau.

5

"My clock says quarter past four," Ptolemy told his great-nephew Hilly Brown.

"It's ten to twelve, Uncle, not four-fifteen."

"If you add forty-five minutes to that," the old man said. "I should be lookin' for you before too much after five. Anyway, it have to be before six."

"Uh, yeah, I guess."

Ptolemy could hear fire engines blaring in the distance. There were floods down south and Beethoven was deaf. Dentifrice toothpaste was best for those hard-to-get places.

Maude Petit died in fire. Ptolemy could hear her screams along with the sirens that cried down the street outside and also in the fire bells that clanged way back then in Breland, Mississippi, when he was five and she was his best friend.

Ptolemy started to rock on his solid maple chair. One of the legs had lost its rubber stopper and so made a knocking sound on the parquet floor. He felt like he needed to do something. What? Save his little playmate, that's what. He was bigger now. He could make it through the fire, if only he could get there.

He could smell the tar roof burning and feel the heat against his face. He rubbed the tears away and then looked at his old weathered hand with its paper-thin, wrinkled skin. Black as that hot tar, black as Maude's happy little face.

Where was Reggie? Where was he?

The clock still said 4:15. It was just like when he used to work for the undertaker and he had to wait for six o'clock to come on the big black-and-silver wall clock that hovered in the hall outside

6

from where he swept the floors around the tables that held the bodies of Maude and her whole family. They smelled like gamey meat cooking in his mother's father's deep-pit barbecue. The firemen threw Maude's dog in the garbage. Maude loved that dog and so Ptolemy snuck around the back of the big green cans they used to throw away everything that the Petit family owned and he stole Floppy's body and buried her down by the river, where Ptolemy had shown Maude his but she was too shy to show him hers.

They were a match for each other, Earline Petit had said.

It was probably a match that started the fire that burned down the house, the fire captain said.

A woman was singing opera in a voice that made Ptolemy think of strawberry jam. He tried to get to his feet by leaning forward and pushing against the arms of the chair. He failed on the first and second tries. He made it on the third. Standing up hurt in three places: his elbow, his knee, and ankle. One, two, three places.

The short refrigerator was humming but empty.

The clock said 4:15.

The lady news announcer was talking about a white girl in Miami who was taken away by somebody that nobody knew. Ptolemy thought about the . . . what did Mama call it . . . the inferno of the Petit's tarpaper home; the yellow fire that waved like tall grass in the wind and the dark shadows that looked like the silhouette of a tall man moving through the rooms, searching for Maude like Ptolemy wanted to do, like he should have done.

The clock must have run down, Ptolemy thought. So how would Reggie know when to come if time had stopped? Ptolemy could be stuck there forever. But even if there was no clock, clock-time, he would still be hungry and thirsty, and how could he find the right bus to take him to the tar pit park if Reggie didn't come?

The knock on the door surprised Ptolemy. He was resting his eyes, listening to a man talk about the money people have to pay for war and school while a trumpet played, a jazz trumpet that carried the sound of black men laughing down the hall in the whorehouse Coydog brought him to when they were supposed to be at the park playing on the swing.

While Coy played poker, or was with his girl, Deena Andrews would bathe Pity, that's what they called him, they called him Pity because Ptolemy seemed like blasphemy, though no one could say why. Deena would give Pity a bath and comb his hair and say, "I wish you were my little boy, Pity Grey. You just so sweet."

The knocking startled him again.

Ptolemy went to the door and touched it with both hands. He couldn't feel anything but hard wood.

"Papa Grey?"

"Who is it?"

"Hilly. Sorry I'm late. The bus got stuck in a traffic jam."

"Where's Reggie?"

"Reggie couldn't come, Papa Grey. Mama sent me to help you go to the store . . . You know, June's daughter."

June was a young woman who went out in hussy clothes on Friday nights when she should have been home with her children. And Esther . . . his sister took care of Hilda, George, and Jason.

"Whose boy are you?" Ptolemy asked the door.

"Marley and Hilda's son," the voice on the other side of the door replied.

Ptolemy heard the words and he knew that they meant something, though he could not conjure up the pictures in his mind. He wanted to ask another question to make sure that this wasn't that woman who came in his house and stole his money out of his coffee can.

Ptolemy strained his mind trying to remember another thing that only a friend of Reggie would know. But every time his mind caught on something—it was a broad rise in Mississippi that had blue mist and white clouds all around. The sun was going down and the heat of the day was giving up to a mild breeze. There were birds singing and something about a man that died. A good man who gave everything so that his people could sing, no, not sing but live life like they were singing . . .

"Papa Grey, are you all right?" the voice beyond the door asked.

Ptolemy remembered that he was trying to recall something about Reggie that the young man through the door should know. He was, Reggie was, Ptolemy's son, or his grandson, or something like that. He was tall and dark, not handsome or slender, but people liked him and he was always nice unless he was drinking and then he got rough.

Don't drink, boy, Ptolemy would tell him. *Drinkin' is the Devil's homework for souls lost on the road after dark.*

"What did I used to tell Reggie about liquor?" the old man asked.

"What?"

"What did I tell him about liquor?"

"Not to drink it?" the voice replied.

"But what did I say?" Ptolemy asked.

"That drinkin' was bad?"

9

"But what did I *say*?"

"I don't know exactly. That was a long time ago," Hilly said.

"But what did I say? To him," Ptolemy added to help the young man answer the question.

"Uncle Grey, if you don't open up I can't help you go shoppin'."

Ptolemy slapped his hands together and backed away from the door. He laid his palms upon the stack of ancient, disintegrating cardboard boxes piled next to the entrance of his one-bedroom apartment. He brought his hand to his bald head and pressed down hard, feeling the arthritic pain in the first joint of three fingers. One, two, three. Then he reached for the doorknob, gripped it.

Just the feel of the cold green glass on his hand brought back that crazy woman into his mind. The woman who came into his house was named Melinda Hogarth, somebody said. She knocked Ptolemy down and made off with his coffee-can bank. She was fifty. "Too old to be a drug addict," Ptolemy remembered saying.

"Get outta my way, niggah," she'd said when Ptolemy got to his feet and tried to pull his bank back from her. "I will cut you like a dog if you try an' stop me."

Ptolemy hated how he cringed and cowered before the fat, deep-brown addict. He hated her, hated her, hated her.

And then she did it again.

"Don't open the door unless it's for me or someone I send," Reggie had told him. And he had not opened that door for anyone but Reggie in three and a half, maybe five years, and nobody had stolen his coffee-can money since. And he never went in the streets except if Reggie was with him because one time he met Melinda down on St. Peters Avenue and she had robbed him in broad daylight.

· · ·

But Reggie hadn't been there in a week and a half by the old man's calculation. He would have had to send somebody after that long. Anyway, it was a man's voice outside, not crazy Melinda Hogarth. Ptolemy turned the knob and pushed the door open.

Down at the end of the long hall a young man was walking away. He was a hefty kid wearing jeans that hung down on his hips.

"Reggie."

The young man turned around. He had a brooding, boyish face. He looked familiar.

"I was leavin'," he said down the long hallway. His expression was dour. It seemed as if he might still leave.

"Did Reggie send you?" the old man asked, holding the door so that he could slam it shut if he had to.

"No," the boy replied. "Niecie did. Mama did."

Reluctantly he shambled back toward Ptolemy's door.

Old Papa Grey was frightened by the brute's approach. He considered jumping inside his apartment and slamming the door shut. But he resisted the fear; resisted it because he hated being afraid.

If you know who you is, then there's nuthin' to fear, that's what Coy used to tell him.

While these emotions and memories fired inside the old man, Hilly Brown approached. He was quite large, much taller than Ptolemy and almost as wide as the door.

"Can I come in, Papa Grey?"

"Do I know you?"

"I'm your great-grandnephew," he said again, "June's grandson."

Too many names were moving around Ptolemy's mind. Hilly sounded familiar; and June, too, had a place behind the door that kept many of his memories alive but mostly unavailable.

That's how Ptolemy imagined the disposition of his memories, his thoughts: they were still his, still in the range of his thinking, but they were, many and most of them, locked on the other side of a closed door that he'd lost the key for. So his memory became like secrets held away from his own mind. But these secrets were noisy things; they babbled and muttered behind the door, and so if he listened closely he might catch a snatch of something he once knew well.

"June, June was . . . my niece," he said.

"Yeah," the boy said, smiling. "Can I come in, Uncle?"

"Sure you can."

"You have to move back so I can get by."

In a flash of realization Ptolemy understood what the boy was saying. He, Ptolemy, was in the way and he had to move in order for him to have company. It wasn't a crazy woman addict stealing his money but a visitor.

The old man smiled but did not move.

Hilly put out both hands pushing his uncle gently aside as he eased past into the detritus of a lifetime piled into those rooms like so much soil pressed down into a grave.

Ptolemy followed the hulking boy in.

"What's that smell?" Hilly asked.

"What smell? I don't smell nuthin'."

"Uh, it's bad." Hilliard Bernard Brown moved a stack of Ptolemy's metal folding chairs that were leaning against the bathroom door.

"Don't go in there," Ptolemy said. "That's my bathroom. That's private."

But the bulbous young man did not listen. He moved the chairs aside and went into the small bathroom.

"The toilet's all stopped up, Papa Grey," Hilly said, holding his broad hand over nose and mouth. "How can you even breathe in here? How you go to the toilet?"

"I usually go at Frank's Coffee Shop when Reggie take me for lunch, and I use my lard can for number one and pour it down the sink every night. That saves water and time and I never have to go in there at all."

"You don't evah take a bath or a shower?"

"Um . . . I got my washrag an' uh . . . the sink. I wash up every three days . . . or whatevah."

"You don't shower an' you pissin' in the sink where you drink water from?" Hilly crossed his hands over his chest as if warding off disease as well as depravity.

"It all go down the same pipes anyway," Ptolemy said. "And the toilet don't work."

"Come on, Papa Grey," Hilly said, closing the door to the bathroom. "Let's get out of here."

"What?"

"It smells in here," Hilly said. "It smells bad."

"I got to get my, my, you know," Ptolemy said. "My thing."

"What thing?"

"The, the . . . I don't know the word right now but it's the, the thing. The thing that I need to go out."

"What thing, Uncle?"

"The, the, the iron. That's it, the iron."

"What you need with a iron?" the young man asked.

"I need it." Ptolemy started looking around the clutter of his congested apartment. It looked more like a three-quarters-full storage unit than a home for a man to live. The television was still on. The radio was playing polka music.

Hilly switched off the radio.

"Don't do that!" Ptolemy shouted, his voice cracking into a hiss like electric static. "That's my radio. It got to be on all the time or I might lose my shows."

"All you have to do is turn it back on when you want to hear it."

"But sometimes I turn the wrong thing an' then the wrong channel, station, uh, the wrong man is on talkin' to me an' he, an' he don't know the right music."

"But then all you got to do is find your station," Hilly said, crinkling his nose to keep the foul odor out.

"Turn it back on, Reggie . . . or Hilly, or whatever . . . just turn it back on."

The young man put up his hood and used it to cover his nose and mouth. He turned the radio on at a low volume.

"Make it have more sound," Ptolemy demanded.

"But you not gonna be here, Papa Grey."

"Make it more."

Hilly turned up the volume and then said, "I'll be out on the front porch waitin', Uncle. It stink too much in here."

Hilly went out of the door, leaving it ajar. Ptolemy was quick to close the door after his great-grandnephew and throw the bolt. Then he moved quickly so as not to forget what he was doing. He scanned the piles of boxes and stacks of cartons, dishes, clothes, and old tools. He looked under the tables and through a great pile of clothes. He shuffled through old newspapers, letters, and books in the deep closet. He looked up at the ceiling and saw a large gray spider suspended in a corner. For a moment he thought about shooting that spider.

"No," he whispered. "You don't have to shoot a spider. He too small for shootin'. Anyway, he ain't done nuthin'." And then Ptolemy remembered what he was looking for. He went to the closet and took out a stack of sheets that his first wife, Bertie, had bought sixty years before. Under the folded bedclothes was an electric steam iron set upon a miniature ironing board. Under the iron lay three un-opened envelopes with cellophane windows where Ptolemy's name and address appeared.

One by one Ptolemy opened the sealed letters. Each one contained a city retirement check for $211.41. He counted them: one, two, three. He counted the checks three times and then shoved them into his pocket and stood there, wondering what to do next. The radio was on. It was playing opera now. He loved it when people sang in different languages. He felt like he understood them better than the TV newsmen and women who talked way too fast for any normal person to understand.

There was a plane crash in Kentucky. Forty-nine dead. It was Monday, the twenty-eighth of August. The spider stared down from his invisible webs, waiting for a fly or moth or unwary roach.

Somebody was waiting for Ptolemy. Reggie. No, not Reggie but, but . . .

There was a chubby young stranger standing on the concrete stairs of the tenement building when Ptolemy came out into the daylight clutching his outside right front pocket. He squinted from the bright sun and shivered because there was a breeze.

"What took you, Papa Grey?" the unfamiliar stranger asked.

"Do I know you?"

"Hilly," he said. "Hilda's son. I'm here to take you shopping. Did you lock the door?"

"'Course I did," Ptolemy said. "It's Monday and you always lock the door on Monday. Monday, Tuesday, Wednesday, Thursday, Friday, Saturday, uh, um, Saturday, and, and, and Sunday. You always lock the door on them days and then put the key in your front pocket."

"Hey, Pete," someone yelled from down the street.

Ptolemy flinched and backed up toward the door, hitting the wood frame with his shoulder.

A tall woman, almost as fat as the stranger who called him Papa Grey, was coming quickly up the block.

"Hold it right there, Pete!" the woman yelled. There was a threat in her voice. "Wait up!"

Ptolemy reached for the handle of the door with his left hand but he couldn't grasp it right. The woman climbed the stoop in two big steps and slapped the old man, hitting him hard enough to bump his head against the door.

"Where my money, bastid?" the woman shouted.

Ptolemy went down into a squat, putting his hands up to protect his head.

"Empty yo' pockets. Gimme my money," the woman demanded.

"Help!" Ptolemy shouted.

When she bent down, trying to reach for the old man's pocket, he twisted to the side and fell over. The woman was in her fifties and dark-skinned. The once-whites of her eyes were now the color of cloudy amber. She grabbed Ptolemy's shoulder in an attempt to position him for another slap.

That was when Hilly grabbed the woman's striking wrist. He exerted a great deal of strength as he wrenched her away from his uncle.

"Ow!" she screamed. She tried to slap Hilly with her free hand.

"Hit me an' I swear I will break yo' mothahfuckin' arm, bitch," Hilly told her.

Almost magically the woman transformed, going down into a half crouch, weeping.

"I jes' wan' my money," she cried. "I jes' wan' my money."

"What money?" Hilly asked.

"It's a lie," Ptolemy shouted in a hoarse, broken voice.

"He promised to gimme some money. He said he was gonna give it to me. I need it. I ain't got nuthin' an' everybody knows he's a rich niggah wit' a retirement check."

"Bitch, you bettah get away from heah," Hilly warned.

"I need it," she begged.

"Get outta heah now or I'ma go upside your head with my fist," Hilly warned. He raised a threatening hand and the amber-and-brown-eyed black woman hurried down off the stoop and across the street, wailing as she went.

One or two denizens of La Jolla Place stopped to watch her. But nobody looked at Hilly or spoke.

The street was narrow, with three-story structures down both sides of the block. One or two of the commercial buildings were painted dirty white but everything else was brown. Apartment buildings mostly—a few with ground-floor stores that had gone out of business. The only stores that were still operating were Blanche Monroe's Laundry and Chow Fun's take-out Chinese restaurant.

Ptolemy pressed his back against the wall and rose on painful knees. He was trying not to tremble or cry, biting the inside of his lips to gather his courage.

"Who is she?" Hilly, his savior, asked.

"Melinda Hogarth," Ptolemy said, uttering one of the few names he could not forget.

"Do you owe her money?"

"No. I don't owe that woman nuthin'. One day a couple'a years ago she squeezed my arm and said that she needed money for her habit. She just kept on squeezin' an' sayin' that and when I finally gave her ten dollars she squeezed harder and made me say that I'd give her that much money whenevah she needed it. Aftah that she come an' push in my do' an' took my money can. That's why I nevah go anywhere unless Reggie come. Where is Reggie?"

"Come on, Papa Grey. Let's go to the store."

Why you shiverin', Uncle?" Hilly asked when they were walking down Alameda toward the Big City Food Mart.

"It's cold out heah. An' they's that wind."

"It's just a breeze," Hilly said. "And it's ovah eighty degrees. I'm sweatin' like a pig as it is."

"I'm cold. Where we goin'?"

"To Big City for your groceries. Then aftah that, Mama want me to bring you ovah to her house."

"You got money?" Grey asked.

"No. I mean maybe five dollars. Don't you have money for your groceries?"

"I got to go to the place first."

"The ATM?"

Ptolemy stopped walking and considered the word. It sounded like *amen*, like maybe the big kid was saying, "Amen to that." But his face looked confused.

"What's wrong, Uncle?" Hilly asked.

Ptolemy looked behind to make sure he knew how far he was from his house. He noticed that Melinda Hogarth wasn't following him like she once did when she knew that he was going to the place.

"You really scared him," Ptolemy said to Hilly, shifting their conversation in his mind. "He slapped me an' knocked me down an' you said, 'Get outta here,' an' he run." Ptolemy giggled and slapped his hip.

"You mean *she* ran," Hilly said. "Not he."

"Yeah. Yeah, right. I mean she. She ran. She sure did." The old man giggled and patted the big boy's shoulder.

"Do you wanna go to Big City?" Hilly asked again.

"I gotta go to the place first."

"What place?"

"The place for in my pocket."

Hilly noticed then that his uncle was holding on to something through the blue fabric of his pants.

"You got somethin' in your pocket, Uncle?"

"That's my business."

"Do you want me to help you with that like I helped you with that bitch slapped you?"

Ptolemy snickered. He would hardly ever use a curse word like that, but he felt it, and the big boy saying it made him happy.

Laughin' is the best thing a man can do," his aunt Henrietta used to say back in the days after the Great War when all the black folks lived together and knew each other and talked the same; back in the days when they had juke joints and white gloves and girls that smiled so pretty that a little boy like Ptolemy (who they called Petey, Pity, and Li'l Pea) would do cartwheels just to get them to look at him.

"Do you want me to help you with what's in your pocket, Papa Grey?" Hilly said again. He reached for Ptolemy's hand but the old man shifted away.

"Mine!" he said protectively, shaking his head.

Hilly put his hands up, surrendering to his great-uncle's vehemence.

"All right. All right. But if you want me to help you, you have to tell me where you want to go."

"The place," Ptolemy said. "The place."

"The ATM?"

"No, not that. Not where they say amen. The place where, where the lady behind the glass is at."

"The bank?"

When the old man smiled he realized that his tongue was dry. He had to go to the bathroom too.

"What bank?" his nephew asked.

This question defeated Ptolemy. How could somebody be so stupid not to know what a bank was? He'd been there a thousand times. And he was thirsty, and he had to urinate. And it was cold too.

"Do you have a bank card in your wallet, Papa Grey?" Hilly asked.

"Yes," Ptolemy answered though he hadn't really understood the question.

"Can I see it?"

"See what?"

"Your bank card."

"I don't know what you talkin' 'bout."

"Can I see your wallet?"

"What for?"

"So that I can see your bank card and I can know what bank you want to go to."

"Reggie knows," Ptolemy said. "Why don't you ask him?"

"Reggie's out of town for a minute, Papa Grey. And I don't know what bank you do business wit' so I got to see your wallet."

Ptolemy tried to decipher what the boy was saying and what he meant. He didn't understand what there could have been in his wallet that this Reggie, no, this Hilly, needed to know. He did fight off that crazy woman. He did know Reggie. And he had to go to the bathroom and drink from the faucet, Ptolemy did—not Hilly/Reggie.

Ptolemy took the wallet from his back pocket and handed it into the young man's massive hand.

Hilly, whose skin was melon-brown and mottled, sifted through the slips of paper and receipts until he came upon a stiff plastic card of blue and green.

"Is your bank People's Trust, Papa Grey?"

"That's it. Now you finally found out what to do," the old man said.

"Hold it right there," an amplified man's voice commanded.

A police car pulled up to the curb and two uniformed officers climbed out, both holding pistols in their hands.

Hilly put his hands up to the level of his shoulders and Ptolemy did the same.

"John Bull," he whispered to Hilly. "They must be lookin' for robbers—or, or, or black mens they think is robbers."

"You can put your hands down," one of the cops, the dark-brown one, said to Ptolemy.

"I ain't done nuthin', Officer," the old man replied, raising his arms higher even though it hurt his shoulders.

"We don't think you've done anything, sir. But is this man bothering you?"

"No, sir. This my son, I mean my grandson, I mean Reggie my grandson come to take me to the People's Bank."

"He's your son or your grandson?" the white cop in the black-and-blue uniform asked.

"He's my grandson," Ptolemy said slowly, purposefully. He wasn't quite sure that what he was saying was true but he knew that he had to protect the young colored man from the cops.

Don't let the cops get you in jail, Coydog McCann used to tell him on the porch of his tarpaper house down in Mississippi, in Breland, when Ptolemy was seven and the skies were so blue that they made you laugh. *Don't evah let a niggah go to jail because'a you,* Coydog had said. *Be bettah to shoot a niggah than turn him ovah to John Bull.*

"My grandson, Reggie, Officer. My grandson. He takin' me to the People's Bank an' to the sto'."

"Why does he have your wallet?" the dark-skinned cop asked.

"He wanted to tell where we was, where it was, you know. Where it was."

"Are you his grandson?" the cop asked Hilly.

"His nephew, Officer," Hilly said in a respectful voice that he had not used before. "He calls me Reggie, who's my first cousin, but I'm Hilly Brown, and Reggie the one usually take care of him. I was lookin' in his wallet because he done forgot the address of his bank."

Ptolemy studied the police as they watched his nephew.

Hilly was his great-grandnephew, he remembered now. He was smaller the last time they'd seen each other. It was at a party in somebody's backyard and there was brown smog at the edges of the sky but people were still laughing.

"Are you okay, sir?" the white cop asked Ptolemy.

"Yes, Officer. I'm fine. Reggie here, I mean Hilly here, was protectin' me from all the thieves in the streets. He takin' me to the bank and the food store. Yes, sir."

The four men stood there on the dirty street for half a minute more. Ptolemy caught the smell of maggots from a nearby trash can. There was danger in the air. Ptolemy thought about Lee Minter, whom he saw run down and beaten by a cop name Reese Loman and his partner, Sam. The cops had truncheons. After the beating, Lee lay up in a poor bed in a tin house, where he died talking to his baby, LeRoy, who had passed ten years before. Lee called the cops fools for trying to arrest him for something they knew he didn't do, and then he ran. The dying man had a fever so hot that you didn't even need to touch him to feel the heat.

The policemen said something to Hilly. Ptolemy heard the deep voices but could not make out the words.

"Yes, Officer," Hilly said to the white cop.

Ptolemy remembered that you were always supposed to speak to the white cop. Sometimes they had black men in uniform but it was the white cop that you had to talk to.

"Come on, Papa Grey," Hilly said after the policemen got in their car and drove off. "We got to get to the bank before they close."

It was a long, crowded room with a high counter down the middle and another one against the window that looked out on the street. Opposite the picture window was a wall of glass-encased booths where women cashed people's checks and took deposit money for their Christmas clubs. Ptolemy used to keep a Christmas club for Angelina, Reggie's daughter . . . or maybe it was William's daughter, yes, William's daughter, Angelina. And he also kept a holiday account for Pecora, even though she never liked him very much.

There were too many people in there. Ptolemy tried to see them but they began to blend together and no matter how many times he saw somebody when he looked around no one was familiar to him. And so he kept moving his head, trying to see and remember everyone.

"Let's go to the counter, Papa Grey." Hilly took his arm but Ptolemy wouldn't budge. He just kept looking around, trying to make all of those faces make sense.

"Don't it bother you?" the older man asked the younger.

"What? Come on."

Ptolemy wasn't going to be pulled around until he could make sense of that room. It seemed very important, almost as much as protecting that boy from the bulls. Didn't he know that you weren't ever supposed to take out your wallet on a street? If the thieves didn't get you the police certainly would. The young people didn't seem to have any sense anymore. They didn't know. All the people on line and at the counters didn't know what to do, and so it was dangerous on the street.

"Come on, Uncle."

One man wearing a bright-blue suit with a long double-breasted jacket stood there talking to a blond-headed black woman who was smiling and wore no wedding ring. The blue-suited man looked very much like the gangster Sweet Billy Madges, and she, blondie, was familiar too. But it wasn't anything to do with Madges and his whores. The blond black woman was like Letta Golding, who lived in a room across the courtyard from which a great oak had arisen.

"That oak," Coydog would say, "is like Christ a'mighty coming up outta the clay, fed by the graves of all the dead souls that believed in him."

"Do you believe in him?" Li'l Pea asked.

"If things goin' good," the wizened old man opined, "not too much. But when I'm in trouble I can pray with the best of 'em."

If he was small enough, a little boy could climb on the limbs of that tree and clear across the courtyard or up or down to the walkways of any of the eight floors of that Mississippi Negro tenement.

Coydog lived there for a while, and Li'l Pea would visit him whenever he could.

"Papa Grey," Hilly beseeched.

Letta was beautiful and friendly. Li'l Pea often found himself climbing up to the seventh-floor window of her apartment because she never pulled down the shade; even if she was naked and in the barrel she used for a bathtub, Letta would stand up and smile for Ptolemy and touch his cheek or kiss his forehead.

"You a nasty boy," she'd say if he came up to her window and she was naked but she'd be smiling and he knew that she wasn't really mad.

"Papa Grey," Hilly said again.

"What?"

"Do you have a check to cash?"

He was still standing in the crowded bank and not in Letta's bathroom. This realization was a surprise for the elder Grey but not a shock. He was used to going places in his mind. More and more he was in the past. Sometimes with his first wife, Bertie, and then later with the woman he truly loved—Sensia Howard. Even when she had been untrue to him with his good friend Ivan, he couldn't get up the strength to leave Sensia—or to kill her.

The next thing Ptolemy knew he was standing at the counter with the three checks for $211.41 in his hand. Hilly was getting him to sign on the back over some other words that the boy had written.

"You stay here, Papa Grey," Hilly was saying. "I'ma go over to the teller and get your money."

Hilly had the checks in his hand but Ptolemy did not remember handing them over. He had signed them and now the boy was on the other side of the dividing table, standing on line at a teller's window.

"That your son?" a woman asked.

She was old but not nearly as old as Ptolemy. Maybe sixty, maybe seventy, but he had twenty years on her at least.

"No. His name is . . . I forget his name but he's my nephew, either my sister's son or her daughter's son. Somethin' like that."

"Oh," the short woman said. "Mister, can you help me?"

"Um, the boy there does most everything for me," he replied, thinking that he should go over on line and stand with, with . . . Hilly.

"I need five dollars more to make my telephone bill," the woman said. She wore blue jeans and a pink T-shirt, black-and-white tennis shoes, and a cap with a long transparent green sun visor.

"I don't take care'a the money," Ptolemy said. "I let the boy do that. I can't hardly see the fingers on my hand and so he count the money so I don't give ya a one instead of a, of a five."

The woman was the same height as he. She once had clear brown eyes that were now partly occluded with wisps of gray.

"My name's Shirley," she said.

"Ptolemy," he said, "but they call me Li'l Pea."

"What kinda name is that?"

"It was Cleopatra's father's name," the old man said. He had said the words so often in his life that they came to his lips automatically. He didn't even know if they were true because it was Coydog told him that and his mother had said, "That Coydog just as soon lie as open his mouf."

"The queen of Africa?"

"What's your last name, Shirley?"

"Wring," she said with a smile. "Double-u ara eye en gee."

"Double-u ara eye en gee," Li'l Pea, Pity, Petey, Ptolemy Grey repeated.

The woman smiled and lifted her left hand, which held the leather straps of a faded cherry-red purse. She placed the bag on the counter and took out a smaller black velvet bag. From this she took a piece of pink tissue paper, which held a lovely golden ring sporting a large, dome-shaped pale-green stone.

"Emerald," Shirley Wring said, placing the delicate jewel on his upturned fingers. "You can hold on to it until I get my Social Security an' then I can buy it back for six dollars."

Ptolemy stared into the sea-green crystal, admiring the flashes of white and yellow from the inner variations as it tumbled between his fingers.

A treasure, he thought. Glee set off in his chest, like the sunlight through the window ignited the jewel in his hand; he felt delight at the reward that Shirley *double-u ara eye en gee* delivered to him even though they were strangers. He experienced a deep satisfaction in the pleasure of her trust in him. He thought about Letta carrying him in through the window and tolerating his presence while she dressed and put on the red lipstick that her boyfriends paid for so dearly.

The excitement became a pain in his chest. Ptolemy, now gazing into the cloudy-eyed woman's brown face, understood that these feelings were strong enough to kill.

He smiled broadly then and said, "Girl, you a beam'a sunshine at the end of a long day of rain."

He put the ring in his pocket. Shirley stared at him, smiling hopefully.

Hilly came up to them then.

"Okay, Papa Grey," he said. "Let's go."

"Gimme my money," Ptolemy said.

"Later . . . at the sto'."

"Now," the old man commanded, "right here in this room."

Hilly handed his great-uncle a paper envelope filled with bills in small denominations.

"This is Shirley Wring," Ptolemy said. "Double-u ara eye en gee."

He was no longer looking around the room, wondering at the changing faces. Ptolemy spread the envelope open and took out a ten-dollar bill. He gave the money to the woman and then took the emerald ring from his pocket.

"Will you take this gift from me, Shirley double-u ara eye en gee?"

Hilly moved his big, heavy head back and forth with a perplexed twist to his face. Shirley smiled. Ptolemy lifted the ring higher.

"You're a sweet man, Li'l Pea," she said, taking her collateral and squeezing it between gnarled fingers.

She put the emerald in its tissue and placed the pink paper in her velvet bag. Then she put the black velvet sack into the faded red-leather purse. Shirley Wring made a movement that was the start of a curtsy and then shuffled off to get on line to pay her phone bill.

"She a friend'a yours?" Hilly asked.

"That's a woman there, boy," Ptolemy replied, thinking about Coydog talking to him when he was young and didn't know a thing.

"Wanna go to the store now?" Hilly suggested, putting his hand on his uncle's shoulder.

"What's your hurry?" Ptolemy asked.

"Nuthin'. We just gotta go."

They went to Big City Food Mart and filled a plastic basket with bologna, store brand Oat Ohs, margarine, sour pickles, a bag of mini peanut butter cups, peanut butter, rye bread, orange juice, Big City brand instant coffee and creamer, and six ripe red apples. The total at the cashier came to $32.37. When they got out of line Ptolemy counted the money he had left: $169.04. He counted it three times and was starting on the fourth when Hilly said, "Come on, Papa Grey, we gotta take these things home."

"Somethin's wrong with my change, Reggie, I, I mean, Hilly."

"Nuthin's wrong," the boy said to Ptolemy's shoes. "That's a lotta money you got there."

They brought the groceries home to the apartment crowded with everything Ptolemy and his wives and his family and theirs had acquired over more than just one lifetime. Hilly put the food onto shelves and into the ancient refrigerator while Ptolemy counted his change again and again, wondering if somehow Shirley Wring had tricked him.

He thought about his trunk and Sensia, the emerald ring and Reggie—where was Reggie?

"Your money's fine, Uncle," Hilly said. "Now we got to get to Mama's house."

"Where?"

"Mama need you to come see her," Hilly said, his brutal face ill-fitting the request.

"What for?"

"She di'n't say. She just said to tell Papa Grey that Niecie need him to come."

"Niecie?" All the floating detritus in the old man's mind sank to the bottom then. The ring and Shirley Wring, the money and Melinda Hogarth, even the fire that killed Maude and the stroke that took Sensia disappeared from his mind.

Niecie. He was only thirty-six when Niecie was born but she was still the daughter of his niece. That's why he called her Niecie, though her mother had named her Hilda. He was her granduncle and her godfather and she was the coppery color of a year-old Indian head penny. Her mother was sitting in the big chair with Niecie on her lap and Charles, June's husband, was standing behind her. He stood just like that, like he was posing for a photograph. But that's the way Charles was: pretty as a picture, and stuffy as a double-starched shirt collar.

"My Niecie?" Ptolemy asked.

"My mama," Hilly said, nodding.

"Is she in trouble?"

"She need to see you," the boy said as he put the nonperishable food in the doorless cabinet. "You got cans on these shelves older than me."

"What fo'?"

"Why you got them cans?"

"Why Niecie wanna see me?"

"She di'n't say, Papa Grey," Hilly whined. "She jes' told me to help you shop and then to bring you ovah. She said to tell you that your Niecie needed to see you."

"Niecie."

The number 87b bus moved slowly in afternoon traffic. Ptolemy sat on a turquoise-colored plastic seat facing across the small aisle, while Hilly hovered above him, holding on to the shiny chrome pole.

A middle-aged Chinese woman and a dark Spanish man sat across the way. Both of them smiled at Ptolemy. People were always smiling at him now that he was so old. Even people who looked old to him smiled because, he knew, he looked even older to them.

He could feel the city move by at his back, could imagine the old Timor Cinema and Thrifty's Drugstore. He thought about jitterbuggers in the juke joints and a small white wooden church that stood on the white side of town.

Sometimes when he'd go by there, on an errand for his mother or a mission for Coydog, he'd stop and gape at the beautiful building with the stained-glass windows of Jesus, John the Baptist, Job, Jonah, and Mary Magdalene. Magdalene was a beautiful name.

One day when he was no more than seven he was standing out

in front of that church with a note in his hand. He couldn't remember on the number 87b bus who that note was for or from but
he could feel the dirt under his bare feet and the hot sun on his
forehead.

"What you want there, boy?" a man asked in a commanding
voice.

Ptolemy was gazing down on the dark Spanish man's brown
leather shoes in the bus but when he looked up he saw that white
man standing in front of the white people's church.

"Lookin'," he said in a small piping voice.

"Is that note for me?" the man asked.

Li'l Pea thought the word *no*, but all he did was shake his head.

The white man wore a white suit with a black shirt that sported
a small square of stiff white cloth where his Adam's apple would
have shown. He wore a wide-brimmed Panama straw hat and glasses
with gold wire frames.

"Speak up, boy," he said.

"No, suh. This note is from my uncle Coy to his brother Lupo
work for the Littletons down on Poinsettia Street," Ptolemy said,
remembering as he did the origins of the note.

"Then why you standin' in front'a my church?"

The sun was above and behind the church spire so whenever
the man in the preacher's uniform moved his head, bright sabers
of light lanced into Ptolemy's eyes.

"It's so pretty," the man, Ptolemy, remembered saying.

The minister paused a moment, his stern visage softened a bit.

"You like this church?" he asked.

"Yes, suh."

"Did you evah look inside?"

"No, suh. I jes' seen the whitewashed walls an' the windahs and the pretty grass lawn."

The minister squinted as people did sometimes when they were trying to make out words that didn't make sense to them. Li'l Pea often wondered how narrowing your eyes could make your hearing better.

"You know that you can never, or none of your people can ever, go into this church," the man said.

"Yes, suh, I know."

"Is that why you lookin' at it so hard?"

"No. It's jes' when I walk by it, it look so pretty like Letta across the way from Uncle Coy's windah. You have to look when somethin's pretty."

The white man turned his back on the boy and looked at his church. He maintained that position for a few moments, allowing Li'l Pea to admire the building a while longer.

When the white man turned around, his face was completely changed, as if he were a different man inside. He held out a hand to the boy. The child didn't know what to do, but he was drawn to the gesture. He grabbed the minister's manicured fingers with his dirty hand and gave them a good shaking.

"Thank you, boy," the minister said. "You've shown me my own life in a new light. It's like, it's like I thought it was day but really there was much more to be seen."

The white man walked away after that.

Ptolemy had often wondered, in the eighty-four years that had passed since that day, what the minister had meant.

"Come on, Papa Grey," Hilly said in a bus a million miles away, "this our stop."

34

. . .

They walked down a long street of sad houses and apartment buildings. There were few lawns or gardens, mostly weeds and broken concrete. Some of the houses had no paint left on their weathered wood walls; one or two seemed crooked because they were falling in on themselves from the ravages of termites, faltering foundations, and general rot.

Ptolemy thought all these things but he couldn't remember how to say them.

"Terrible."

"What, Papa Grey?"

"Terrible."

"What? You hurt?"

"My knees hurt when I walk."

"That's too bad."

"But it's not terrible," Ptolemy said.

"Then what?"

The old man glanced across the street and saw a big sand-brown woman sitting on a stoop. She was smoking a cigarette and between her fat knees were huddled two toddlers in diapers and nothing else.

"Her."

Two blocks away they came to a small house that was once painted bright blue and yellow, Ptolemy remembered, but now the colors were dim and dingy. There were cars parked in the driveway and at the curb at the house across the street. Men and women in their

Sunday best were standing on the brown grass and up beyond the cars.

"What's today?" Ptolemy asked Hilly.

"The fifteenth," the young man replied.

Four rose bushes had died under the front window. A fifth rose was still alive. It had nine or eleven bright green thorny leaves and a bud that might one day blossom. Ptolemy noticed a spigot behind the struggling plant and realized that it was a leak that made it possible for that rose to survive.

Hilly held Ptolemy's elbow as they went up the wooden stairs that had worn down into grooves from the heavy foot traffic over the years. As they approached the screen door, Ptolemy could see that there was a party going on. Dozens of people were crowded into the living room, talking and smoking, drinking and posing in their nice clothes.

Hilly reached for the screen door but it flew inward before he touched it.

"Pitypapa!" a woman yelled. "Pitypapa, I ain't seen you in six and a half years."

Big, copper-brown, and buxom Hilda "Niecie" Brown folded the frail old man in a powerful yet cushioned embrace. For a brief span that extended into itself Ptolemy was lifted out of his pained elderly confusion. He floated off into the sensation of a woman holding him and humming with satisfaction.

She kissed his forehead and then his lips. When she let him go he held on to her arm.

"Oh, ain't that sweet?" Niecie said. "You miss me, Pitypapa?"

Ptolemy looked up at her face. Her skin was smooth and tight from fat. Her mouth was smiling, showing two golden teeth, but in spite of the brave front Niecie's eyes were so sad that he felt her agony. He raised his hands through the pain of his shoulders and placed them on the sides of Niecie's arms.

"Niecie," he said. "Niecie."

"Come on in, Pitypapa. Come on in and sit with me."

The crowded room smelled of food, cigarettes, and booze. Four children were playing on a green couch but Niecie shooed them away.

"Sit with me, Papa," she said. "Tell me how you been doin'."

Ptolemy sat looking around the room, remembering the house. He had come here for Niecie's wedding and later, when her mother, June, had died. June was his oldest sister's child, he remembered. She died of pneumonia, the doctor said, but anyone could have told you that she really died because she went wild with drink and dance after Charles had died.

"You remember my house?" Niecie asked.

"I only remembah it bein' old," he said. "I was already old when you got married. There ain't nuthin' here young or childish."

Even Niecie's smile was sad now.

A short girl came up to stand next to Niecie. She was dark-skinned; not as dark as Ptolemy but almost.

"You remember Robyn?" Niecie asked. "But maybe not. Maybe she came here to live wit' me since the last time I seen you. Her mother died an' me an' Hilly took her in."

Robyn was no more than eighteen and she was beautiful to Ptolemy. Her almond-shaped eyes looked right into his, not making him feel old or like he wasn't there. And there was something else about her: she didn't remind him of anyone he had ever met before. Usually, almost always, people looked to him like someone he'd already met along the way. That was why he found it so hard to remember who someone was. Faces usually made him want to remember something that was lost. He felt sometimes that he had met everyone, tasted every food, seen every sky there was to be seen.

"I seen it all," old Coydog used to say, "but that don't mean I seen everything."

Ptolemy understood now because Robyn was someone, something, new to him.

"Hi," she said with perfect lips that smiled briefly, showing off her strong white teeth.

"You grinnin', Pitypapa," Niecie said. "All the men here be grinnin' after Robyn."

"I have never seen anything like you, girl," Ptolemy said.

Robyn put out a hand and he took it, staring at her.

He was suddenly aware that somewhere a woman was crying. The faraway, muted sobs were pitiful. For some reason this made Ptolemy remember.

"Where's Reggie?" he asked Robyn.

With her eyes she indicated someplace behind Ptolemy. He tried to turn his head but his old joints wouldn't cooperate.

"Why don't you go with him, Robyn?" Niecie said.

Ptolemy was still holding her hand. She pulled gently and he got up with a minimum of pain in his knees. Robyn was just about his height. He grabbed on to her elbow and she guided him through the mob of guests in the living room. They went into a narrow hallway that made the house seem larger because it was so long.

They passed a room from which came the sad sobbing. He removed his grip from Robyn's arm. Gently she took the hand in hers.

"Why she's cryin'?" Ptolemy asked.

"She been like that for hours," the girl answered.

They came to a brown door that was closed. Robyn opened the door and stood aside for Ptolemy to pass through.

It was a very small chamber, only big enough for the single bed and an open coffin. The pine box fit Reggie's hefty proportions perfectly. The tall young brown man's waxy hands were crossed over his chest. His face was calm but the smile that the mortician had placed there was not any expression that Reggie had in life.

Ptolemy turned to Robyn with his mouth open—screaming silently. He forgot how to breathe or even how to stand. Falling forward into the child's arms, the old man cried, "No."

"Didn't Hilly tell you?" Robyn asked.

Ptolemy heard the question but didn't remember. Maybe the boy had said something. Maybe he wasn't listening when he did. Maybe if he had listened Reggie wouldn't be dead.

Ptolemy pushed against Robyn's shoulders and turned to see the boy. Big oily tears came down his face. He leaned over the low-standing coffin, putting his hands against Reggie's chest, tears falling upon his own knuckles and Reggie's. The young man's chest felt like the hard mattress that Coydog slept on in his room at the back of Jack's Barber Shop, where he lived after they kicked him out of his apartment for not paying the rent.

Reggie had a long face with a small scar at the corner of his mouth. His eyes were closed. His black suit was new.

"I don't know why I gotta buy him a new suit t'get buried in," Ptolemy's father, Titus Grey, complained when his wife, Aurelia, had demanded they get good clothes to bury Titus's father in. "He never even came by once when I was growin' up. Not so much as one hello to his son and now you want me to spend a month's wages on a new suit he only gonna wear once."

"It's not for him," Aurelia had said. "Look here."

She touched Titus with one hand and with the other she gestured at Li'l Pea. Ptolemy thought that he was maybe five at that time.

"You see your son?" Aurelia asked.

Titus looked but did not speak.

"When you pass, how do you want him to remember you?" she asked her husband. "He watch you day and night. He practice talkin' like you an' walkin' like you. So what you gonna show him to do when he have to lay you an' me to rest?"

That night he was lying in his bed with his eyes open, thinking about his grandfather lying on the undertaker's table. From the darkness came candlelight and the heavy steps of his father. The huge sharecropper sat on the boy's cot and placed his hand upon Ptolemy's chest.

"I love you, boy," he'd said.

There was a whole conversation after that but Ptolemy couldn't remember it. There was something about his grandfather's death, about men who love their sons . . .

Ptolemy didn't remember sitting down on the bed across from Reggie's coffin, but there he was. Robyn was seated next to him, holding his hands. Maybe he had told her the story of his grand-father's death or maybe he was just thinking about it. They had been talking; he was pretty sure about that.

He noticed that the yellow wallpaper had slanted red lines that were going opposite ways, almost meeting each other to form un-connected capital T's. Seeing this, recognizing the pattern, made him smile.

"When did your father die?" Robyn asked.

"A long time ago," he said. "I seen a lotta people die. Dead in bed, and lynched, but the worst of all is when some stranger come to the do' an' tell ya that your father is dead an' ain't nevah comin' home again."

"You have big hands, Mr. Grey," Robyn said. She was squeez-ing the tight muscle between the forefinger and thumb of his left hand. "Strong."

The pressure hurt and felt good at the same time.

"He stoled my money," he said.

"Who did?"

"I had three checks at the place but he only give me the money for one. I give ten dollars to this woman had a green ring and then thirty-two dollars and thirty-seven cent fo' my groceries. But now all I got in my envelope is a hunnert an' sixty-sumpin' dollars and a few pennies. That adds up to two eleven, but I had three checks for that much. I know 'cause I save 'em up so Reggie only have to go to the bank with me once ev'ry three weeks. We put one check in a account for my bills to be paid and we spend one on groceries."

"Reggie stoled your money?" Robyn asked.

"Yeah . . . I mean no. Reggie wouldn't steal. It's that big boy, that, that, that . . ."

"Hilly?"

"There, you got it."

So much talking and thinking exhausted Ptolemy. Then remembering that Reggie was dead and that they'd never go to the bank again made him sad.

Robyn squeezed his hand and tilted her head to the side so that he'd have to notice her.

"Don't you worry, Mr. Grey," she said. "It's all gonna be all right."

"How?"

"Reggie gonna go to heaven an' Hilly gonna go to hell."

"Are you sure?"

"Yes I am," Robyn said, her young features set with grim certainty.

Such serious intentions on a child's face made Ptolemy smile. His smile infected her and soon they were giggling together, holding hands, sitting next to Reggie's corpse.

After a while the girl stood up, pulling Ptolemy to his feet. Together they left the dead man and went back down the long hall. When they approached the room where the woman cried, Ptolemy asked, "Is that the girlfriend?"

"They been married for three years."

"His wife?" Ptolemy remembered that Reggie was gone for four days once because of his wedding. Then he'd gotten a job at a supermarket and would bring him strawberry jam and old-fashioned crunchy peanut butter almost every week.

Robyn nodded. "And their children. She sat down in Niecie's room on the way back from seein' Reggie an' now she cain't stop cryin'."

Ptolemy pushed the door open and walked in.

The room was filled with yellow light. The walls and the floor were dark, dark blue. A high-yellow woman was slumped across the blue sheets of the bed, crying, crying. Lying next to her head was a toddler girl in fetal position and sucking her thumb. Next to the girl sat a five-year-old boy who was turning the pages of a book. Both children were much darker than their mother.

The boy looked up when Ptolemy and then Robyn came in.

"You readin' that book, boy?" Ptolemy asked slowly as if each word was a heavy weight on his tongue.

The boy nodded.

"What's it say?"

The child shrugged and looked back at the book.

"His name is Arthur," Robyn whispered.

The boy looked up and said, "It got pictures of people with no skin an' pictures of hands and feet and other parts."

"Aunt Niecie was goin' to nurse school for a while," Robyn said. "It's prob'ly one'a her schoolbooks."

Arthur nodded solemnly and scratched his nose.

"Nina," Robyn said then. "Nina, this here is Mr. Grey, the one that Reggie helped out."

The woman raised her head from folded arms. Ptolemy could see that she was young, in her early twenties, no more. Her face was devastated and beautiful; far more lovely, Ptolemy thought, than Robyn. But he still liked Robyn better. He liked her way around him. She knew how to speak when he needed her.

Nina rose up and put her arms around Ptolemy. Again he felt lost in a soft hug. It was like sinking into a warm tub at the end of a hard day.

"He loved you so much, Mr. Grey," Nina said. She smelled sweet from perfume. Too sweet.

"What happened to him?" the old man asked, pulling away as he spoke.

When Nina fell back on the bed the toddler whined and Arthur put his hand on her cheek. She embraced her brother's fingers with her head and shoulder. This gentle show of affection seemed to make the room clearer to Ptolemy. It was as if he was seeing something the way that minister had, in front of his white church so long before.

"They shot him down," Nina said.

"Who shot him?"

"Drive-by."

"Who's that?"

"Nobody knows," Robyn said. "Somebody jes' shot him when he was sittin' on a porch of a friend'a his."

"But they say his name was Drivebee."

"No. The men drove by in their car and jes' shot him."

The little girl was crying. Arthur lay down behind her and put his arms around her shoulders.

"Why?" Ptolemy asked.

"Nobody knows."

Ptolemy squinted, trying to see with his mind's eye the reasoning behind Reggie's murder. He remembered his hidden box and a promise he'd made Coydog before the old man was dragged off and killed like some wild animal. It was something that happened to colored men and boys ever since they left the land of Ptolemy, father of Cleopatra.

There came the sound of heavy feet down the hall.

"Nina?" a man's voice called from outside the room.

Ptolemy turned just in time to see a man come through the door. It was a freckle-faced, strawberry-brown man with straightened, combed-back hair. He was handsome but had a wild look to him as if there were something or someone right behind him, ready to strike. The man was tall and wore a purple shirt that was open down to the bottom of his chest. He wore a thick gold chain that held a pendant which formed the name *Georgie*, written in slanted letters.

Reggie's wife rose from the bed like a creature coming up out of the water. Her movements were fluid, graceful. The idea of dancing came into Ptolemy's wandering mind.

"Alfred," she said.

They grabbed each other, kissed on the lips, and then pressed their cheeks and bodies together.

"Who's that, Mama?" Arthur asked.

"Who's this?" Alfred asked, looking at Ptolemy.

"This is . . ." Nina began saying but she had forgotten the name.

"Mr. Ptolemy Grey," Robyn said, snipping her words to their shortest possible length. "Reggie's great-uncle."

"Who's that, Mama?" Arthur asked again.

"Oh," Alfred said. "Hey, Mr. Grey. I'm sorry for your loss."

"If your name is Alfred, how come you got a sign sayin' Georgie hangin' from your neck?"

A flash of anger crossed the haunted man's face.

"He don't mean nuthin', Alfred," Robyn said. "It's just a question."

"Georgie was my brother," Alfred said angrily. "They shot him down."

"They shoot your brother too?"

"What?" Alfred said, jutting his head toward Ptolemy.

Robyn moved between the men.

"He's a old man, Alfred," she said. "He sit all day in his house listenin' to German music and readin' old papers."

"He bettah get some news, then," Alfred said threateningly.

Nina went to Alfred's side and took his arm.

"We bettah get outta here, Alfie," the grieving widow and mother said.

But Alfred was not finished staring at the old man.

Ptolemy thought it was funny that a fool like that would try and intimidate him. He wasn't afraid. He wasn't afraid hardly at all.

"Yeah," Alfred said. "I come to take you and the kids back to your house."

"Okay," Nina said. "Come on, babies."

Arthur and his sister started crying. They didn't say that they didn't want to go or even shake their heads. They just cried.

For their daddy, Ptolemy thought.

"Why'ont you let the kids stay here with Big Mama Niecie?" Robyn suggested. "She feed 'em an' stuff."

"Do you wanna stay here, Artie? Letisha?"

Arthur nodded and Letisha put her head in her brother's lap.

"You sure?" Nina asked. "Okay. Mama's gonna go home and sleep now. She's tired."

The baby girl whimpered for her mother but would not leave her brother's lap. Nina kissed them both on their foreheads and then moved as if she wanted to kiss Robyn. But the younger girl leaned away. Nina played it off, putting her hand on Robyn's shoulder.

All the while Alfred glared at Ptolemy.

The old man stared back, trying to understand what was happening, what had happened.

Nina turned away from her children and left under the protective arm of the handsome Alfred. Nina glanced back at her children as she went through and past the doorframe. Ptolemy listened to their shoes on the hardwood floor of the hallway.

"Where they goin'?" he asked.

"Who knows?" Robyn said. "You hungry, Arthur?"

"Tisha is."

"What she want?" Robyn asked with a smile.

"Cake."

"Did you have some dinner?"

"No, but we want some cake."

"Okay," Robyn said, "but jes' this one time now."

"Okay."

"You wait here with your sister and I'll get Big Mama Niecie to bring you some'a the cake Auntie Andrews brought us."

She held out her hand and Ptolemy took it. They walked down the hall, back into the crowded room where people had come to mourn and laugh, give their condolences and eat and drink. Ptolemy's skin hurt as he passed through the confused and confusing mob.

When Robyn told Niecie that Nina had left with Alfred Gulla, the older woman sucked her tooth.

"The kids said they want some cake," Robyn added.

"I get it. Poor angels. Did you get somethin' to eat, Pitypapa?"

"I have to go to the toilet," he said.

"I'll show you. After that you want me t'get Hilly to take you home?"

"I'll take him," Robyn said. "I gotta get outta here anyway."

Niecie kissed the girl and smiled.

"You are a blessing, child."

They walked down the street together, hand in hand. The sun was hot and Ptolemy had so many thoughts in his head that he couldn't say very much. But Robyn, once she was out of the house, talked and talked. Ptolemy heard some of what she'd said. She'd come from down south somewhere when her mother died. Robyn's mother and Niecie were good friends and so Niecie offered to take the orphan in. They weren't related by law but Niecie felt like they were blood and let her sleep on the couch in the living room.

"Who's Alfred?" Ptolemy asked after a long spate of listening to the calming words of the child.

"He's Nina's boyfriend."

"But I thought she was Reggie's . . . I mean, I mean . . . his wife."

"He did too. But Nina kep' on seein' Alfred from back when she went out with him years ago. I think he went to jail or sumpin' an' Nina met Reggie an' got pregnant with Artie an' so she stayed with Reggie, but when Alfred got outta jail she was still seein' him too."

They came to a sidewalk where three blue-and-red taxis were parked.

"Can you tell the driver how to get to your house, Mr. Grey?"

"I guess so," he said. "I think I remembah."

They held hands in the back of the cab.

"How old are you, Mr. Grey?"

"Ninety-one year old. Some people don't think I can keep count, but I'm ninety-one."

"You don't look that old. Your skin is so smooth and you stand up straight. It's like you're old but just normal old, not no ninety-one."

She walked Ptolemy to his apartment door and watched him use the key on the topmost of four locks.

"I only lock the top one when I go out," he told the girl. "That way I can remember the copper key. But when I go in, I lock 'em all."

When he was just about to turn away, Robyn kissed him on the cheek and whispered something that he didn't hear.

The TV news was on and a piano concerto was playing. He turned on a light and shuffled through the papers and boxes until he found a picture of Sensia taken before she divorced her first husband to marry Ptolemy. Her heart-shaped brown face was tilting to the side and she was smiling the smile of someone who had just made a suggestion that he would have liked.

· · ·

Bombs went off across Baghdad this morning," said a pretty woman in a blue jacket wearing red lipstick. She was a light-skinned Negro woman but looked more like a white woman trying to pass for colored to Ptolemy. "Thirty-seven people were killed and one hundred and eleven sustained serious injuries."

A man with a deep, reassuring voice was talking on the radio about Schubert, a German musician who'd had a hard life long ago and made beautiful music, some of which no one ever heard in his lifetime.

"Three American soldiers died in the attacks. President Bush expressed his regrets but said that we were making progress in the Iraqi peace initiative."

Ptolemy had been searching for Coydog's treasure for days. He knew that he'd put it away somewhere amongst all the furniture and tools, newspapers and broken toasters, books, magazines, clothes, and sealed cellophane bags containing plastic cutlery wrapped in ancient paper napkins.

His deep closet was piled high with boxes of papers that went all the way back to his grandfather's handwritten birth notice on the Leyford rice plantation in southern Louisiana. There were also his wife's old clothes and shoes, and box after box of photographs that he'd taken, collected, and gathered from family members and the children of old friends.

"Why you keep all this old junk, Uncle?" Reggie used to ask him.

"It's my whole family, boy," he'd once said. "Everything about them. Without they papers they, they . . . you know what I mean."

"No, Uncle. It's just moldy old clothes you ain't nevah gonna wear and papers you ain't nevah gonna read again. I could get you a storage space and put it all in there. Then you could walk around in here."

"What if your mama wanted to put you in a, in a . . . a sto' place?"

"My mama's dead, but I'm alive, Papa Grey."

Patting the door to his deep closet Ptolemy said, "All my stuff is livin' too."

Someone knocked and the news announcer stopped making sense. Ptolemy turned his head toward the door and stared at it. His legs wanted to get up and go but his mind said stay down. His tongue wanted to call out, "Who is it?" But his teeth clamped shut.

Ptolemy's dark features twisted in the attempt to remember why he wasn't going to answer.

The knock came again. He once had a doorbell but it broke and the landlord wouldn't fix it because he was mad that he couldn't raise the rent and so he said that he wasn't going to fix anything.

"I'm losing money on this place and that's not why I own it," he shouted at Reggie one day.

"Get the fuck outta here, man," Reggie had said, and the white landlord, Mr. Pierpont, got the cops.

The police threatened Reggie, but then Pierpont tried to make them get rid of Ptolemy too.

"You're trying to evict this old man?" one of the cops had asked.

"I'm losing money on this place," Pierpont said, as if Ptolemy had stabbed him.

"If I was this young man I would have done more than threaten you," the cop said. The police left, and potbellied Joseph Pierpont never came back, or answered any calls.

Now the doorbell no longer worked and people had to knock. And when they'd knock, Ptolemy would get up and go to the front and ask, "Who is it?"

But not this time. This time he stayed in his seat, listening to the newsman's gibberish and music that scratched at his ears.

The knock came again and Ptolemy remembered why he stayed in his chair. That big boy Hilly had been there and knocked and said that he wanted to come in. He'd come three days in a row and each day Ptolemy told him that he didn't need him and that he would call if he did.

"But you don't know my numbah, Papa Grey," Hilly said through the door. "You haven't called up in years."

"I know how to phone for a operator. All you have to do is dial oh. I call her if I wanna talk to you."

"Mama told me to come help you," Hilly, the thief, beseeched. "She be mad at me if I don't."

"I don't need no help."

"How can you go to the sto'?"

"I walk there."

"What about the bank?"

"You stoled my money, boy. You stoled it at the bank."

"I didn't."

"I don't need yo' kinda help," Ptolemy said, and after three days he no longer even asked who it was. He just stared at whoever was giving the news and waited for the caller to go away and for the words to make sense again.

The first time someone knocked on the door after Reggie's wake it wasn't Hilly.

"Who is it?"

"Mr. Grey?" a man's voice said.

"You Mr. Grey too?" Ptolemy asked.

"No," the man said patiently, "you're Mr. Grey. Open the door, please."

Ptolemy almost obeyed; the voice was that certain.

"Who are you?"

"Antoine Church, Mr. Grey. Your nephew, Reginald, applied to the social services office for a doctor for you a while ago. Is Reginald around?"

"Reggie's dead."

"Oh. I'm sorry to hear that. Is someone else taking care of you?"

"I don't need no one to take care'a me. Reggie's dead and now there's just me."

The radio was playing a march and someone on the TV was laughing. Ptolemy pressed his ear against the door.

"I've found a doctor who wants to see you, Mr. Grey," Antoine Church said. "He's a memory specialist, and he has a grant, so his services are free."

"I'm not sick. I don't need no doctor."

"Let me in, Mr. Grey," the voice said. "Let me in and we can sit down and talk about it."

"I don't wanna talk. Go away and leave me alone."

There came a spate of silence filled in by electronic babble.

"Mr. Grey?"

"Go on now."

"I'm putting my card under the door. If Reginald or someone else comes by to help you—"

"Reggie's dead. Drivebee killed him. Now, you go away."

Again Ptolemy pressed his ear against the door. There came a soft rustling and then a sigh. After that he heard footsteps going away down the hall.

On the floor at the old man's feet was a bright white card. Using the wall for support, he leaned down and picked it up. Putting Antoine Church's business card in his pocket was reflex more than anything else.

Hilly kept coming by but after three days Ptolemy never opened up or even asked who it was. Sooner or later they all went away.

The knock came again.

He concentrated on the TV to keep the person on the other side of the door out of his mind.

". . . the convicted killer was found innocent. The DNA test did not match the blood found at the crime scene," the woman was saying.

"Mr. Grey," a girl called.

Ptolemy leaned forward suspiciously, wondering if somehow the TV had learned how to talk to him.

"Mr. Grey, it's me, Robyn."

Robins. They gathered in the trees outside his parents' house in September and October and sang a sweet song to the cool winds that eased the last heat of summer. If Ptolemy sat still enough with week-old breadcrumbs scattered on the ground, the robins and other birds would gather around him in the grass next to the cypress tree.

"That food gonna attract rats," his father would say, but Li'l Pea didn't believe him.

The knock came again.

"Mr. Grey, are you all right in there?"

That was the right question. Hilly had never asked how he was. Hilly was a thief and even though he had saved him from Melinda Hogarth he still stole his money and then lied about it.

Ptolemy used to give Reggie money. Reggie wanted to help him. But then Reggie got lynched.

"Mr. Grey, if you don't talk to me I'll have to go call the police. I'm afraid that you might be hurt in there."

Ptolemy opened his mouth to tell the girl that he was okay but he hadn't spoken in days and his voice was gone. He got up and coughed, took a step, coughed again.

"I'm here," he rasped.

"What?"

"I'm here."

"It's me, Robyn, Mr. Grey. Can I come in?"

"Who?" he wheezed.

"Robyn. You remembah, I took you in to see Reggie's coffin. Then we took a taxi here."

The image of Reggie's body came up out of the floor at Ptolemy's feet. He gasped and sobbed, remembering the death of his beloved son or nephew or great-grandnephew, yes, great-grandnephew.

He took the chain off its hook and flipped the four locks Reggie had installed. He opened the door and Robyn stood there in a little black dress with an ivory locket hanging from her neck. Her hair was tied back and her eyes saw things that he wanted to see.

"Hi," she said.

Ptolemy smiled because this was the girl that didn't look like anybody else he ever knew.

"Robyn," he said.

"Can I come in?"

He nodded, not moving.

The child swiveled her head and moved toward him; then, just as she came close, she kissed him on the cheek. He moved backward, grinning and touching the place she had kissed.

When Robyn moved around him Ptolemy turned with her, feeling as if he were dancing with Sensia at the big band shell at Pismo Beach.

"Dog!" Robyn said as she came into the congested room. "Where do you sleep, Mr. Grey?"

He pointed at the oak table against the southern wall of the room. It was piled almost to the ceiling with brown boxes.

"In them boxes?"

"No. Under."

She stooped down, putting her hands on her bare knees and turned her head to see the thin mattress and sheer olive blanket.

"You sleep on the floor under a table?"

He nodded, suddenly shy and ashamed.

"What about rats and roaches?" she asked.

Smiling, he was reminded of red-breasted robins singing brightly, thanking him for their breadcrumbs.

"You wanna sit down, girl?"

"Where?" she asked, her left nostril rising.

"There's chairs everywhere," he said. "But I gotta special one for guests that I keep in the kitchen."

He walked there feeling but not minding the pain in his knees. He'd found the aluminum garden chair set out in front of a house with six cars parked on the lawn.

"They got so many cars, they don't have room for no outside furniture," he said to himself as he dragged away the lightweight chair with the threaded seat of sea-green and aqua nylon ribbons.

"You use patio furniture?" Robyn asked when he returned dragging the chair behind him.

"I got them oak chairs over there," he said, "but they too heavy now, an' there's all that stuff stacked on 'em. This here's a lawn chair, but it's comfortable, though."

After the lovely young girl was seated, Ptolemy got his folding wood stool from under the east table. Reggie had brought it for him. It was composed of light pinewood legs held together by rainbow-colored cotton fabric. Ptolemy opened the stool and sat down in front of the black-clad black girl.

"How old are you?" he asked.

"Seventeen."

"You should be in school, then."

"I dropped out when I was fifteen but then I went to night school and got my GED. Now I'm gonna start goin' to community college in the fall," she said, adding, "An' I'm almost eighteen, anyway."

They were quiet for a while, looking at each other. She cast her eyes about the room while he wondered where someone like her might come from.

In the background a man was talking about Palestinians. This brought the image of Egypt into Ptolemy's mind. Egypt—where his name came from.

"He had what they say is a Egyptian name," Coydog had said, "but Ptolemy, Cleopatra's father, was a Greek—mostly."

"Is that music German?" Robyn asked.

"It's from Europe," he said. "Classical."

"Oh."

"How come you here, um, um, Robyn?"

"I came to see you."

"Why the most beautiful girl at the whole party gonna come to a old man's house smell like he ain't clean it in ten, no, no, twenty-three years."

Robyn sat forward on the lawn chair and took hold of one of Ptolemy's big fingers. She didn't say anything.

Ptolemy noticed that her skin was actually as dark as his but it had a younger tone. He wanted to say this but the words fishtailed away, eluding his tongue.

"Niecie wanted me to come and make sure you was okay, Papa Grey."

He took a deep breath into his large nostrils and smiled.

"What is that smell?" Robyn asked him.

"I don't know. There's parts'a the house I cain't get inta any-more. The bathroom, half the kitchen. I ain't been deep in the bedroom since before what's-his-name, uh, Reggie, would come."

"You got a bedroom an' you sleepin' under a table?"

Ptolemy pulled his hand away from hers and tried to get up but couldn't on the first try. Robyn grabbed the corroded metal handles of her chair and moved next to him.

"I'm sorry, Mr. Grey. I didn't mean to embarrass you. I was just surprised, that's all." She took his hand again. "Niecie axed me to come here an' be wit' you."

"Niecie?" Ptolemy said, remembering as if for the first time in a long time the existence of his grandniece.

"Uh-huh. Because Hilly told her that you wouldn't let him in an' he wanted her to come here an' talk to you. But she's takin' care of Arthur an' Letisha an' the funeral an' all. She aksed him why you wouldn't let him in." Robyn squeezed Ptolemy's hand. "I knew why but I didn't tell her 'bout Hilly takin' your money 'cause Hilly live in that house too an' he's a thug. So I said I'd come ovah an' see about you an' she said okay."

"Niecie send you?"

"Uh-huh."

Robyn's face was only inches from Ptolemy's. Her eyes were asking for something, pleading with him. He didn't understand. He didn't know how to ask her what she wanted. But he knew that he would have done anything for that child. She was his child, his baby girl. She needed his protection.

"Niecie send you here to me?"

"Yes, Mr. Grey. Hilly said that you get these retirement checks an' that you would let me an' him cash 'em but I told him that I was not gonna steal from you."

"And then Niecie send you?"

"Yeah." Robyn sat back in her chair still holding his fingers.

"President Bush today said that America was a safer place than it was five years ago, when terrorists crashed two passenger jets into the World Trade Towers," a female news anchor said in between the silence of the new friends. "Democratic leaders in Congress disagreed . . ."

Don't go in there," Ptolemy said when Robyn opened the door to the bathroom.

"I got to, Mr. Grey," she said. "If I'ma be comin' here an' lookin' aftah you I got to have a toilet to go to."

While Ptolemy tried to think of some other way he could have Robyn's company and keep her out of the bathroom, she opened the door and went in.

"Oh my God," she said. "What is this?"

A large wad of blackened towels flew out from the doorway and landed with a thump on the small bare area of the crowded floor.

Ptolemy covered his face with his hands.

"You got suitcases in the bathtub," Robyn called out. "An' there's black stuff growin' in the commode. There's, oh my God, oh no . . ."

Ptolemy went to sit next to his big cabinet radio so that the woman singing opera would drown out the sounds and complaints coming from the girl.

As the singer professed what sounded like love in her sweet, high voice, Ptolemy allowed himself to drift. He was adrift in a boat in a city in Italy where all the streets were rivers. Coydog had told him about that town.

"Men stands at the back'a long boats with long sticks they push to the bottom to move 'em down the way," the old liar told him.

"You been there, Coydog?" the boy asked. Ptolemy remembered then, so many years later, listening to opera and ignoring Robyn, that he never called Coy Mr. McCann, which was his name. It was just mostly *boy* for Li'l Pea and *Coydog* for Coy.

"I been there in my mind," Coy McCann told the boy.

"How you do that?"

"Read," he said, stretching out the vowel sound like the singer did with her notes.

"How you learn that?"

"A, B, C," Coy said, wagging his forefinger like the white conductor did on odd Thursdays in the summer when the white people's marching band stopped in front of the town hall and performed old southern favorites.

That was the beginning of Li'l Pea's informal education. From A to L were accomplished that very afternoon.

After he could say all the letters, Coydog stole some paper from the country store and showed his student how to make the sounds with pencil lines.

"Ain't it wrong to be stealin' that paper from the white man's sto'?" Li'l Pea asked his aged friend.

"Wrong?" the wiry little man exclaimed. "Hell, it ain't wrong, it's a sin."

"But if you do a sin, ain't you goin' to hell?"

"That all depends, boy." Coy's long dark face cracked open at his mouth, showing his strong, stained teeth. "The Catholics profess that all you got to do is say you're sorry and the Lord will forgive. Other peoples say that Saint Peter's got a scale where they put all the bad you done on one side and all the good on t'other. An' if the good outweigh the bad they got a cot for you in heaven.

"So if I steal this here tablet an' pencils but then I teach you how to read an' write an' from there you invent a train that go from here to Venice . . ."

The German alto was warbling about love and Ptolemy remembered the name of the city with rivers for streets. He wanted to go to the bathroom and call the girl out to tell her what he'd accomplished but Coydog wouldn't stop talking.

". . . well, if I do that, then maybe the good beat out the bad."

Ptolemy recalled watching his friend study him with a calculating eye.

"But you know, boy," Coy said, "I don't believe any'a that."

"What do you believe?" the boy asked, the ABC's whirling around his head.

"I think that there's a long line up there in heaven an' yo' place in that line is predicted by what you done wrong. The worser thing you did puts you that much further to the back of the line. The people done the lesser is up toward the front.

"Now, the line start in downtown heaven and goes all the way to the barracks of hell because the two places is connected, just like good an' evil in the same man. So anyway, when you die you get a number that stands for what you did wrong. So if you had two mens, a black one and a white one, and the black man stole the white man's pig to feed his kids and then the white man shot the black man's son because he couldn't find the thief . . . well, the white man gonna get a much bigger number for murder than the black man will for stealin'. So, forgettin' any other misdemeanors, the white man will have a hotfoot at his place on line and the black man will hear harp music comin' from just up the way."

"But what about the boy?" Li'l Pea asked.

"What boy?"

"The one that the white man killed."

"Him?" Coydog said with a pained grimace. "They ain't no special numbahs for the victims. Just 'cause they grabbed you and chained you, just 'cause they beat you an' raped your sister don't mean a thing when it come to that line. God don't care what they did to you. What he care about is what you did."

Ptolemy was Li'l Pea looking up at the man who had just opened the alphabet for him, the man who stole for him, sacrificing himself to the judgment of the great beyond.

"Mr. Grey?"

The newscaster was talking about a criminal in a cornfield somewhere, a woman was singing sweetly, and his name came in between the two.

"Mr. Grey."

Looking up from his place on the floor in Coy's room, no, in his own apartment, looking up, he saw Robyn, her short skirt hiked up even higher, her hands holding unidentifiable gelatinous masses of blackened rot.

"Uh-huh," he said.

"Are you lookin' at my legs, Mr. Grey?" she asked with surprise but no anger in her tone.

"Yes, ma'am."

"You think I'm pretty?"

"I think pretty is your ugly little sister," he said, repeating a compliment that he'd heard Coydog use a thousand times.

It worked on Robyn just like it had on all the young women that Coy had courted.

"That's sweet. You a playah, huh, Mr. Grey?"

"What's that in your hands?" he asked.

"It come out from under the sink an' in the bathtub. It's a mess. How do you go to the bathroom at all in there? The toilet don't even flush."

"For number one I use a coffee can and I . . ." He hesitated. "I pour it down the sink."

"An' what about numbah two?" Robyn asked, neither ashamed nor disgusted as far as the old man could tell.

"I usually wait for Reggie to come by. He usually take me to Frank's Coffee Shop for breakfast or lunch an' aftah I get my coffee I go."

"So you ain't been to a toilet since you was at the wake?" she asked.

"I guess not."

The girl was staring at the old man while he inspected the floor.

"You really let this place fall apart," Robyn said.

"I'm sorry 'bout that. It was just that when Sensie passed I stopped doin' things, movin' things around, makin' 'em bettah."

"Do the sink work in the kitchen?" Robyn asked.

"Uh-huh. There's stuff all around it, but it works."

He was having trouble leaving Coydog's lectures behind him so that he could give the girl and her lovely strong legs the proper attention. He wanted to get up on his feet but there wasn't enough strength in his arms to lift him.

While Ptolemy thought about standing up, Robyn went into the kitchen. He began listening to the singing again but there came a loud crash and the old man found the strength to push himself up and grab on to the ledge at the top of his console radio.

He went through the kitchen door and found the girl throwing piles of pots down from the sink onto the floor. Hundreds of roaches of all sizes and breeds were scuttling madly from the wild woman's attacks. The black gunk from her hands was coming off on the pots and pans and and even the dishes that she was putting on the floor.

"Stop," Ptolemy said, but Robyn didn't even slow down.

"I can't, Mr. Grey. I gotta wash my hands and clean this house and get rid'a all these roaches an' shit."

"But you the one messin' it all up."

"It's already a mess, Mr. Grey. It's already messed up," Robyn said. "Look at all the junk just piled up and moldin'. Look at all these bugs."

"They only out 'cause you th'owin' everything around," the old man argued.

By this time the sink was clear enough that Robyn could turn on the water and wash her hands.

"Oh no," Ptolemy said, feeling as if maybe the walls would fall down or a fire would erupt from the stove. "This is bad."

Turning to him, smiling, her hands dripping because there was no dry towel, Robyn said, "We have to clean up this place, Mr. Grey. You can't live like this with a house full'a garbage and bugs."

"But it's too much. Too much stuff. We should just leave it and go to the store. I don't have to cook."

Robyn whipped her hands back and forth through the air to get off the excess water and then came to Ptolemy and put her arms around him. She hugged him to her chest and put her cold hand on the top of his bald head.

"Shhh," she whispered.

65

He realized then that he was crying.

"It's all right, baby," Robyn said. "I can clean up all'a this mess in a week or two. I could have your whole house set up for you. Don't you want your house clean and neat? Don't you want a nice bathroom and a bed to sleep in?"

"No."

Robyn moved back a few inches, still holding on with her face there close to his.

"Why not?"

"My things," he whined.

"But most of this stuff is just old junk an' trash."

Ptolemy lifted up his hands, resting them on the girl's chest beseechingly.

"In between the garbage and the trash is all the things I have. Keys and lockets, pictures and money . . . treasure. One time Reggie tried to clean up but he just took a armful'a stuff an' th'owed in the thrash. There coulda been anything in the middle'a that."

"I won't do that," Robyn said with the solemnity of a much older woman. "We will go through every newspaper and rag, lookin' for all your li'l trinkets. Okay? I won't th'ow away nuthin' before we go through it."

Ptolemy realized where his hands were and pulled them back to his own chest.

"I'm sorry," he said.

"Don't worry, Mr. Grey. I know you don't mean no harm."

"Really?"

"Of course I do," she said. "You a sweet old man. There used to be a man like you lived next do' to me and my mama before my mama died. He used to give me peaches in the season. He said that

66

I was a smart little girl and I needed peaches to make me smarter. It didn't mean nuthin' but it was nice.

"You still got that money Hilly got you, Mr. Grey?"

He nodded and smiled, feeling gratitude for no reason he could have explained.

"Well then, get your wallet and show me where the sto' is. We gonna get you some soap and steel wool and a mop an' broom. We gonna get a big box of trash bags an' shake out ev'ry newspaper, rag, and old shirt until we done emptied out the whole bathroom."

On the walk to the market Ptolemy swiveled his head from side to side again and again.

"What's wrong, Mr. Grey?" Robyn asked him. "You lookin' for somebody?"

"Melinda Hogarth."

"Who's that? Your girlfriend?"

"She the one gonna rob me if she sees me."

"Rob you? You mean you think she gonna try an' take yo' money?"

Ptolemy nodded, feeling disgraced by what felt like a lifetime of weakness and fear.

"Don't you worry, Mr. Grey," Robyn said. "I got me a six-inch knife in my purse and I know to use it. My mama told me that I always had to have a li'l sumpin' extra 'cause I'm short and a girl. You know I stick a mothahfuckah in a minute they try and mess with either one'a us."

It was her grimness that gave Ptolemy confidence. He glanced up at the sky, thinking, *This is everybody's ceiling. This blue roof belongs to me just as much as anyone else.* They were words he'd heard along the way somewhere. He remembered them, and they held him like an anchor, like that young girl, that Robyn, held his hand.

They didn't see Melinda Hogarth that day. Robyn spent seventy-three dollars of Ptolemy's retirement check on cleaning supplies. They stopped by a McDonald's hamburger place and had french fries and chicken salads. After two cups of black coffee Ptolemy spent half an hour in the restaurant's men's room.

All afternoon Robyn cleared out, scrubbed, and rinsed off Ptolemy's bathroom. She brought out every rag, box, towel, and doodad, showing it to her guardian's great-uncle before throwing it almost all away in big black garbage bags. There were stains on her little black dress, and her hair was getting wild. But she laughed a lot and seemed to enjoy reporting to Ptolemy.

"Do you want this old toothbrush, sir?" she asked with a knowing smile.

He had to study everything she brought to him. At first he didn't know what it was he was looking at, and then, when he identified the object, he'd get lost trying to remember where it came from.

"That bresh was Sensie's, I'm pretty sure," he said. "She got it at the Woolworth's . . . No. Maybe not. I don't know where she got it at."

"But do you want to keep it?" Robyn asked again.

"I guess not. No. You can th'ow it away . . . I guess."

Hours and hours Robyn cleaned, taking breaks now and then to discuss bits of detritus found in Ptolemy's bathroom. She filled five thirty-nine-gallon lawn bags with the debris from just that one room. She scrubbed and swept and mopped, and then scrubbed and swept and mopped again.

Once she found an old sepia photograph way down under the sink. It was the picture of a huge brown woman holding the hand of a skinny, frowning little boy.

"Who is this, Mr. Grey?" she asked, coming out to see him.

Ptolemy had set his folding stool right at the door so that he could see everything the teenager was doing.

"Oh, don't throw that away. No, no."

He took the crumbling photograph in his hand. It had once been five inches by eight but now the corners and sides had been eaten away by damp rot. The woman's face was water-stained, as was the bottom half of the boy's body. He held the picture gently, as if holding a wounded creature.

"That's my mother," he whispered, "and her son . . . me."

"Let me put that away someplace safe so we can take it to the drug sto' copycat to see if they can make a good print of it," she said, taking the fragile memory from the man's thick black fingers.

After a while Ptolemy stopped watching Robyn's every move. He could see that she knew what was important and that she looked into every corner and fold.

"Come on in, Mr. Grey," Robyn called in the early evening.

The bathroom was sparkling, neat and clean. The blue tile floor was eroded in places, and there were stains and dings on the blue porcelain sink, but the bathtub was glistening white and the walls were a lovely if faded aqua.

"There's water damage on the ceiling," she said, "and I can't wear no dress the next time I come. And look . . ."

Robyn pushed the white ceramic handle on the toilet and the stained commode flushed for the first time in many years.

"You fixed the toilet?" he asked. "You must be like a plumber too."

"No, I just cleaned it out and turned on the water, that's all. It worked once it was clean."

This made sense to Ptolemy. He went to sit on the edge of the tub and ran his fingers over the smooth white porcelain.

"There's some leaks and stuff, but we can get somebody to fix all that."

"Landlord won't fix nuthin'," Ptolemy said, peering closely enough at the porcelain to see the barest reflection of his dark face in the deep whiteness.

"I gotta go, Mr. Grey. It's gettin' late."

"I never seen nuthin' like this," he said. "I don't even remembah half of what it looked like in here. How did you know?"

"I jes' cleaned. But I gotta go. Now you can go to the bathroom in your own house. I'll come back day after tomorrow and we'll start on your bedroom."

"Oh no," Ptolemy said. There was a big black moth fluttering in the center of his heart. "No. Best to leave well enough alone."

"You need a bed, baby. A place where you can sleep up off the flo'."

"No."

"Uh-huh," she sang. "Day aftah tomorrah I'm'a come back and we gonna tackle the bedroom together. Don't worry, I won't th'ow out nuthin' you don't want me to."

"But this is enough, don't you think?" Ptolemy asked, still running a hand over the cool ceramic rim.

"I got to go, Mr. Grey. Okay?"

"Okay."

At the open door of the apartment Robyn and Ptolemy stood face-to-face. They both seemed a little confused. Finally she put her arms around him and kissed his cheek, after which he put his hands on either side of her face and curled his fingers like clawless paws.

Ptolemy couldn't speak because he had more than one thing to say. The first was that he didn't want her to go into the bedroom. He didn't need a bed. He didn't want to be in that room, not ever. But he also wanted Robyn to come back and be there with him. Maybe she could clean the bathroom again.

She kissed him a second time and then walked away down the hall. When she got to the front door of the building she turned and waved before going out the door. He stood there for long minutes with the news and medieval recorder music behind him. He watched that closed door with many people on his mind: Robyn, and Coydog, and Reggie, who had been coming to his house for more than five years.

Then Reggie the man was standing next him in the hall but next to them was Reggie the corpse in the whitewashed pine coffin. The children were on the floor. Ptolemy wanted to call to them but couldn't remember their names.

"Children shouldn't be in the room wit' dead peoples, Reggie," he said into the empty corridor but also, in his mind, he was in the small bedroom of Niecie's house where the dead man lay.

The front door to the hall came open and a woman the color of dark redwood came in carrying a bundle of envelopes and magazines. She looked familiar.

"Mr. Grey?" she said, walking toward him.

He usually slammed the door and threw the locks when someone came in the building but this time Ptolemy hesitated.

"Miss Dartman?"

Approaching him, the tall colored woman said, "I haven't seen your face in almost two years, Mr. Grey. Sometimes I be droppin' the mail in your slot and I think, 'Maybe he's dead in there.'"

"Not me. Old Man Death done lost my numbah, I think."

The phrase was used by Coy McCann when someone hadn't seen him for a while and assumed that he'd died. Almost all of Ptolemy's automatic coherent sentences came from his old friend Coydog.

The tall woman smiled and handed Ptolemy a bundle of mail.

"I was outta town seein' my brother for the last few days so I didn't get the mail. Maybe I should give you back the key so that nice grandnephew of yours could collect it for you."

"Reggie got hisself killed."

"No!" Miss Falona Dartman cried. "How did that happen?"

"They lynched him. A mob drived by and kilt him."

"I'm so sorry, Mr. Grey. He was . . ." she said, and then sighed. "He was such a nice young man. Oh no. What are they doin' to our young black men?"

"Killin' 'em," Ptolemy said. "What they always done."

"Who's gonna come take care of you now, Mr. Grey? You can't be here all by yourself."

"My great-granddaughter Robyn come from down Alabama,

or someplace, to he'p me out. She cleaned up my bafroom today. Worked all day at it. All day long she cleaned and th'ew away garbage. But I'ma miss Reggie."

"Was he married?"

Ptolemy nodded. "An' they had some kids."

"Oh no."

Ptolemy placed the mail in a neat stack on Robyn's lawn chair. Then he went into the bathroom, put the top lid down on the commode, and sat there. Robyn had brought new lightbulbs and screwed them into the seven sockets above the sink. The light was so white in there that it made him laugh. He was happy sitting on the toilet and watching the bathtub.

Now and then a curious roach would dart in and then scurry away again, daunted by the brightness of the room. Four times he went to the sink and turned the corroded spigots, just to see the water run. There was a leak at the base of the hot-water faucet, but the water dripped into the sink, causing no problem.

At midnight he took a shower. The nozzle could only muster a few sprays but it was enough to wash his body clean. He used an old T-shirt for a towel and another one for a bathrobe.

That night when he wrapped himself in the thin blanket under the south table Ptolemy had a feeling of giddiness that kept him up for what seemed to him like hours. He thought about Robyn's ability to clean and polish and throw out things without hurting him or those things that he needed to keep. She was better than Reggie at understanding what was important.

A flute was playing on the all-night classical program and the newsmen and -women droned on. Ptolemy had trained himself not to listen when he was in his bed, but this night the background racket was a bother to him.

On other nights, before Robyn had come, Ptolemy shared space with the music and news. They were as much a part of the room as he was. His mind was like an open field over which these sounds and opinions passed unhindered. But on that night Ptolemy was thinking about the tragedy of Reggie and the blessing of Robyn. She was an orphan taken in and protected by, by, by Niecie. And the boy and baby girl were orphans too.

The flute scratched at these thoughts. The news commentators seemed to be trying to talk him out of the value of Reggie and Robyn, the boy and his baby sister. In the dimness he cursed the radio and the flittering shadows cast by the TV. Rage opened up in Ptolemy's breast. The anger took over his mind like a swarm of biting fire ants. And then, when he was angry enough to break something, the passion ebbed away, leaving that old familiar open field.

It reminded him of a portal at the end of a long corridor behind the pulpit of Liberty Baptist Church. When he was a child and the minister's sermon went overlong, he'd sneak away from the pews and walk down the long hall to that doorway. It was always ajar, emitting a cool breeze year-round, even in the summer heat. There was almost no light in there, but Li'l Pea could see the dim image of a white cross in the depths of the chamber. It was leaning against something dark and massive.

The child called Pity would walk up to the threshold of the sacred room and strain his eyes, trying to glean its tale.

Remembering this important, spiritual moment in his history, Ptolemy Grey drifted off into sleep.

In the dream he was trying to pull Reggie up out of his coffin, to shake his shoulders until the boy woke up. All around the casket were women seated in white folding chairs and dressed beautifully, mournfully, with hats and handkerchiefs and black gloves. Robyn and Niecie, Letta Golding and Shirley Wring and many others whom he knew but could not remember their names—all of them watched him. They hummed as he beseeched the boy to get up and walk and live. Beyond the casket was a window that looked out on a green lawn where the children Arthur and Letisha played. They laughed and chased each other. "Fall down! Fall down," they sang.

In the morning Ptolemy ate one of the small pop-top cans of tuna that Robyn had brought back with the cleaning supplies. He visited his bathroom for over an hour, trying to think of how he could keep Robyn from going into the bedroom. He closed the bathroom door to keep out the sad viola solo and weather report. Then he sat on the commode, rubbing his hands and looking at the aqua walls.

Sitting there, he experienced what he called eternity. It was whenever he was in one place by himself and didn't have to go anywhere else or answer to anybody.

"A moment like that," Coy McCann had said, "like when you

fishin' or after you done made love with your woman and you smokin' a cigarette while she sleep . . . that's the kinda time that's just so wonderful. That's when you can think because you ain't hungry or lustful or in it with somebody wanna waste yo' time. You could be just sittin' there by yourself and you see what you need to do, the way God do in eternity."

These words came back to Ptolemy decades after Coydog was murdered and gone.

Ptolemy knew exactly what he had to do.

On the sink in the kitchen was the flimsy little box that held the plastic lawn bags Robyn used to throw out the detritus of Ptolemy's bathroom.

When Ptolemy picked up the box a huge gutter-roach fell out and onto the sink. The black and brown and russet-red insect flipped from his back onto his legs and stood there on an old plate that Ptolemy hadn't used or cleaned in over a decade. The old man slapped his hand down hard on the bug, but when he pulled back, the roach leaped in the air, spread his beetle-like wings, and flew toward the back of the kitchen.

Watching the strange bug flapping its way toward the towering boxes on his porch brought about a flutter in Ptolemy's chest. His breath came quickly and he had to squat down so that he didn't fall. He could feel the sweat sprouting on his brow and between his fingers. A painful burp brought the strong flavor of tuna up into his throat.

Ptolemy concentrated on the pain in his left knee.

"The great man say that life is pain," Coydog had said over

eighty-five years before. "That mean if you love life, then you love the hurt come along wit' it. Now, if that ain't the blues, I don't know what is."

The ache in Ptolemy's knee felt deep and bloody. He ignored the quick breath and racing heart. All he knew was the pain and Coydog's words.

"Why you always hang around that old man?" Titus Grey had asked his son on the porch one morning when the boy was going off to meet Coy to go fishing.

"He teachin' me my ABC's."

"He don't know no alphabet."

"Yeah, he do."

"Are you contradictin' me, boy?" Titus asked.

"No, sir."

"Then put down that pole and come on with me up in the woods. This is yam season and you don't have time to be a fool."

Hearing these words in his *yester-ear*, Ptolemy stood up straight. His knee and chest were fine. The huge roach was still flying, batting its head against the small patch of window that was visible above the big boxes on the back porch. Music played and some man was talking about something far away, and Ptolemy went about searching for what he needed under the sink.

After a while he forgot what he was looking for. And so he went back to the living room and stood at the bedroom door, trying to remember what was so clear to him in the bathroom, before his war with the cockroach.

Finally he decided that the only thing to do was open the door to see if there was a clue inside.

The bedroom was dark, as it had been years before when he

closed it up in order to forget about his life with Sensia. She was dead and buried but that room had been her memorial. She was put to rest in a whitewashed pine coffin like the one Niecie had for Reggie. Niecie's mother, Ptolemy remembered, had gotten Sensie's coffin and put her in the same room where they had Reggie for his wake . . .

There was a gray tarp covering the contents of Ptolemy's abandoned bedroom. It loomed like a shifting desert under a cloudy, moonless night. Ptolemy stared at the fabric, remembering his true love. Thinking about her, he remembered what it was that he needed.

He went back into the kitchen and started pulling out furniture. Two small benches, a stone-top chrome-stalk table, a walnut tabletop and various boxes, bags, satchels, and one Hopalong Cassidy cowboy lunchbox that Reggie's father had when he was a child.

After dragging all that junk into the living room, Ptolemy went into the closet and got his oldest possession: an oak yardstick that Coydog had given him when he was only five.

"This here yardstick will be the measure of your life, boy," the old man had said.

"The what?"

"As long as you keep this here span wit' you, I will be wit' you."

Ptolemy had never broken that three-foot rule. The name in red letters, BLUTCHER'S BUTCHER MARKET, had mostly rubbed off. The numbers and most of the increment lines had faded also. There was a chip at one corner of the dark wood and dents and gouges throughout. But Coydog's gifts to Li'l Pea, both gifts, he had kept through the years.

With his stick in hand Ptolemy yanked open the door under the sink. He stuck the yardstick in there and pulled out the strong spiders' webs laden with greasy dust. After rubbing the webs off on an old curtain that lay in a forgotten corner, Ptolemy reached in and took out the old steel ice hook he had from seventy years before. It was a vicious-looking device used to hook twenty-pound blocks of ice in the days before refrigeration was available in poor homes. Ptolemy and Peter Brock worked on a truck, driving up and down city streets delivering ice to the customers of Brock's father, Minister Brock.

"What church your daddy preach at?" Ptolemy asked Peter on their first day.

"He ain't no preacher," Peter said. "My grandfather named him that so if you used his first name you had to respect him anyway."

With his full strength Ptolemy swung down on the big plastic tarp covering Sensia's room. The triple hook sunk deep. Using both hands, the ninety-one-year-old man began to pull. At first there was no give. It was as if he were pulling on the knob of a locked door. But Ptolemy Grey would not give up. He twisted his shoulders for torque, let his weight work against the heft of the covering. He pulled and yanked and tugged in staccato snatches.

All the while there was a symphony playing and a sports report spouting meaningless numbers and names.

Ptolemy didn't listen. He went down to his knees, using all the strength in his spindly shoulders. He was about to take a rest when the plastic sheet begin to give. He stood up and away from the door, using both his strength and weight, and the tarp began to flow outward from the long-abandoned room.

The dry plastic gushed into the crowded living room like a huge reptilian tongue. Ptolemy pulled the hook out and sank it in again, dragging more of the gray sheet from the bedroom.

Again and again he dug his fang-shaped hook into the tarp, the plastic hissing like lizard skin against itself and along the floor. Ptolemy, sweating and laughing, his heart beating fast, pulled the entire covering from the bedroom. He fell to the floor under the mist of dust that had been raised. He hacked and laughed, sneezed and chuckled, rubbed his irritated eyes and tittered to himself.

"I did it," he announced triumphantly. "I pulled that bastard outta there."

For a while Ptolemy Grey lay there, half on the floor and half on the dusty gray tarp. He was breathing hard and laughing to himself, remembering people and things randomly, haphazardly. There was the time he and Keith Low shoveled coal on a steam train from Jackson to Memphis to pay their fare.

After Coydog had died Pity stayed in bed for two weeks. Sheriff Walters had come to ask Li'l Pea what he knew, but he didn't say anything except that he didn't know anything. It was all he could do to keep from crying while looking at the ugly blue veins that crossed back and forth over the sheriff's nose.

"You know that I'm here to find them that killed your uncle, now, don't ya, boy?" the middle-aged, portly white man asked.

"Yessuh."

"You know that it's crime to lynch a man no mattah what color he is?"

"Yessuh," Ptolemy remembered saying while he caught his breath on the dirty floor, half on and half off the gray tarp.

"All you gots to do is tell me who did it and I won't tell nobody you did."

Walters had closed the door to Ptolemy's back bedroom but the boy knew that his father and mother were on the other side with his sisters and little brother.

"I don't know nuthin', Sheriff Walters," Ptolemy said.

"Then why you snivelin' an' lookin' at the floor?"

"Because my friend is daid, suh. He daid an' he was the person I loved the most in the whole world."

Ptolemy got to his feet in his apartment on La Jolla Place across the street from the laundry and Chow Fun's Chinese restaurant and takeout. The tears falling from his eyes onto the plastic tarp sounded like solitary raindrops on a lonely dark afternoon.

Moving toward the door, he saw the piles of clothes and photo albums, chairs, rolled-up sheets, covers, and carpets; there were broken straw baskets and suitcases, paperback books tied into bundles, bottles, dirty silk flowers, paintings, balls of twine, tape, and packages that had never been opened. Over it all swarmed insects of various kinds. Ants, silverfish, roaches, beetles, spiders, and even a few flying bugs. A mouse or two leaped from box to bed or floor to basket.

A fast piano piece was playing and 111 people had died in Baghdad. Ptolemy remembered Coydog telling about Ali Baba and the Forty Thieves, and then he remembered the old man with a noose around his neck, standing on tiptoes on a wooden box that wasn't tall enough to keep him from choking a little; and all the white men and boys standing around, laughing; and then the man pouring kerosene on Coy's feet and lighting it so that the old man couldn't stand still to keep from hanging himself; and then Coy dancing in the air, his feet and pants on fire and all the white people laughing. Coy's head moved from side to side and his tongue stuck out like he had something caught in his throat that he was trying to cough up.

Li'l Pea looked away.

Ptolemy slammed the door on the teeming, swarming insects and rodents. He pressed the edges on the tarp against the gap at the bottom so that the bugs couldn't get into the rest of the house. Then he went into the bathroom, closed the door, pressed towels into the cracks, and turned the lights on. He filled the tub with hot water and stood at the ready to throw it on bugs or lynchers or ghosts if they should come.

Ptolemy didn't know how much time had passed. Robyn had wound his clock and it was the kind that you had to prime only once every two weeks. The right time was just on the other side of the bathroom door, but Ptolemy couldn't bring himself to go out there. All his worst memories were out there: Sensie dead and her grave covered with maggots and worms. Now all he had was the dripping water of the bathroom sink to count the time away. He sat on the floor, watching the towels, to be sure that no maggot or worm found its way to him the way his father said that the worms made their ways into Coydog's eyes after his brother, Lupo, had cut him down and buried him in a pauper's grave behind the barbershop without even a stone to mark his passage.

He sat upon the tile floor, counting the drips and thinking about Reggie and Coy; both men lynched and buried and made food for bugs.

Whenever Ptolemy got hungry he would drink from the faucet. After a while the hunger went away. Through the door he could hear soft music and voices that he couldn't understand. Underneath these calming sounds he thought he could make out the scuttling of bugs and the titter of rats. If he paid too much attention to these noises his heart pumped harder and his head got light. Sometimes, when he got too frightened, he'd fall asleep and then wake up from a dream with imagined worms trying to crawl their way into his tightly shut eyes.

Ptolemy had no idea how much time had passed. He sat in the bright room listening, feeling light-headed now and again, and drinking water to kill his hunger pangs. The classical music was broken, tinkly. The news reporters made no sense. Reggie and Coydog were dead, and that girl would never find her way to him.

"You ain't got to be afraid'a nuthin', boy," Coydog would tell him. "We all gonna die. We all gonna get some hurt. I mean, when a woman bring a child outta her big belly it hurt like a bastid. But that girl ain't nevah been happier than when she hurt like that."

"Why she be so happy?" Li'l Pea asked.

" 'Cause she know that baby gonna be the love of her life, and that would be worf ten times the pain."

At first Ptolemy was soothed when he thought about his old friend and mentor. But then his thoughts drifted back to that last fiery dance, and then to little Maude Petit. And when he thought about his loved ones being lost to fire his heart thundered and he fell asleep to dream the dreams of the dead.

Papa Grey?" a voice called.

Ptolemy was in his coffin. It was pitch black and the worms were wriggling between his fingers and toes. He opened his eyes, expecting to see nothing, but instead he found himself in the white bathtub under brilliant light. Someone was knocking at the bathroom door.

He remembered draining the tub and lying down in it the way Reggie was laid to rest in his pine box.

"Papa Grey?" she called again.

"Who is it?"

"It's Robyn, Papa Grey. I took the keys to your front do' but the bathroom do' don't have a key."

"Robyn?"

"Yeah. Open the do'," she said.

The old man fumbled with the lock for a minute or more. He panicked once or twice, fearing that he was locked in, but he got the door open at last. Robyn was standing there in dark-blue jeans and a light-blue T-shirt. There was a yellow ribbon in her hair and big bone-white earrings dangled on either side of her jaw.

"I died," Ptolemy Grey said. "I died and was in my grave with worms and Coydog McCann. I was dead and gone like Sensie and Reggie and other names that I cain't even remembah no mo'."

Robyn put her arms around Ptolemy's neck.

"It was a dream," she said, cocking her head to the side and humming with the words.

"No, no, no," he said, pushing his savior away. "It wasn't no dream. Come on out here in the room and I can prove it to ya."

"What's this big plastic sheet out here, Uncle?" she asked. "It's dirty."

"It don't mattah," he said. "Just push it aside and, and, and pull up some chairs."

Robyn did as he requested, frowning at the dust rising from the faded tarp. She sneezed and got his stool and her lawn chair set up in front of the door.

"Mr. Grey, can I turn off the TV and the radio so I can hear you?"

"Sure. I don't care," he said.

They sat down facing each other. Ptolemy's eyes were bright. There was a grin on his face. He took the child's left hand in his and gazed deeply, even thoughtfully, into her eyes.

Robyn stared back, seeing a face that she knew with a different man inside.

"Some things," Ptolemy said. "Some things is in the world and in our hearts at the same time."

He went silent, waiting for more words to come, the words and the ideas behind them that were coming slowly but steadily from his mind.

Robyn nodded, her head like a pump priming a well.

"I had a tarp," Ptolemy said, "this one right here, over all the things in my bedroom. All the books and carpets and clothes and glass jewelry. That was Sensia's room, the wife that I loved the most . . ."

Pitypapa Grey was aware of the silence in the room. The music had been hushed and the men and women talking about crime and killing were quiet at last. It occurred to him that before now, before this moment, the content of his mind was the radio and the TV, that he was just as empty as an old cracked pecan shell—the meat dried up and crumbled away.

"Papa Grey?" Robyn asked.

"Yeah, baby?"

"You just sittin' there."

"What was I sayin'?"

"That some things is in the world and in our hearts at the same time."

He looked at her lovely young face and let the words wash over his parched mind.

"Yeah," he said with a smile. "That tarp. That tarp was like the pall in my mind."

"The what?"

"The pall. It's a shroud what undertakers put over the dead until they get put in the coffin."

"And this plastic sheet is like that?" Robyn asked.

"It was over that room, and at the same time it was in my head, coverin' up all the things that I done forgot, or forgot me."

The idea turned in on itself and Ptolemy lost his way. He brought his hands to his head and tried to remember. It was all there but not quite clear. Things jumbled together: Coydog's funeral next to Artie and Letisha; the iron-banded oak box with its treasures and promises, its curses and death——hidden but still a danger; Reggie laughing and eating french fries in the sunlight through the restaurant window.

Robyn took his hands from his face.

"Look at me, Mr. Grey," she said.

There were tears in his eyes.

"I got to get my thoughts straight, girl. I got to do sumpin' before that damn pall is th'owed ovah me."

"When's the last time you et?" she asked.

Ptolemy understood the question but the answer was the white tail of a deer flitting through the trees. He shook his head and wondered.

"First thing we gotta do is get you sumpin' to eat, Uncle," she said.

"I had a can'a tuna day before, day before yesterday."

The cheeseburger tasted good, better than any food he'd had in a very long time. They sat in the window seat at the fast-food restaurant, watching the black people and brown people walking up and down the sidewalk, driving up and down the street. The faces didn't confuse him anymore but he was still confused. Not so much that he'd get lost in Coydog's lessons down near the mouth of the Tickle River, where they had alligators that would carry off little boys and girls sometimes. He'd remember the purple skies of fall evenings without getting inside them, but he couldn't recall where he'd put the treasure; he couldn't put words to the one lesson that Coydog taught that he needed to know.

"What you do in school?" Ptolemy asked Robyn.

"I'm not in school right now, Uncle."

"I know. I know that. I mean, what you *gonna* do when you go back again?"

"Maybe be a nurse or a schoolteacher."

"Why not a doctor?" the old man asked.

Robyn stared at her newly adopted relative.

"Bein' a nurse is good," she said.

"A doctor is a king and the nurse is like the five of hearts. You at least a queen, Reggie, I mean Robyn. I'm sorry."

"Don't be sorry," she said.

Robyn put her fingers on his forearm. "We got to bomb your house, Uncle," she said.

That day they went to the bank to cash two checks that Ptolemy had received in the mail. The old man was looking from face to face, examining each one.

"You lookin' for somebody, Uncle?"

"Double-u ara eye en gee," he said.

"What?"

"Double-u ara eye en gee. That's a friend'a mines."

"If you say so."

They bought groceries at Big City and insect bombs at Harold and Rod Hardware. There were seven of them like Roman candles held up by Popsicle-stick crosses, which were bonded by rough dabs of white glue.

"You only need one for every one and a half rooms in the house," the salesman told Robyn.

He was a redheaded young black man with pinkish-brown skin and big brown freckles. Ptolemy wondered how many white men had been that boy's forefathers. This seemed very important to him, but then the thought got lost in the young people's conversation.

"How long before we can go back in?" Robyn asked.

"Twenty-four hours, no matter what," he said. "Then you go in an' open the windahs, let it air out a hour or two and it'a be fine."

"You got windahs, Mr. Grey?" the girl asked.

"Out on the back porch. Sensie an' me'd open the back windahs and the front do' in summah an' it was bettah than air conditionin'."

"What's your name?" the freckled clerk asked Robyn.

"Chili Norman," she said easily. "I live in that green house ovah on Morton."

"You gotta phone?"

"Uh-uh," she said coyly. Smiling as she did so. "I'll take two'a those little electric fans you got on sale. And I'ma need some wide tape too."

"How come you don't have no phone?" the goofy boy asked.

"Money."

"Could I come by and knock on the door?"

"Ain't no law against that," the lying child said.

From there they went to Baker's Inn on Crenshaw. It took three busses and more than an hour to get there. They had to walk six blocks at either end of the long ride. At first Ptolemy carried one of the three bags they had, but he started slowing down and Robyn took his load too.

They paid for two nights at the motel in cash up front and left the groceries in the room. There was a small refrigerator for the milk and beer and butter they'd purchased.

"You can stay here if you want, Uncle Grey. I just got one thing to do and then I'll come back."

Ptolemy looked around the motel room. It smelled of chemicals, and the two beds looked like the slabs in the undertaker's room where he swept up the dust that collected around the dead. The ceiling was low and he was again reminded of a coffin.

"How long you be gone?" he asked.

"I don't know. Couple'a hours at least."

"I'll come with ya. No need just to sit in here. I don't even know how to work the TV."

Robyn carried the fans and the insect bombs in three white plastic bags. She and Ptolemy didn't talk much on the walk to the busses or on the rides. Young men talked to her. Older men did too. She smiled at them and told lies about her name and address. She gave them phone numbers but Ptolemy didn't think that they belonged to Niecie.

On the last bus a young man came to sit opposite them. He was dark-skinned and pretty the way young men can be. He was no more than thirty and could have passed for twenty-two.

"Mr. Grey?" he said after staring for a moment.

Ptolemy looked at the young man. His face was familiar, but that was nothing new; almost all faces looked both familiar and strange to him.

"I'm Beckford," the man said, "Reggie's friend."

"I know you," Robyn said then. "You used to come by on Thursdays when you worked on that fishin' boat. You smelled bad."

"Robyn, right?" Beckford said. "The cute little girl Reggie's aunt took in."

As the bus turned, the young man stood up and let the gentle centrifugal pull swing him across the aisle until he was on the seat next to Ptolemy.

"Yeah," he said as if someone had just asked him a question. "I was up in Oakland for the last two years or so. I remember one time me an' Reggie went to your house, Mr. Grey, and you bought us a pizza. How is Reggie?"

"He daid," Robyn said, showing no emotion. "They kilt him in a drive-by not two blocks from his house."

"No," Beckford said. "Who did?"

Robyn shook her head.

"Damn." Beckford sat back in his seat. "Damn. Why anybody wanna kill Reggie? He ain't in no gang. He ain't mess wit' nobody."

The bus driver hit the brakes and Ptolemy swayed into the young man's shoulder. In that moment he was back in the little room that Coydog called home behind the colored barbershop. Coydog was talking and through Ptolemy the words came out. "Don't worry, boy," he said. "Man do sumpin' wrong, man pays for it. There ain't a surer truth on God's green earth."

"Niecie still live at the same place?" Beckford asked.

"Uh-huh," Robyn said, and then she added, "We gettin' out here."

She helped Ptolemy to his feet and they went toward the exit.

"Nice to see you, Mr. Grey, Robyn," Beckford called after them.

The old man waved. Robyn was holding his other hand and watching his feet while negotiating her three bags and so did not speak to Beckford.

That was a nice boy," Ptolemy said as they walked toward his house.

"Yeah," Robyn replied, "we'll see."

"Pete!" a familiar voice bellowed from across the street.

Melinda Hogarth came at the man and girl like a freight train that had jumped its track at full speed. She had a broad grin on her face and her mannish hands were balled into big hammer-like fists.

"Oh no," Ptolemy whispered. His sphincter tightened and his chest ached. He didn't run but he wanted to. He didn't fall to his knees but his legs shivered.

"That her?" Robyn asked when Melinda was half the way to them, roaring in the middle of the street like a wild beast that just caught the scent of blood.

Ptolemy nodded and Robyn moved to stand between them. The teenager turned so that her left shoulder was pointed at the approaching juggernaut. Melinda was wearing blue jeans under a faded navy-blue dress that came down to her knees. She was two and a half times the size of Robyn, the color of a wild bull, and three sheets to the wind. Robyn could smell the alcohol when the woman got near.

"Move out my way, heifer," Melinda Hogarth cried, and then Robyn swung, starting from her hip. The bag holding both of the electric fans moved in a small quick arc, slamming the drunken mugger in the center of her forehead. The first blow set Melinda back a step. The second put her right knee on the ground. The big woman was on both knees and an elbow, screaming, by the fourth swing. That was when the bag tore open and the broken fans went flying.

Robyn reached into her shoulder bag. Ptolemy put a hand on her forearm. He didn't have the strength to stop her, but Robyn stopped anyway. She turned her face to the elder.

At first sight she looked like a demon to the old man. The slants of her eyes were reminiscent of horns, and her teeth showed without making a smile. And then she changed. She was the sweet girl again, a mild worry showing in her eyes and on her mouth.

"Don't worry, Uncle," she said. "I know what I'm doin'."

Ptolemy took a step backward and Robyn pulled out her six-inch knife.

"Look up here at me, bitch!" Robyn commanded.

The pile of quivering womanhood made sounds that were like the snuffling cries of a wounded animal.

Robyn kicked Melinda Hogarth's fat shoulder.

"Look at me or I'ma stab you up," Robyn promised.

Melinda threw herself away from the threat, landing on her backside. Her eyes were wide with the fear and the possibility of death.

"What's your name?" Robyn said, moving closer.

The prostrate woman was too frightened to speak.

"Tell me your name or I'ma cut yo' th'oat right here."

"M-m-m-melinda."

"Linda," Robyn said. "Linda, if I evah see you talkin' to my uncle again, if he evah tell me you even said a word to him, I'ma come out heah wit' my girls an' we gonna cut yo' titties right off. You hear me?"

Melinda Hogarth didn't answer the question. She walked backward on her elbows and heels until somehow she was on her feet. Then she ran down the street, screaming high and loud like a woman miraculously transforming into a fire truck.

After a long minute Robyn put her knife away. She picked up the fans. Now they were just blue and silver plastic pieces.

"Damn," she said. "Now we got to go back to that hardware sto' an' that yellah niggah gonna start slobberin' on me again."

"I got a fan on my back porch," Ptolemy said.

"Why the hell didn't you tell me that in the first place?" she said angrily.

"You didn't aks me, girl. I didn't know what you was doin'."

With some effort Robyn smiled again and reached for Ptolemy's hands. He took a step backward.

"Don't be scared'a me, Uncle," Robyn said. "I just wanna make sure you can stand out on the street and not be beat down by that crazy woman."

Ptolemy's mind was scattered over nearly a hundred years. His mother and father, Coy's lynching, the one brief battle he fought in during World War Two. He saw Melvin Torchman fall dead in a barbershop in Memphis, and he was waking up again to Sensia dead in the bed next to him. And then a million bugs swarmed over her . . .

"Uncle?"

Robyn was holding his hands. He looked into her eyes and she was a friendly child again.

"Don't do that no mo', okay, baby?" he said.

Robyn kissed his big knuckle and nodded.

After dragging the huge gray tarp out to the curb, Robyn cleared two places in each room and placed an insect bomb candle in each space. She only put one bomb in the bathroom.

"You go wait in the hall, Uncle," she told Ptolemy, "while I set these bad boys off."

He stood outside in the dilapidated marble-and-oak hallway. It was once a nice building that people kept up. That was in the old days, when black people came to Los Angeles to make a life away from the Jim Crow South. He hadn't stood in that dark hall for many years. He'd walked down it ten thousand times; between two and a dozen times a day when he was younger. But he hardly ever just stood there.

Once there was a young man stabbed and killed at the front door of the building. He'd pressed Ptolemy and Sensia's bell, but when nobody responded to the intercom they went back to bed. He was already old and she was fragile by then. They'd been burglarized and had put up the chain gate on the back window and door.

Hey, Mr. Grey," Robyn said.

She'd come into the hallway, dragging one of his pine chairs with a small suitcase lying in its seat. The slight scent of sulfur and smoke came with her. She also had a sheet of paper and the roll of masking tape they got from the hardware store. Using the chair to stand on, she put tape all along the cracks of the door. She put many layers of tape, one on top of the other, to make an air-tight seal against leaking poisons. Then she taped the paper to the door.

"Insect bomb," Ptolemy read. "Stay away."

"You can read, Mr. Grey?" the child asked.

"Sure I can read. Anybody can read an' write they name."

"Can you read a book?"

"Hunnert pages, two hunnert pages, two fifty."

Robyn smiled and put her hand on his shoulder.

"Let's go to the motel," she said.

The thought of a new house tickled Ptolemy. He walked briskly toward the front door of the building, happy, unafraid of Melinda Hogarth for the first time in years, and looking forward to the day outside, and a new man in the bathroom mirror.

Are you lookin' at my legs, Uncle?" Robyn asked coyly.

She took one of the single beds and the old man lay down on the other. He'd gone into the bathroom to change into his sleeping clothes. Robyn had brought his navy-blue sweatpants and a gray T-shirt. When she changed, all the teenager did was tie up her hair and put on a T-shirt over her panties.

The TV was on a show about three young black women who lived together in an apartment and argued all the time. Now and then Ptolemy would swivel his head to catch a glance at Robyn's strong brown legs.

"I guess so," he said.

"Are you a dirty old man, Uncle?"

"No, but . . . you sure do remind me of somethin'."

"What's that?" Robyn shifted on the bed but she didn't hide her legs. She was smiling at Ptolemy as if she was telling him something.

"Cover up them things, girl," he said. "You know I'm a old man but I still remember how much a girl can hurt you. I'm past ninety but that don't mean you could play wit' me like that."

Robyn slipped under the blankets and buried her head in the pillow.

The women on the TV program were screaming and running around a couch where a man sat with a perplexed look on his face. Ptolemy didn't understand what they were saying.

He got up from the bed and pushed buttons on the side of the box. The first button made the volume go up and then down. The second one changed the channel and suddenly there was a naked couple having loud sex with everything showing.

"Fuck it harder!" the woman cried out, and Ptolemy, his heart thumping in fear, pressed another button, which shut the TV off.

The TV was the only light on and so the room went dark.

He made his way gingerly to the bed and climbed in. The blankets were tangled but he finally got himself mostly covered.

In the dark he lay awake. From time to time he'd forget where he was and fear would thrum in his ears. He'd wanted to jump up but the angry face of Robyn beating Melinda Hogarth would come to him and he'd grab on to his blankets, determined to wait for sunup to go home.

"Uncle?"

"Yeah?" he said, relieved that she sounded like the nice girl he'd met.

"I'm sorry," she said.

"'Bout what?"

"Dancin' around half naked in front'a you. I know I shouldn't'a done that."

"No. I mean. Baby girl, you are my angel. I, uh, I love you, you . . ."

"What?"

"God done send you down here to me. He send you to help me save them chirren."

"Letisha and Artie?"

"Yep."

"How you gonna do that, Uncle?"

"With your help, baby. With your help."

"What can I do?"

"You got to, got to . . . help me remembah what it is I'm thinkin'."

For a while after that they lay in silence.

"Is that true, Uncle?"

"What?"

"Do you love me?"

"When I think about you my heart hurts and laughs."

"That's why you din't wanna see my legs?"

"That's why I don't even wanna think about your legs."

The next day they had breakfast at a diner and went to the La Brea Tar Pits park, where Reggie used to take Ptolemy sometimes.

"When Reggie was a boy he loved the dinosaur bones," Ptolemy told Robyn. "The museum was on'y one buildin' then and they had dinosaur bones in a buildin' like a hole. When Reggie grew up he didn't like this place no mo' but I wanted to come so's I could remembah . . ." Ptolemy drifted off, staring at the large clouds passing overhead.

"What you remembah, Uncle?"

"What it used to be like in my head before things got confused."

"What's that like?"

"It's like they's a jailhouse in my mind," he said, "an' I'm in the prison an' they's all these people I know outside yellin' to me but I cain't make out what they sayin'."

"Hey, girl," a male voice sang.

Ptolemy swiveled his head to see a young black man in a red jumpsuit.

"What you doin'?" he asked. He had a sneer on his lips that had more anger than friendliness to it.

"Niggah, get away from me," the other, angry, Robyn said. "Cain't you see I'm takin' care'a my grandfather?"

"Let me help you guys," the young man offered, smiling and touching her shoulder.

Robyn jerked away from him and clutched her purse close to her breast.

"You gonna treat me like that?" he said as if he were truly insulted.

"Fuck you, niggah."

Ptolemy could see that Robyn was ready to grab her long knife. He had known women like this before: wild and violent, sweet and loving. He'd never had a girlfriend like Robyn, but Coy had had more than one.

"A woman like that could turn on a dime," Coydog McCann used to say.

The young man in the red exercise uniform sneered and took a step forward. Robyn shoved her hand into her purse and he stopped.

"Bitch," he said, and then he spat on the ground.

Robyn stared death at him and he walked away across the lawn of the park.

"Come on, Uncle," she said. "We should get back."

They ate at the small diner again.

Ptolemy was exhausted from his day in the city. He lay down on top of the covers, falling asleep without even undressing. He felt Robyn take off his shoes and socks and fold the blankets over him.

There was no TV announcer, no classical music. He was in a coffin again and the earth was cold. He was dead and couldn't move. He couldn't even shiver against the chill.

"What you gonna do wit' my treasure?" Coydog asked him suddenly, shockingly—out of nowhere.

"I'm cold."

"I give up my life and my dignity for you," Coy said.

"I'm dead."

"You don't even know what dead is. Dead is havin' a noose around your neck an' yo' feet afire. You just restin' while my treasure go to waste."

"I cain't, Coydog! I cain't even see. If they catch me they gonna lynch me too. They gonna kill me too."

The cold settled into Ptolemy's bones like it must have in the old pharaoh after whom he'd been named. The chill hurt his joints and his marrow. He wasn't breathing and instead of a heart there was a drum being played by a dimwitted monkey who couldn't keep the beat any better than a drunkard.

Suddenly warmth enveloped him. It was as if he were lowered into a hot tub of salted, scented water. The heat went through him and Coydog walked away in disgust. Now only his hands and feet and nose were cold. He was floating in the Tickle River in late August.

"When the water runs as hot as the blood of a woman in love," Coydog said as he walked from the tomb.

Ptolemy woke up held from behind by Robyn. He realized that he must have been shivering in the night and she held him to warm him as his mother had done in the winter months when he was a boy.

Ptolemy sat up and Robyn rolled on her back.

"Mornin', Uncle."

"What you doin' in my bed, girl?"

"You were so cold that you was cryin' in your sleep," she said. "I hope it was all right."

"What we doin' today?" he asked, unable to condemn or condone her gift of warmth.

"Gettin' some breakfast and suckin' the poison out yo' house."

"Ain't Niecie wonder where you are?" Ptolemy asked, realizing as he did that he could connect Robyn and Niecie and Reggie in his mind. He knew that Reggie was dead and not coming back and that he had something that he had to do.

"I told her that I was gonna stay at your place till it was cleaned up. She trust me. Do you trust me, Uncle?"

Trustin' a woman is like walkin' in California," Coydog would say. "You know there's bound to be a quake sometimes but you just keep on walkin' anyways. What else could you do?"

I'm a man dyin'a thirst an' you the on'y water in a thousand miles," Ptolemy said, repeating a phrase that had been in his mind for at least seventy-five years.

Robyn crinkled her broad nose and sat up to kiss her faux uncle.

"I trust you," she said.

While Ptolemy sat on the pine chair outside his door, Robyn made it to the back porch, set up the fan, and opened the back door through the protective gate.

Three hours later she was filling up bags with old newspaper, clothes, bills, and general trash. She swept up thousands of dead insects, some suffocated rodents, and few creatures that neither she nor Ptolemy could identify.

Ptolemy followed her around, looking through every paper and blouse that she threw out. He was very excited by a large iron key that she found between the mattress and box spring.

For four days they filled trash bags, swept, and discarded.

The strong girl also lugged chairs and tables and even the broken bureau out to the street.

At night Robyn slept on the mattress roll under the south table and Ptolemy slept on Sensia's bed, which Robyn had covered with plastic casing and unused sheets she had found in a closet. Sometimes the girl would come to him and hold him for a while until his teeth stopped chattering and he no longer cried in his sleep.

On the fifth day the apartment was mostly clean. The junk that Ptolemy wanted to hoard was stacked neatly in the deep closet. There were chairs in the living room and laundered blankets on the bed. The kitchen had been swept and scrubbed and disinfected until it almost seemed as if someone might cook in there.

"Uncle?" Robyn asked one day. She had just returned with a basket full of clothes from the laundromat across the street.

"Yeah?"

"What's this card? It's got a name and number printed on one side and on the other somebody wrote, 'For the doctor you requested' by hand."

"I don't . . . I don't remembah no card. And I ain't sick, either."

"It says that this man, this Antoine Church, is a social worker," Robyn said. "Maybe he gotta doctor help you remembah things like this."

Grey," a woman called. "Pee Toll My Grey."

"That's us, Uncle," Robyn said.

"That ain't my name," he said, stubbornly anchored to the

blue armchair in the hall at social services. "I mean, that's my last name but she must be callin' somebody else."

"Please," his young guardian whined.

"That's not my name," Ptolemy said again.

"Please."

He allowed the girl he thought of as his child to lift him by the forearms and lead him through the scuffed and stained brown door.

It was a small office with no bookcases or books. The desk was made from pressboard and covered in plastic walnut veneer that had started peeling at the corners.

Mr. Antoine Church was a prissy young black man with straightened hair and a picture of Jesus on the wall. He wore a tan suit and brown calfskin gloves.

"What you got gloves on for on a hot day like this?" Ptolemy asked.

"Germs," he replied.

"Why'ont you sit down, Uncle?" Robyn said.

He didn't want to, but the busses and the walks to get to the government office had tired him out. Robyn stood behind the chair.

"How are you two related?" Church asked Robyn.

"My friend Niecie is his grandniece, and she asked me to take care of him."

"But why call him 'uncle' if he's just a friend?"

"I call my boyfriend 'honey,'" she said, visibly holding back her anger, "but that don't mean I'ma put him in my tea."

"You got germs in here?" Ptolemy asked.

"What?" Church said.

"You got them gloves for germs you say. That mean I'ma get sick in here?"

"No," Antoine said in an exaggerated, almost yawning, tone.

"Then why you got them gloves on?"

"Why are you here, Mr. Grey?"

"I . . ."

It was like falling into a dream for the old man. He wanted Coydog McCann to fish with, and Reggie smiling naturally in his grave. He wanted to show the children how to fly kites and sing songs that Jesus might not want to hear.

Ptolemy sat there in Church's uncomfortable metal chair, thinking that he'd like to move without his joints aching and to have one full thought all the way through without stumbling over the words and getting distracted by the slightest thing. He didn't want people to call him *old man* anymore or for social workers like Antoine Church to have power over him.

He wanted a job and driver's license and a hard-on with a girlfriend like he was sure that boy Beckford wanted with Robyn.

Before Robyn came to stay with him, before Reggie came and before Sensia died, Ptolemy might have said these things. He might have talked about going to the bathroom and having sex. But now he just sat there, lost in the jumble of ideas. He knew that somebody like Church wouldn't understand his words.

"Uncle wanna go to the kinda doctor help him remembah how to think," Robyn said.

She was wearing her charcoal-gray dress with the high hemline and black hose under that. Sporting a hint of makeup, she carried a small red purse that was too small for her fighting knife.

"Your nephew came to see me a few months ago," the social worker said. "He told me that you were having trouble with your memory and communication skills."

"Reggie's dead."

"I know. I'm sorry."

The tone of Church's voice jabbed at Ptolemy's mind like the cut of a rusty chisel. It made him want to sneer and spit. He wanted to tell that man that he was an idiot, a stupid fool.

"Are you still having trouble thinking?" Church asked.

"No. I think just fine," Ptolemy said. "It's just that I got some trouble rememberin' things I used to know. I mean, I know you got them gloves on 'cause you think there's a germ in here. I know that this girl here is my granddaughter. But I don't remembah where I put things a long time ago, an' I cain't, I cain't . . . things I need to find."

There was so much he couldn't do. Sometimes he'd stand over the toilet for five minutes waiting to urinate. Sometimes when the phone would ring he'd go to the door and ask, "Who is it?" and when Robyn told him that it was the phone he'd get so embarrassed that he'd go into the bedroom just so he wouldn't have to see her feeling sorry for him.

"Well," Antoine Church said, smiling. "The reason I dropped by your house and left that card was because I found out about a man who might have just what you're looking for."

"What you laughin' at, boy?" Ptolemy asked.

"I'm not laughing," the grinning man said.

"Yes you are. Are you laughin' at me?"

"No," Church said, managing to approximate a sober look.

"You gonna be old too," Ptolemy told him. "You gonna be sittin' in this chair and a young man gonna be tellin' you sumpin'. I got a family needs me and I cain't walk down the street wit'out this child here to he'p me. I'm just askin' for that, for that. That, that thing."

Church scribbled in tiny script on a small slip of paper, which he handed to Robyn.

"Call this doctor and tell him that I referred you," the prissy man said. "And if you have any problems you can call me. Maybe we can work together to help your uncle."

"Thank you, Mr. Church," Robyn said, smiling.

Mothahfuckah," she whispered when she and Ptolemy were a few steps down the hall.

Dr. Ruben, who answered his own phone, said that he didn't have a free appointment for three weeks.

"I'm traveling to India," he said, "to Mumbai for a conference, but I'd be happy to see Mr. Grey when I return."

Robyn didn't argue with him. She made the appointment and then sat in the lawn chair that Ptolemy wouldn't let her throw out.

"Do you want me to move back to Aunt Niecie's house now that yo' place is clean?" she asked her *uncle*.

"Do you wanna go back?"

"I wanna have a place with a bed up off'a the floor and a chest'a drawers."

"I could buy you all that."

"Honey, you only get two hundred and eleven dollahs a week," she said. "That's more than you need to live but it ain't enough for no new bed and chest'a drawers."

A door opened in Ptolemy's mind and he smiled, then grinned.

"Wha?" Robyn said.

"Go in the closet an' pull out that brown suitcase I made you leave in there."

"That big heavy thing?"

"That's it."

The girl went in and dug under the mounds of picture albums and books and shoe boxes filled with letters, small tools, and what Ptolemy called "his remembrances."

She dragged the heavy leather bag out to the center of the living room.

"Now bring me that jar with all the keys we found in it," the old man commanded.

"Yes, Uncle."

As the days had gone by, Ptolemy had gotten more and more bossy. He'd tell Robyn how to cook his eggs and where he wanted his books, even what clothes he'd like her to wear.

Instead of getting angry, the child almost always acquiesced to his demands. In his heart he knew that she was the one who made the important decisions, and she knew that he wanted in the worst way to be in charge.

"Here you go, Uncle," Robyn said. She was wearing tight red jeans and a pink T-shirt. Her tennis shoes were pink too.

Ptolemy dumped the keys out on the table that once stood at the south wall, the table that he'd slept under for more than twenty years.

The small brass key was for his locker at the Y that they tore down in 1962, or maybe 1963. The big skeleton key that Robyn found under Sensia's mattress was to the lost treasure. The three master keys on one ring were to various padlocks that he kept in the bottom drawer in the kitchen. The tin key was the one he wanted. He set it aside and placed all the rest, one by one, back in the old mustard jar.

"You could put these back," he said, pushing the jar toward Robyn.

"Ain't you gonna want to put that key back after you unlock the bag?" she asked.

Questions like that gave Ptolemy the most problems. When he was alone with his TV and radio, nobody asked him anything and he didn't have to put together any responses. People talked in his head, and on the TV, but there were no questions that he had to answer.

He blinked and tried to understand all the various things she meant.

"Why don't I just put it in my pocket and hold it for you, Uncle?"

"I can put it in my own pocket," he said.

"Should we open it now?" she asked.

"Let's get it up here on the table," he said.

Together they lifted the heavy bag until they got one corner of it on the battered ash top. Then Robyn pushed until it was fully on.

Ptolemy had to study the lock. He tried different ways to put the key in. It had been a few months since he'd opened the case but finally he got it right.

"Goddamn, Uncle," Robyn said, standing up from the aluminum and nylon chair and putting her hands to her face. "Shit!"

"You mad, baby girl?" Ptolemy said, leaning away from her, remembering the way she had looked when she beat Melinda Hogarth until blood flowed from the addict's forehead.

Robyn was staring at the suitcase filled with ones, fives, tens, and twenties. The money was stacked in some places. In others it was piled, just thrown in, and all mixed around. Robyn dug both hands in, lifting a shovelful of cash, and coins rained down from the jumble of bills.

"Uncle," Robyn said.

"I been savin' that for years," he said. "It's almost ninety-four thousand dollars. Ninety-four thousand . . . almost."

Robyn sat down again. Her face was indecipherable to her adopted uncle.

"Did Reggie know you had all this?" she asked.

"He knew I didn't cash but two checks every three weeks. He'd put one in a account that paid my bills and I'd put my leftovers in the trunk. When I wanted to tell him where I put it he said that he didn't wanna know. He said that he might start borrowin' and not know when to quit."

Tears were coming down Robyn's left cheek. She had dropped the cash and now her hands were picking at each other.

"We could use this money to buy you a bed and a dresser," Ptolemy said. "An', an', an' if there's enough, maybe a nice dress."

Robyn stared at the suitcase full of money and shook her head.

"Is this the treasure you always be talkin' 'bout?" she asked at last.

"Naw," he said. "That ain't treasure. That's just Social Security an' retirement money. Nobody died for that. You know a pirate's treasure have to be cursed with blood."

Robyn moved as far away from the table as she could get. Ptolemy got to his feet and went over to her. He put his hands on her strong shoulders.

"What's wrong, baby?" he asked.

"Why you wanna show me that?"

"You my girl. You my blood."

"No I'm not. You don't even know me. You don't know what I did 'fore I got here. I could steal this money from you."

"You want it?" he asked.

"What?"

"You want it? I could give it to you, baby. You know, I only need ev'ry fourth check an', an' once a mont' or so I get a li'l bit from Social Security. That's all I need. You could have this. You could, you could take it and buy you a bed."

Robyn jumped away from her benefactor and ran to the door.

"No!" she yelled as she rushed into the hallway and out to the front door of the building.

By the time Ptolemy got to the threshold she was gone. He stayed there for a while but she didn't return and so he went back to the ash table. He considered separating out the various denominations. There were a few hundred-dollar bills in there, he remembered. He wanted to stack all the like notes, but there was too much cash and so he closed the suitcase and locked it. Then he went to the TV to turn it on but he couldn't remember which button did the job.

Finally Ptolemy Grey went to the bathroom and sat on the edge of the tub, trying to remember.

For a long while nothing seemed to work. All he could think about was how angry Robyn was. And she was so pretty in red. He wanted to tell her that by giving her the money. After all, it wasn't a treasure, just some cash. His rent was set at $185 a month, and the bills, which Reggie had the bank pay, were low.

"Money ain't the root of all evil," Coydog had told the boy Li'l Pea, "but it get a hold on some people like vines on a tree or the smell'a fungus on damp sheets. They's some people need money before love or laughter. All you can do is feel sorry for someone like that."

"But money is what makes you rich, Uncle Coy," the child said. "My daddy said that if he had enough money he'd be a rich man."

"Rich man is the man live in his own skin," the old thief countered. "Black as oil, white as cane sugah, yellah like gold—that's riches for ya, boy. All the rest is jes' wastin' time."

Ptolemy felt pain in his joints and weakness in his muscles. Robyn running away the way she did hurt more than seeing Reggie in his coffin. Or maybe it wasn't more, but added on to Reggie's death, Robyn's departure was a weight too great to bear. He didn't cry but he wanted to. He didn't run out in the street looking for her but he would have if it wasn't for Melinda and the fact that he got lost if he wandered beyond his own block.

"I got to think," Ptolemy said clearly. "I got to get my mind movin'."

With these words he stood up from the commode and went out into the newly ordered and cleaned living room. He brought his rainbow stool and sat it in front of the TV. Robyn had wanted to throw the stool away, along with a dozen other chairs that she put out on the street on trash day.

"No, no, baby," he remembered saying. "This here is my move-anywhere chair. I could sit anywhere in the house or outside with this here chair. Whenever I get tired or need to get down and study sumpin' close to the ground, this chair will work for me."

"Okay, Uncle," she'd said.

"You got to understand, this chair is like a extra leg or a tool I can have and carry anywhere. It's light like a feather, and so it ain't nuthin' for a old man like me to pick up."

"Okay, Uncle," Robyn said again, "we can keep the chair."

"Reggie got it for me," Ptolemy continued as if he hadn't heard. "An' the minute I seen it I knew that it was mine and I could use it anywhere, for rest or to study sumpin' close to the ground . . ."

Robyn took his wrists in her hands and moved her face close to his.

"I hear you, Uncle. You don't have to keep on explainin' it. I'm gonna do what you tell me to do."

That was the clearest evidence to Ptolemy that he was losing his mind. Even though the girl had said yes, he still wanted to explain over and over why he needed that chair. All he could think about was how important that chair was; that and how much he wished he could stop that thought from going again and again through his mind.

So he set the stool up in front of the TV and stared at it—the green screen that bulged out some, and the flat buttons along the side. There was a box on top of it that had a red number in lights: 134. That was his station. That was where the news came from. He didn't want to change that number, just get the TV to turn on.

He sat there for a long time, or at least what seemed like a long time. He didn't want to push just any button. And he didn't want to turn the TV on by mistake—he wanted to *know* what the right button was so that he knew that it was his mind that made the light. There were four flat, dark buttons. One said *vol.* and another said *I/O*. Two others had no letters to describe them, just symbols that made no sense at all.

"A, B, C," Ptolemy said, "D, E, F, G, H." He stopped there and wondered a moment. "I, J, K . . ."

The letters didn't tell him anything. They were just sounds that had nothing to do with slashes or periods or letters that didn't make words that he knew.

"Double-u, ara, eye, en, gee," he said, and smiled. He knew those letters. He knew what they meant. But he couldn't find Shirley Wring. He couldn't find the bank or even remember the bank's name to ask somebody how to get there.

"Uncle?"

Seeing Robyn in her red clothes brought an even broader grin to Ptolemy's lips, brought him to his feet.

"I'm so sorry," he said, meaning many things that he couldn't say.

"Sorry for what?" the child replied, tears in her voice.

"For whatevah I did to make you leave. I just wanted . . . wanted you . . . I didn't mean to make you mad."

They fell together in an embrace that made them both shudder and cry.

"It's okay, Uncle."

"It's okay, Robyn."

"I ain't leavin'," the girl said.

"You could have my bed and I could sleep under the table again," he said. "There ain't no more roaches hardly and the mice is all gone."

"You want me to turn on the TV for you, Uncle?"

"No, baby. No. I wanna figure it out for myself. I wanna use my mind again. I wanna remembah."

"Remember what, Uncle?"

"I don't know exactly, but it got to do with them babies and, and, and you."

"You remembah me, don't you?"

"But not what I'm meant to do."

"Don't cry, Uncle. You make me sad."

"You was on'y gone for a hour or sumpin'," Ptolemy said, "but I felt that I lost you like I lost Maude Petit in that fire."

"What fire, Uncle?"

Robyn pulled up a chair next to the old man, in front of the silent and dark television set. She listened as he told her the broken story of a child stalked in the flames by a huge shadow and a man, or maybe a coyote, that danced on fire. There was a dead dog and a dead man in a tuxedo, the ABC's that didn't work anymore, and Reggie, hanging like an anchor from Robyn's leg.

She didn't question nor did she understand exactly what her aged friend had said. She held his hands and nodded now and then. He asked her questions that she had no answers to and told her stories that made him laugh and shake his head.

At one point he looked up and asked, "Why you run away like that, girl?"

Robyn heard this question and understood its meaning. She brought her hands to her throat and made a sound that had feeling but no meaning.

"I sleep on a sofa, Uncle," she said. "Hilly try to be gettin' up in there wit' me almost ev'ry night he home."

"That boy's a thief."

"Niecie nice," Robyn said. "She took me in, but nobody evah offered me a bed and open they doors and showed me their money and said take whatevah you want.

"I loved my mama, but she was wit' just about ev'ry man she met. Sometimes she tell me to go stay wit' my friends 'cause she didn't want her boyfriends lookin' at me an' thinkin' she was that old."

"I don't know why not," Ptolemy said. "You a lovely girl. They cain't help but look at you."

"I wanna stay here an' live wit' you, Uncle."

"Me too. I wanna stay here wit' you too."

"An' I want you to buy me a bed an' some sheets an' pillows and blankets, but I don't want your money. We gonna start puttin' your money in a bank account and get you a special bank card so you can buy the bed and then I can sleep in it."

"But you got to wear clothes so I cain't like your legs like I did at that other place," Ptolemy said.

"You don't like to look at my legs, Uncle?" Robyn said, the sly smile returning to her lips.

"I don't like to like to look at your legs, child. That was a long time ago, and now is now."

So, Mr. Grey, you wish to start a debit account along with the accounts you already have?" Andrea Tolliver asked, her smiling black face as insincere as the white sheriff who wanted Li'l Pea to testify against the men who had lynched his uncle. She was a dark-skinned black woman with bronze hair and golden jewelry around her neck and wrists and on at least three fingers.

"Whatevah Robyn say is what I want," Ptolemy said in a tone that he knew made him sound sure and smart.

"But do *you* want a debit account?" the banker asked. "You already have an account that automatically pays your bills." She glanced at the computer screen before her. "It is overdrawn, however."

"I need to buy a bed, an' Robyn tell me that you just cain't take all your money into a sto' an' put it down 'cause there's thieves all around you."

Ptolemy took a moment to look around the room from his seat at the bank officer's desk.

"Are you looking for someone, Mr. Grey? Maybe some teller you know?"

"Shirley Wring," he said, a smile rising to his lips. "Double-u ara eye en gee."

"No . . . no Shirley works here."

"My uncle been savin' his extra money in a box in his closet," Robyn said then. "I told him that that wasn't safe and that he could maybe get a little bit'a interest if he brought it here. I'm taking care'a him but it's his money and so I brought him to his bank."

Ptolemy watched the bank officer's eyes scrutinize the girl. He'd seen older black women do this to young ones before.

Andrea Tolliver was older now and she didn't have to lie to young men on the street about her address and telephone numbers anymore. She knew that Robyn could talk an old man out of his money.

"Miss?" Ptolemy asked.

"Yes, Mr. Grey?"

"If this child wanted to steal my money we wouldn't be here."

Watching her watching him, Ptolemy knew that he had read her right, that he had said the right words.

"We can put the money in your savings account, Mr. Grey, and issue you a debit card. Do you want your, um, niece to have a card too?"

"No," Robyn said. "No. I don't need one. This is for my uncle, not for me."

Ms. Tolliver smiled at the child then. It was her last test to make sure that the girl was not trying to rob an old man.

Ptolemy gazed paternally at Tolliver, and then he grinned.

"Something funny, Mr. Grey?" the banker asked.

"Here we all are," he said, repeating word for word something that Coydog McCann had said long ago, "somebody gettin' on the boat an' somebody gettin' off, and a captain in the middle makin' sure we all get where we goin' to."

Robyn took Ptolemy's hand and smiled for him as Tolliver frowned, wondering what he meant.

M̲r. Grey. Mr. Grey."

Robyn turned quickly on the crowded street. She put her hand in her purse, ready, Ptolemy knew, to protect him with her edge, her six-inch blade.

He heard his name and wondered back through the voices that called him and the things they had to say.

"Mr. Grey," Felix Franz the German baker would say to him every morning when he came in to buy his coffee and coffee cake on the way to the maintenance office where he and his partners got their orders for the day.

He just said the name and that was the greeting. But this was the voice of a woman, not a German man; not Melinda Hogarth or Sensia or proper Minister Brock.

He turned to see the name-caller and laughed.

"It's okay, Robyn. That's my friend. Double-u ara eye en gee."

She wore tapered black slacks today and a turquoise T-shirt. She still had the green sun visor and the faded cherry-red bag.

"Mr. Grey," she said again.

"Shirley Wring," Ptolemy said, gleeful to see her and reveling in the fact that he could remember a name, a face, and something he wanted. "Robyn, this is a woman who offered me a treasure."

"Uh-huh," Robyn grunted, and he could see in her the suspicion that had shown on Tolliver's face.

All around them black and brown people were moving. Shirley Wring's occluded eyes were gazing at Ptolemy.

"This is Robyn, my niece," Ptolemy said.

"Your uncle is the treasure," Shirley said. "He helped me out when I couldn't pay my phone bill and wouldn't even take my ring for a guarantee."

"You could pay him back now," Robyn said rudely.

"She don't have to pay me," Ptolemy said. "She offered me a treasure. You know that was on'y the second time in all my life that somebody offered me a true treasure."

"I could take you two to lunch," the small, gray-brown colored woman offered.

"We got to go home."

"No, baby," Ptolemy said. "Shirley here, she, I mean, I been comin' ovah here . . . lookin'."

"Oh," Robyn said, and then she smiled apologetically. "I'm sorry, Miss Wring. Uncle been lookin' for you for a long time. He been havin' me comin' down here just about ev'ry other day, hopin' you show up."

Shirley Wring smiled shyly, looking at the man who had been looking for her.

"I ain't had a man searchin' me down in quite a while," she said. "Old woman like me lucky somebody don't run her underfoot."

"So we all gonna have lunch, right?" Ptolemy asked, looking into the brown and gray eyes of Shirley Wring.

They had sandwiches at a Subway chain store. Shirley paid for the meal.

She talked about when she moved to Los Angeles from someplace up north. When Ptolemy asked her if she was from

California she looked away from him and said, "No. I'm from some-place else."

"You talk real nice," Ptolemy said, realizing that he had asked an uncomfortable question. "Did you come here to go to school?"

"My mama wanted me to get a education but I met this high-yellah fellah named Eric and I couldn't think about nuthin' else."

"Robyn gonna go to college in the fall," Ptolemy said, his voice loud to cover all the things he didn't know.

"Junior college," Robyn said.

"Junior college is college too," Shirley declared.

"That's right," Ptolemy added. And he and the woman Shirley Wring smiled for each other across the bright-yellow plastic table.

"We got to get back home, Uncle," Robyn said finally, to fill in and end the silence.

The days passed in a new kind of harmony for the old man. The TV stayed off unless Robyn wanted to watch her shows at night. Ptolemy refused to have her leave it on for him or turn to his news station. He wanted to run the TV himself without any help. If he couldn't do that, then he wouldn't ever be able to find his treasure and save his family; he would fail the way he failed Maude Petit and Floppy in that tarpaper house on the outskirts of town.

For the same reason the radio stayed off.

Sometimes Robyn would go out with Beckford Ross, Reggie's old friend. Some nights she didn't get in until hours after Ptolemy fell asleep. But the old man did not chastise her. Robyn was looking after him, and she needed to be free, like the birds his father didn't want him to feed.

Twice a week for three weeks Shirley Wring came over in the afternoon to sit with Ptolemy and converse.

The talks always started pretty well. Ptolemy would tell her about his mother and father and their poor sharecropper's farm; he'd talk about Coy and a treasure that was lost and her green ring. But after a while he could see in her eyes that he wasn't making sense. She didn't frown or get bored, but her smile became soft and her dim eyesight focused on something other than what he was saying. At this point he'd offer her tea and she would say that it was time for her to get home, "before the sun goes down and the thugs come out."

During this time Ptolemy received a letter from his bank. The letter contained a plastic card that had his name printed in gold at the bottom. Robyn took him to a machine that had a TV screen in it in a shopping mall on Crenshaw. There she put the card in the slot and asked him, "What is the favorite name you like to spell, Uncle?"

"Double-u ara eye en gee?"

"Can you press those buttons?"

He did it twice and the card came back out of the slot.

"From now on all you got to do is remember those lettahs and this machine will give you money," the child told the old man.

"For free?"

"Naw, Uncle. They take it outta that bank account we started."

"Oh yeah," he replied, not remembering and disgusted with himself for the lapse.

. . .

At a store called Merlyn's, in the same mall, using his new bank card, Ptolemy bought Robyn a white wooden bed that sat atop three big drawers with pink handles. There was a padded board at the back of the bed that could be folded up to make the bed into a couch. They also got new sheets and blankets, pillows, and bright-red cushions for when the bed would be used as a couch.

When the bed was delivered the next day, Robyn grinned at the men assembling it.

After they left she took her uncle by the hand and pulled him until he was sitting next to her on the well-made bed.

"Are you gonna marry Shirley Wring and kick me outta here, Uncle Grey? I don't care if you do. I mean, it's your house and you could do what you want, but I nevah had no nice new bed before, and I'd like it if I could take it with me if you told me I had to go."

"You wanna go and here we just got your bed?"

"No. I thought you loved Shirley Wring."

"I'm too old for that. At this age I can only love chirren . . . like you. I love you."

Robyn got down on her knees, took her faux uncle's hands, and pressed her face against them.

They stayed like that for a long while, the man sitting up straight and the girl on her knees.

"Are you gonna leave me, Robyn?"

"No, not nevah, Uncle Grey. Not nevah."

· · ·

Robyn cooked and cleaned and slept in Ptolemy's living room every night after that. They took walks in the neighborhood and never once saw Melinda Hogarth.

Niecie called twice.

"Pitypapa is sick an' I got to take him to the doctor and give him his medicine," Robyn told her guardian. "But I'ma come home when he bettah."

"Bless you, child," Niecie said.

Things went along like that for three weeks, until it was time for their appointment with Dr. Ruben.

The office was a block north of Melrose, on the west side of town. They took the bus and Ptolemy hummed to himself while one young man after another tried to get Robyn's attention. She smiled and lied and sometimes just ignored them while Li'l Pea and Coy McCann fished almost a century before in the old man's mind.

The doctor had a room in a courtyard of professional offices that surrounded a beautiful rose garden. The roses were white and gold, red and bright yellow. Ptolemy smiled while Robyn led him along.

"It's beautiful here," he said. "What is this place?"

"The doctor's, remembah?"

"Oh yeah. Yeah."

There was no nurse or receptionist, just a large room with a desk on one side and an examining table on the other. Robyn and Ptolemy sat in cushioned chairs before the desk.

Bryant Ruben was a white man of medium height, age, and

build. He had a great mustache that made Ptolemy smile and beady green eyes that were not at all off-putting. The doctor's voice was clear and strong. This made Ptolemy think that even if they were across the Tickle River from each other, he would still be able to understand the smiling doctor's words.

It started with a memory test.

The doctor would recite a list of words, like *apple, tomato, pinecone, orange, sparrow,* and *stone,* and then ask Ptolemy to repeat them.

"*Orange stone* and, and, somethin'," he answered on the first try.

After eight lists, Dr. Ruben smiled.

"I'm going to ask you to strip down to your shorts and sit on the examining table, Mr. Grey. Would you rather your niece wait in the garden?"

"No. She could see me right here. I don't mind. I'm too old to be worried about bein' naked."

Ruben examined Ptolemy from head to toe with a rubber hammer, a stethoscope, and a pair of magnifying glasses that had double lenses and sat on the end of his nose.

"Ninety-one, eh, Mr. Grey?"

"Yes, sir."

"You're in wonderful physical condition for a man your age. You can put on your clothes and we'll talk at the desk."

Robyn helped her charge with his pants and shirt and then got down on her knees to tie his brown shoes.

"Those shoes is older than you, girl," Ptolemy said, and Robyn stood and kissed his cheek.

. . .

Your uncle is in the early stages of dementia," Ruben said to Robyn. "Maybe a little bit further along than that, but not much. He can converse with difficulty and has some trouble with immediate memory. I believe, however, that the damage is not so far along that it can't be ameliorated."

Ptolemy didn't mind the doctor explaining to the child. She was his eyes and ears in a world just out of reach. She deciphered what things meant and then told him like a busboy in a restaurant that runs down to the waiter and then comes back with information for the cook.

"What does that mean, Doctor?"

"He's losing the ability to use his mind to solve problems, remember things, and to communicate. His language skills are still pretty strong, but his cognitive abilities are weakening."

"What's cognitib—?" Robyn asked, frowning, trying to understand what she could do for him.

"It means thinking."

"I wanna make it so that I could think good for just a couple mont's, Doc," Ptolemy said then. "I got some things to remembah, and relatives to look aftah. And, you know, if I . . . if I mess up, then it's all lost, my whole life."

"What will be lost?" the mustachioed man asked.

"I, I . . . well, I don't have the words right now," Ptolemy said. "You see? That's the problem." Ptolemy placed his fingertips on the edge of the doctor's desk, as if the image of his words were there.

"There are medicines in general use today," Ruben said, listing five or six names. "None of them are very effective. I mean, something might be able to keep you the way you are without getting worse for a while, but . . ."

"Uncle wants his mind back," Robyn said, a look of surprise and anger on her lovely face.

Ruben smiled.

"And I'm pretty sure he got medical insurance," the girl said. "We found some insurance papers when I was cleanin' up his apartment. He's a veteran and the army will probably be able to pay sumpin'."

Ruben's smile extended into time.

"Well?" the girl asked.

"Mr. Grey," Bryant Ruben said, like the baker that used to greet him.

"Yes sir, Doctor."

"Do you want to live to see a hundred?"

A hundred years. Ptolemy thought back over all the time that had brought him to that patient's chair.

"Time is like a river," Coydog had told the boy. "It come up behind ya hard and just keep right on goin'. You couldn't stop it no more than you could fly away."

Ptolemy's river had been rough and fast, rushing over stones, throwing him around like a half-dead catfish. More than once he'd opened his eyes on a day he'd wished he'd never seen.

"No, Doctor. I on'y need a few months."

Ruben smiled again.

"Robyn?" the doctor asked.

"Uh-huh?"

"Medicine isn't perfect. Many times, especially with new drugs, they cause as many problems as they solve. They only get better by way of trial and error."

"Uh-huh."

"You know what I mean by that?"

"That if I take some new pill that ain't been tested a lot I might could get sick?"

"You might could die," the doctor said, managing not to insult the girl.

Robyn nodded. Ptolemy nodded too.

"This is too much for a child," the old man said.

"She brought you here, Mr. Grey."

"If we gonna talk about death, she could wait outside."

Ruben smiled again. "You're just about half mad," he said, "not quite. I'm the other half of that."

"You like the crazy white doctor down in Adamsville used to come down an' help colored men get shot and stabbed when the hospitals turnt them away?"

"I'm more like the gunshot or the knife wound."

Ptolemy heard these words clearly, and he understood, even though he could not have explained this knowledge.

"You want my life, Doctor?"

"There's a drug," Bryant Ruben said. "They make it in a town in Southeast Asia where there are fewer laws governing research. A group of physicians from all over the world that work there, remotely, are testing a medicine that might be able to help you."

"A trial-and-mistake medicine?" Robyn asked.

"Yeah. It's dangerous, and would be illegal if the FDA knew

about it. It doesn't always work, and when it does, it burns bright for just a little while. We need subjects who have not deteriorated so much that they have lost too much, so that we can tell where we went right and where we went wrong . . . after the subject dies."

"Dies?" Robyn stood up, putting her hand on Ptolemy's shoulder. "Let's get outta here, Uncle."

But Ptolemy Grey didn't stand. Instead he bowed his head and pressed his fingertips against the bones of his skull. He'd caught a few of the doctor's words. He'd grasped at them something like when he was a child chasing chicken feathers floating on the breeze.

"Come on, Uncle."

Ptolemy raised his head; staring into those beady green eyes, he realized with a shock that he was staring into the face of the Devil.

"Devil a angel just like all the rest," Coydog had told him more than once. "Devil came to the Lord and demanded more. His wings was singed an' he was th'ow'd down, but he still a angel, and you got to give him his due."

The two men, Dr. Ruben and Ptolemy, looked at each other across the desk. There was the heavy scent of roses drifting in from the open door. Robyn's hand was on Ptolemy's shoulder.

"Do I sign something?" Ptolemy asked the Devil.

"A form willing your body to a university I have a relationship with. It says that upon your death we can examine your remains."

"Uncle Grey, we don't have to listen to this man."

"Do you promise that it woik?" Ptolemy asked, a slight smile on his dark lips.

"Not always. There are three phases . . ."

The doctor explained but Ptolemy did not care, or even try, to comprehend. He watched the fallen angel's expressions and gestures, looking for signs and portents. There was a rushing sound in his ears and his heart ran fast.

". . . that has been the last phase," Bryant Ruben was saying. "We've changed the cocktail, hopefully to alleviate this symptom, but I'd be lying if I promised you anything."

Devil the most honest man walk the earth, Coydog had said. *He offer you his treasure and take your soul. They call him the Prince of Liars, but he ain't no different than a bartender: you pays your nickel and drinks your poison.*

"Uncle."

"If I drink yo' medicine, that will be for you, right?" Ptolemy asked, picking over the words carefully, slowly.

"You're likely to find relief from your cognitive issues."

"But you wanna pay me, right?"

"I would give you a sum of cash . . . twenty-five hundred dollars."

It was Ptolemy's turn to grin. The back door of his mind was open for a moment. He didn't understand most of what either of them was saying but he could follow anything the doctor said with an answer that he knew must be true.

"Keep yo' money, Satan," he said. "Gimme the poison for you, but I don't need no money."

A deal was struck, over Robyn's protests. Papers were signed, plans were made, and the men shook hands. Ruben saw them both to the door.

"You paid Antoine Church for this?" Robyn asked at the door.

The green-eyed Devil-doctor smiled for her, barely nodding. She sucked her tooth at him.

Ptolemy laughed on the bus ride home.

"Uncle, we cain't do this," Robyn said.

"It's already done, baby."

"But you don't have to go through with it."

"I already done the hard part."

"What's that?" the dark child asked.

"I done played the Devil an' beat him at his own game. On'y way he could take my soul is if he give to me. But I tricked him. I made a fair trade wit' him. I give 'im my body but not my soul."

"Uncle, you crazy."

"Not for long."

Olga Slatkin, a young woman of Lithuanian origin, came to the apartment the following Monday.

"I vas told by my agency to come here and give Mr. Grey these antibiotic shots for five days," she said to Robyn.

"That was Dr. Ruben?" the girl asked.

"No. No, I do not know this man. I vork for a voman named Borman."

Olga was young and unattractive but still Ptolemy liked her face.

She gave him one injection in his left arm and then another in his right.

"Why he got to have two shots?" Robyn asked, hovering behind the nurse.

"One is the medicine, and the other is for what the medicine might do."

"Like what?" Robyn demanded.

"Fever, nausea, diarrhea, pain," the Eastern European said, her face flat and her voice matter-of-fact.

"Uncle, I don't think that you should be doin' this," Robyn said after the nurse had gone.

"It's okay, baby. It's the only chance we got."

"But you old," the child complained. "You might could get so sick that you might could die."

"I'ma die anyways," he said. "But this way I won't get so lost when I look around the room, I'll have my double-u ara eye en gee for myself, and then I could turn on the thing, the thing, the thing . . . That thing there," he said, pointing at the television.

Robyn knew what Ptolemy got like when he spoke too long or got excited. If he went on much longer he'd stop making any sense at all and get frustrated and then sad.

"Okay, Uncle Grey," she said, "but that doctor said that this medicine would probably kill you."

Ptolemy was looking at his hands by then. He was wondering once again why words failed him after just a few sentences.

That night the place on his left arm where the nurse had injected him started to burn. He didn't tell Robyn, though. He knew that the girl could stop the nurse from coming if she really wanted to.

Olga came again the next day, and that night Ptolemy's arm seethed all the way to his shoulder.

"Did you live on a farm?" he asked her on the third day as she injected the medicine.

"Yes," she said, smiling. "How did you know that?"

"You could see the country in people's eyes," he said. "It's like deep skies and long times'a bein' quiet."

Olga Slatkin smiled at her charge and then frowned.

"How haff you been feeling, Mr. Grey?"

Robyn was in the living room, watching the TV, because she didn't like seeing him given his medicine.

"My arms burn some," he said.

"Do you vant me to stop?"

"No, baby. I could take the pain. I seen Coy dance on fire, but he never told, never."

By Thursday the pain was in both arms, his chest, and his head too. On Friday, when Shirley Wring came for a visit, Robyn had to turn her away.

"Uncle Grey got a fever," Robyn told the older woman. "He says that maybe you could come back next week. He's real sick and cain't get out of bed."

Shirley Wring took in these words as she stood there, staring at the teenager.

"Why don't you like me, child?" Shirley asked at last.

"He really is sick," Robyn complained. "I ain't lyin' to you."

"I believe you, but you still don't like me and I don't know what it is I done to make you hate me."

"I don't hate you, Miss Wring. I don't even think about you at all."

"See? Now that's just rude. Why you wanna be rude to me? I'm your uncle's friend."

"He not my real uncle," the woman-child said to the woman. "But that's what it is. He don't know who he lookin' at or what he sayin' half the time. People wanna take his money or his things. He paid your utility bill and now you come by all the time."

Shirley Wring smiled then and nodded. She walked into the living room, noticing that the door to Ptolemy's bedroom was closed.

"I told you that he cain't get outta his bed," Robyn said, a strain of grief in her young voice.

"I ain't gonna bother him," Shirley told the girl.

The older woman sat down on a maple chair in front of a TV tray that Ptolemy sometimes used as a table for intimate teas with his friend.

"It was my phone bill," Shirley said. "I asked him for five dollars and he gave me ten. But I offered him this to hold."

She placed her faded cherry-red purse on the TV tray and took out a smaller black velvet bag. From this she took the piece of pink tissue paper which held a lovely golden ring sporting a large green stone. This she handed to Robyn.

The girl could see that the metal was gold and the stone was precious. She had seen nice things in magazines, on TV shows, and through thick, bulletproof glass.

"Cabochon emerald," Shirley Wring said.

After fondling the stone a moment or two Robyn held it out to Shirley, but the half-blind woman would not take it.

"My great-grandmother stoled it outta her ex-master's house in 1865, when Abraham Lincoln's bluecoats freed the slaves," Shirley said in a tone of voice that was obviously quoting family lore. "She told her son that even though the ring was worth a whole lifetime for a poor black family that he should keep it as a treasure that stood for our freedom. My grandfather was named Bill Hollyfield, but he changed his name to Wring to honor his mother's gift to him.

"I want you to give that ring to your uncle and tell him to get bettah and that I want him to be well because he has been like a real man to me when I was down past my last dollar."

Robyn felt the gravity of the old woman's gift like a stone in her chest. She wanted to return Shirley's family name and history but the old woman's wounded eyes stopped her.

"I cain't take this from you, Miss Wring."

"It's not for you, sugah. It's for Mr. Ptolemy Grey. It's me tellin' him how much that ten dollahs he give me meant."

"But this precious," Robyn said. "This is worth much more'n that."

"No it ain't, baby."

Shirley rose and touched the girl's cheek.

"If he get real sick an' might die, will you let me see him?"

These words brought Robyn to tears. She sat down on the well-made white bed, crying on the emerald ring in her hand. When she finally raised her head, Shirley had gone and closed the door behind her.

. . .

J ust after Olga Slatkin gave Ptolemy his final injection Robyn had to help her hold the old man down. He was delirious, shouting unintelligible words and writhing in his big bed.

"Coy! Coy!" the old man shouted.

"What's he sayin'?" Robyn cried as she held down his surprisingly strong right arm.

"He's not making sense," the Eastern European woman said. "Hold him for a moment and he vill calm down."

A minute later Ptolemy slumped down in his bed, unconscious, hardly breathing.

"It is always like this after last shot," Olga said. "They go to sleep for three or four days and then they wake up, most of the time."

"What do you mean, 'most of the time'?" Robyn cried.

"He is sick. This medicine is supposed to help, but vit some people it does not vork."

"He wasn't sick before you give him these shots."

"But vy vood Dr. Borman tell me to give shots if he vas not sick?"

While the women talked, Ptolemy awoke on a grassy hill above a stream that flowed over big stones and made the sound of children's laughter. He smiled and stood up without pain or strain. He wasn't old or young or concerned with being old or young. The sun shone brightly upon his head and there were white clouds here and there. The sunlight was so powerful that it burned his face, but he didn't care about that. The day was a particular one he remembered from his childhood. The river was the Tickle, and Coydog McCann was just a ways up from where he now stood.

"He wasn't sick," Robyn said somewhere beyond the blue, "before you give him the shots."

"I cannot tell you anything more than vat they told me," the plain-faced European country girl replied.

When Ptolemy scratched his head his fingers found hair up there. This seemed odd to him, but what difference did hair make anyway?

Coy was sitting on a tree stump by the water, holding a home-made bamboo pole with a twine line.

When the old man (who didn't look nearly so old anymore) looked up, he frowned for a second and then smiled. Ptolemy had forgotten the two canine teeth that his friend had lost. It made his smile seem deeper than the average man's grin.

"Is that you, L'il Pea?" the old man asked.

"Yeah, Uncle Coy. Yes, sir."

"You come all the way back here just to see me?"

"I'ont know," said the old man who was no longer an old man. "I just saw a white nurse from somewhere around Venice an' she gimme some shots an' then I woke up on the rise ovah on t'other side'a the hill."

"I only got one pole," Coy McCann said in apology.

"That's okay. I could just sit next to ya if you ain't just wanna be alone."

"Hell no. I been waitin' for ya."

"Really?"

"Oh yeah. You owe me a debt, and I been waitin' till I get released."

Ptolemy knew what the old man meant. This knowledge made him silent and so he sat down next to the fisherman and peered into the water.

The sun was bright but not bright enough to illuminate the shadows that lay between and underneath the large stones in the river. Catfish and crawfish and other creatures hid down under there in darkness, where bears and cougars and coyotes couldn't get at them; where even the long-necked, elegant gray herons' beaks could not go.

But Ptolemy's mind could climb down there with the fishes and algae. The darkness was cold like night, black and deep . . . sleep . . .

Wake up, boy, wake up," he said in a whisper that was both soft and sharp.

Little Ptolemy opened his eyes and squinted from the pain. He could tell that it was the early hours of the morning, even before the time that his father and mother got out of bed to work in the fields. His brother and sisters were sound asleep as only children could be, and his parents were asleep in the front room of their two-room shack.

"Daddy?"

"Shh!" Coy commanded, putting his fingers to the boy's lips. "Come with me."

Coy pulled the boy out of bed and through a flap in the tar-paper wall and all Ptolemy had on was a nightshirt.

The moon was crescent and an owl passed above them. Crickets chattered and tree frogs chirped. Ptolemy had rarely seen the depth of night. He had never been outside this late, moving along the path behind his family's shack.

"Where we goin', Coydog?"

The old man stopped and turned, putting his face very close to the boy's.

"Shet your mouth or we both be dead. You unnerstand me, boy?"

And with that he clutched Li'l Pea's right forearm and dragged him deep into the woods. They traveled for a long time, until they came to Hangman's Knoll, and climbed up past there through a deep wood until they reached Mourners' Falls. Ptolemy wouldn't have been able to find the falls on his own, even in daylight, but Coy's steps were sure and certain, quick and desperate.

The falls were forty feet high and constant because all the water that came down from the hills drained here. Coy took Pity on a winding path of big stones that led up to the cascades and then around to the cave hidden behind the blind of water that was barely visible in the weak moonlight.

Ptolemy's nightshirt was soaked by the time they got inside the cave. Coy let go of his arm and the boy went to his knees on the stone floor, shivering from cold.

Coy lit an oil-soaked torch, illuminating a stone space that was about the size of the worship hall at Liberty Baptist.

"I'm cold," the boy complained.

"Come back here," Coy replied, stalking to the far end of the huge shale and granite chamber.

Something in the old man's voice, something that the child had never heard before, made him obey in spite of his own suffering.

All along the back of the cave were big flat rocks that had fallen from the roof, broken or shattered.

"This one up next to the north corner," Coy McCann said, waving his torch over a big flat stone that was black except for a white swath at the right side. "Under here is where I hid the treasure. Under here is what I want you to take just as soon as you strong enough to lift it. Go on now, try an' lift it away from the wall."

Ptolemy grasped the edge of the rock, which was much larger than him, and strained to push it away from the wall. But he couldn't budge it at all.

"Good," Coy said, smiling for the first time that night. "You too young, and this is too soon for you to get at it. But later on, when you get to be a young man, I want you to move that stone or break it and take that treasure and make a difference for poor black folks treated like they do us."

Later on they were out under the threads of moonlight that wavered between the branches of pines and oaks.

"I got to go to my place before I run," Coy told Ptolemy. "But I'm ascared to do it."

"Why you scared, Uncle Coy?"

The old man knelt down and brought his leathery hands to the sides of the boy's face.

"You know Jersey Manheim?"

Ptolemy knew and hated and feared the evil white man. He was one of the wealthiest men in their whole community and he treated black people like slaves. He owned the land that Ptolemy's parents worked and kept them so far in debt with his community store and loans for their tools and supplies that they couldn't ever leave or save one thin dime.

"One time when he was drunk as a skunk he told me," Coy said, "that he had a pot'a gold. That him and his fathers before him had put away a gold coin for every week since thirty years before the Civil War. I did my numbers and figgered he had to have nearly five thousand coins. Now, that's some money right there. You know I been thinkin' on them coins for years. And finally, just a few hours before I got to you I went in his house and lugged 'em out to his wagon. I brung 'em up here, heaved 'em under that rock I showed ya."

"How come he didn't wake up when you went in his house?" the child asked.

"'Cause when I came by earlier to give him your daddy's rent I poured some laudanum in his gin when he wasn't lookin'. You know he drink that gin ev'ry night. An' when I was sure that he was paralyzed, I come on in an' searched the house until I fount the treasure chest under a trapdo' under his bed."

"An' he was sleep?" Ptolemy asked.

"Yeah." ·

"So he don't know you took it."

"That don't mattah to the white man. He don't have to know. All he got to do is remembah that I was the last niggah he saw. I was the last he saw and so I'ma be the first he go to."

"So you gonna run?"

"Damn right I'ma run. I'ma run all the way to New York City with the twenty coins I took for myself. I'ma go up there an' I won't see another cotton plant ever again in my life."

At these words Li'l Pea Grey started to cry. Coy was his closest friend.

"Sometimes we got to make a sacrifice, Pity," the old man said. "Now, come go wit' me to my house so I could get my things and make it outta the county before sunup."

They moved on back-road paths through the night headed for the lean-to shelter that Coy McCann had called home since the barber took over his room for his new wife and child. Ptolemy didn't think anymore about his feet or the cold. He didn't worry about the white people that might be after him or his uncle. He felt as if he were a soldier now, fighting on enemy ground, like in the stories he and Coy read down by the Tickle when the fish weren't biting.

"Stay here," Coy told Ptolemy at a stand of live oaks on a rise that looked down on the old man's shelter.

"How come?"

"I wanna see you every minute I can before I'm gone forever," Coy replied, "but this is my most dangerous moment. I got all my things in a bag in the house. I couldn't take it with me because of how heavy the gold was gonna be. And I had to get you and show you where the gold was before I left. So now I just got to hope that old Jersey drunk enough drug to keep him sleepin' through the night. But if it don't, I don't want him to find you down there wit' me."

Ptolemy slipped behind a tree as his uncle spoke, feeling both afraid and ashamed of his fear. He watched as Coydog McCann loped down the hill to his home. Just when he was at the tarp entrance, someone yelled and white men jumped out from all over the place.

The first white man cuffed Ptolemy's friend, and the boy shouted, unable to keep the pain out of his mouth. But no one heard him because they were all shouting and hollering and beating Coy mercilessly, throwing him from man to man.

The sun was a red strip above the farthest hill.

Shouting loudly, Jersey Manheim asked Coy again and again where he had hidden his money. And for a long time Coy was silent. He was surrounded by thirteen men who meant to kill him, but Coy took the blows. Finally he shouted out something; the only words Ptolemy could make out were "*. . . bottom of the well . . .*"

Mercifully the vision of the lynching passed by the fevered dreamer's eyes quickly. He only caught a glimpse of the hanging man dancing on fire while the white men laughed and raised their firebrands in the half darkness of dawn.

Twenty-six-year-old Sensia Howard was married to Ezra Bindle when Ptolemy, a man of forty-five years, met them at a barbecue in Griffith Park. Her yellow dress made its own party, and Ezra's powerful arm held her so tightly about the waist that they might have been grafted like that.

Sensia was medium brown with dark hair that shone in the

L.A. sunshine. Her eyes were different colors of brown and her smile made Ptolemy happy.

He mentioned a book he'd been reading and how much he liked going to the library on Avalon.

"You live near there?" Sensia asked innocently.

"Across the street. In a big blue boardinghouse," Ptolemy said. "It's funny that the house is so big 'cause my room the size of a two-cent postage stamp."

"I own my own house," Ezra said then. He was twice Ptolemy's size, the color of aged red brick, and proud. "I keep my woman here in nice clothes, and I feed her steak three times a week."

"What kinda book you readin', Mr. Grey?" Sensia asked.

"Called *Night Man*. It's about a man who live in darkness and who nevah see the light of day."

"Nevah?"

"What you do for a livin'?" Ezra asked Ptolemy.

"I used to 'liver ice off a truck, but now I do cleanup for the county."

"How much they pay you for that?"

"How does he go to the bank?" Sensia asked, obviously talking about the protagonist of Ptolemy's book. "How does he go to the post office?"

"He does all his bankin' by mail," Ptolemy said. "An' he, an' there's a twenty-four-hour post office he go to a lot."

"That's so interesting," the young beauty said. "A man that's just different from everybody else."

"We gotta go, Sensie," Ezra Bindle said. "Rex an' them want us to have a drink together."

"Can you come with, Mr. Grey?" she asked.

"They didn't invite him," Ezra said before Ptolemy could say yes.

"Then I'll stay here an' talk to Mr. Grey about his book while you go guzzle that beer," she said, pushing out from the grip as she spoke.

"You are coming with me," the big red-brown man said to his young wife. And he dragged her off.

Ptolemy had been married, started a family, and gotten divorced by that time. His children were almost grown, living with their mother, and he felt like an old man, except for a moment there under the scrutiny of Sensia Howard's eyes.

But Ezra dragged her away through the parking lot and out past the baseball field, where uniformed white men in some amateur league played their game.

Ptolemy watched them go: Ezra pulling on her arm and Sensia struggling to get free. He felt almost as if the brute had pulled out one of his organs and was running away with it, leaving him wounded and sore.

Ptolemy was flying above the park then. It was really more like a small forest than a manicured lawn. It gave him a giddy feeling seeing all the various people and hidden animals, paths and clumps of trees.

He was flying above Los Angeles, and every once in a while he'd turn his gaze upward, where the blue was so intense that it made him feel as if he'd burn out his soul with the vision and so he had to look away, back to earth, where life was pedestrian and shabby.

He was flying in his sleep, rising higher and higher until he remembered that men were not made to fly and that sooner or later he would come crashing back down to the ground. The sudden fright woke him and he sat up in the bed in his windowless room in the big blue house across the street from the public library.

Ptolemy considered the dream of flying and fear of the fall. He thought about the picnic he had been to the weekend before with his friends who knew Ezra, who had a wife named Sensia.

It was 6:45 in the morning.

Someone knocked at the door.

There are times in your life when things line up and Fate takes a hand in your future," Ptolemy remembered Coydog saying. "When that happens, you got to move quick and take advantage of the sitchiation or you'll never know what might have been."

"How do I know when it's time to move quick?" L'il Pea asked.

"When somethin' big happens and then somethin' else come up."

Ptolemy got out of the bed, laughing at the foolishness of his childhood. He'd loved his uncle and cried for days after the old man's demise but he had come to understand that Coy McCann was a dreamer mostly and that his lessons were either useless or dangerous.

He opened the door, expecting a rooming-house neighbor who needed help of some sort. Everybody in the Blue Bonnet, as they called their home, was up early to go to work at some job cleaning or carrying, cooking or breaking stone.

When he opened the door and saw Sensia Howard standing there, all Ptolemy could think about was Coy and how well he understood even the incomprehensible. Coy became Ptolemy's religion on that morning, standing in front of the most beautiful woman he had ever known.

Ptolemy gawped at the girl, who now wore a green frock that made her brown skin glow like fire.

"Are you gonna put on some pants, Mr. Grey?" were her first words to him.

He was standing there in boxer shorts, expecting some normal person who shouldn't expect him to get dressed after being dragged from bed.

"Yeah, yeah," he said. "Hold on." And he went back to his closet and pulled out a pair of brown trousers and a yellow shirt.

As he dressed he remembered that he hadn't asked her in. Maybe she'd think this was an insult and leave. And so he went back to the door without putting on socks and shoes.

Sensia was there, waiting.

"Come on in," he said.

He only had one chair, and that had a book, a glass of water, and three stones he'd found that day at the park on it. They were blond stones, a color he'd never seen in rock and so he picked them up and brought them home, to be with them for a while. He wondered what Coy would have said about those pebbles as he removed them, the book, and the water glass from the chair.

"Where do you want me to sit?" Sensia asked.

"What are you doin' here, Mrs. Howard?"

"Howard's my maiden name and I'm not married no more. At least not as far as I'm concerned."

"You not?"

"What day is it?" she asked.

"Thursday."

"And what day did we meet?"

"Sunday. No, no . . . Saturday."

She smiled, studied the seating arrangements, and sat on the straight-back pine chair.

"You go sit on the bed, Mr. Grey."

He did so.

She beamed at him and nodded. "It was Saturday, because I left Ezra on Sunday, the day after he manhandled me."

Ptolemy felt like a bug fixed in amber, caught forever in brilliance and beauty beyond his understanding.

"Mr. Grey?"

"Yes, Miss Howard?"

"Can I come sit next to you on your bed?"

He gulped, which gave the impression of a nod, and so she moved from chair to bed, putting her hand on his knee.

"My mama always told me," she said, "that a woman must have at least three days between men. Three whole days or people could say that she was loose."

Ptolemy said, "Monday, Tuesday, Wednesday," and they kissed lightly.

"Why you shakin' your head, Mr. Grey?"

"Because I'm almost forty-six, will be in two months and a half, and I have never seen you comin'."

"I'm twenty-six," Sensia said, and then kissed his cheek, "and I been waitin' to find you every day I been alive."

"Me?"

"I saw you at that barbecue party and I knew that you would read to me and hold me if I had fever. I knew that you would ask me how I was today and hear every word I said. A year later when I had forgot, you'd still be there to remind me. My man."

"And that's why you left Ezra?"

"No. I left Ezra because he pushed on me and grabbed at me. But he did that because he knew how much I wanted to be with you."

With that, Sensia stood up and took off her green dress and Ptolemy knew that Coy was right.

"Are you gonna take off them pants?" she asked him, and the dream shifted while someone in the room moaned, either in ecstasy or pain.

He woke up to find her dead twenty-two years later. She hadn't put on a pound, smoked, or drunk to excess, but she died of a stroke in her sleep while he dreamed of waking up to her smile. She wasn't yet forty-nine, would never be. She'd had lovers and times away, but Ptolemy couldn't bring himself to leave her (except once), nor could he bar her from their door. In the decade before she died she had begun to hoard things: suitcases and clothes, newspapers and books. She'd go to secondhand stores and buy hat racks and jewelry boxes, furniture and musical instruments that she meant to learn to play but never did. The kitchen had fallen into disrepair and they ate take-out food from pizza kitchens and Chinese restaurants that were no more than holes in the wall. Ptolemy would get up every morning and buy them coffee in Styrofoam cups at the diner two blocks down.

And he loved her.

"What do you think about this dress," she'd ask him, twirling about in something new or used that she'd bought with money he made working for the county maintenance department.

He'd look at her posing, knowing that no man could get between this. She might meet someone now and then that distracted her; like Harlan Norman, who asked her to go to Hawaii with him. They spent a month, and all of Harlan's money, on the islands, but then she came back, alone, with a big black pearl for Ptolemy.

There were many days that Ptolemy wanted to kill Sensia. He'd bought a short-barreled .25-caliber pistol once when she didn't come home for the weekend. But then, on Tuesday, she walked through their apartment door and smiled for him. He forgot his mission and they made love and she said she was sorry.

One day she told him, "I will nevah cheat on you again, Papa," and as far as he knew she hadn't.

When he woke up that morning next to her corpse he cried for an hour; cried calling emergency; cried while the ambulance drivers tried to resuscitate her.

"Stroke," the Asian paramedic said.

"She nevah did you right, Pitypapa," Niecie said.

"Eleven hundred dollars," the funeral director said.

"Amen," the preacher said to a room filled with men and women that had been her lovers over the years. Even Ezra Bindle was there. He had a portly wife and seven portly children but he came to say good-bye because Sensia was the kind of woman that lovers pined after even when they no longer felt the love.

Ptolemy was already an old man. He read to Sensia at night and asked her about her day. He made her chicken soup when she was ill—and she was often ill. She was never out of his mind since the first day he'd seen her and she shook off the grip of Ezra Bindle to be his woman.

"Even if I wander, I will always find my way back home to you," she'd told him.

He'd put those words on her tombstone, sold two of Coy's doubloons to pay for it and for the flowers to be put on her grave every Valentine's Day, her favorite holiday.

"Wake up, Uncle," Robyn said from somewhere beyond the blue, blue sky above the graveyard.

Things began to happen quickly after the death and burial of Sensia Howard: Ptolemy saw himself as a young man with a stout lever under the light of an oil-soaked brand, moving the dark stone that hid the double-thick canvas bags filled with old gold coins; he was working, working, working cleaning out buildings set for demolition, or empty lots where the city planned to build, or the sidewalks in front of courts, office buildings, and police stations; he was talking to Coy in life and death, loving Sensia, missing his children (Rayford and Rayetta), who despised him after their mother had taken them away; and wondering what a treasure could do to save black folks who had been crushed down by a whole epoch of restrictions and pain.

. . .

Uncle Grey?" Robyn said for maybe the thousandth time.

"Yeah, babe?" he replied with his eyes still closed.

"Are you awake?"

He raised his lids then, like the curtain from a stage at the beginning of a play that he had wanted to see for many, many years. Robyn was sitting next to him, holding his hands in hers.

"Right here," he said. "How long?"

"Four days," Robyn said. "I called Dr. Ruben but his phone was disconnected. I wanted to tell somebody but I didn't know who. Niecie been wantin' to come ovah, but I told her that the doctor said that you had this bad flu, that anybody breathe yo' air could get sick."

"Help me to sit up."

He looked around the old bedroom, the room where he awoke to find Sensia Howard dead. He no longer felt the pang of loss when thinking of Sensia, whom he had loved unconditionally. She was gone, off in a lovely dream.

"Help me stand up."

"I thought you was gonna die, Uncle," Robyn said as she half-supported him into the living room.

He sat down on the rainbow hammock of his stool and stared at the TV. He reached out and pressed the *I/O* button and smiled as some comedy show came into view. His fingers felt hot, alive. He could sense the old bones beneath his leathered skin. He could feel the air and smell the sour odor rising from his body. He looked around.

It had been decades since that room had been so clean and neat.

"Robyn?"

"Yeah, Uncle?"

"You are a gift from God, you know that?"

"Are you okay?" she replied.

"Nevah bettah, nevah once in all my years."

"Yo' skin is hot," she said.

"Burnin' bright," he said with depth to his raspy voice.

"Maybe we should see a doctor."

"We already seen the doctor," he said. "What we gotta do is make things right, make things right . . ." He stalled for a moment, then found the thread of his thoughts again. "Because there's a lot to do for you and Reggie's kids, for Niecie and black folks all ovah the world."

"Like what?"

Instead of answering, Ptolemy looked at his child savior. She didn't have the magic of Sensia or the deep, crazy accuracy of Coydog, but Robyn was the best of them . . . Ptolemy dawdled over this thought a moment. Here he was, sitting on a folding chair in his home after years of sadness and careless loss. His mind had fallen in on itself like an old barn left unmended and untended through too many seasons.

"What, Uncle?" Robyn asked.

"A gift from God," he said again. "Without you I wouldn't even be here."

"Somebody else woulda come," Robyn said, bowing her head.

"Yeah. They'da come, but I still wouldn't be here. It's me that's the lump'a clay and you that's the hand of God."

. . .

Pitypapa!" Niecie exclaimed when Ptolemy and Robyn showed up at her door three days later.

He'd needed twenty-four hours to recover from the weakness four days in bed had put on him. The next day he bathed and pondered, read a book called *Real Time*, and listened to jazz on the radio. Then he went to a small men's store on Central and bought a dark-blue suit with a deep-brown shirt and a yellow tie and black shoes.

"That the way you used to dress when you was a playah, Mr. Grey?" Robyn had asked him while he stood before the store's triple dressing mirror.

"No, baby. That's Coydog McCann I see in the mirror—the classiest man I evah knew."

After donning his new clothes Ptolemy took Robyn to the ladies' shop next door, and then to the taxi stand on Normandie. From there they went to Niecie's home.

"Hey, Niecie," the old man said in a tone he hadn't known for decades. "How you doin', sugah?"

Niecie stopped there in the desolate living room, cocking her head to try and get a bead on the voice she was hearing.

"I'm all bettah now, Niecie," Ptolemy said. "Robyn done took me to a doctor near about killed me, but then he pulled me back from the night."

"You can, you can think bettah now, Pitypapa?" Niecie asked, stumbling on her own tongue. "Like when you was young?"

"Mmmm," Ptolemy said, smiling and nodding. "But I'm still old in my bones, so you gonna offah me a seat?"

. . .

After Robyn got the lemonade from the kitchen, big-bodied Hilliard came back from a run to the store with Letisha and Arthur in tow. The big thief frowned when he saw Ptolemy sitting there with his legs crossed and a glass of lemonade in his hand.

"Boy," Ptolemy greeted. He wasn't mad at the young man anymore.

"Name's Hilly, not *boy*."

"Hilliard, you will speak respectfully to elders in my house," his mother said.

Hilliard glowered.

"Why you wouldn't let me in your house when I come all the way ovah there to see about you, Papa Grey?"

"You know why."

"'Cause you old an', an', an' senile."

"Hilliard!" Niecie said.

"It's true."

"Maybe I was a little forgetful," Ptolemy admitted, "but I could still count up to three with the best of 'em."

"You see, Mama? He talks crazy."

The angry young man's tone was aggressive. Robyn put her hand in her purse as Ptolemy smiled. The children huddled next to their auntie Niecie's chair, staring at Hilly as if he were some dangerous stranger.

"I ain't so crazy I don't know how to make you listen," Ptolemy said.

He put his hand inside his breast pocket and came out with a roll of twenty-dollar bills.

The sight of money hit Hilly like a slap.

"What's that, Pitypapa?" Niecie asked.

"Yo' boy took me to the bank with three checks, got my signature, but only gave me money for the one," Ptolemy said. "That's why he blusterin', 'cause he feel guilty. But I had Robyn bring me ovah here to bury the hatchet."

He leaned over, handing the roll of cash to his grandniece.

"That's six hunnert dollahs, Niecie. I wanna make sure that these kids is gettin' what they need. I'ma give you sumpin' like that ev'ry mont'. Lucky I didn't give yo' son my passbook or I might not have nuthin' left ta give ya."

"My boy does not steal," Niecie said, clutching the wad in her lap. "You gettin' old, Pitypapa. You just made a mistake thinkin' you give him three checks but it was only one."

Ptolemy noticed then that she was wearing a maroon dress with pink flowers stitched into it. It was faded and worn.

"Madeline Richards made that dress for you, didn't she?" Ptolemy asked.

Robyn grinned when she saw the surprise on her one-time guardian's face.

"How did you know that?"

"Sensie introduced you to Maddie. An' Maddie made clothes for a livin'. She always was partial to flower patterns, an' when she couldn't find no cloth with a flower she sewed some on."

"I remember meetin' Maddie," Niecie said. "She made this dress maybe fifteen years ago."

"When you was a li'l girl your uncle Roger called you Betty Boop because you loved to watch that cartoon on the TV. If you'd sing her boop-boop-pe-doop song he'd give you two nickels."

Hilda "Niecie" Brown frowned and cocked her head again. Her eyes narrowed to slits, and after a moment or two she nodded.

"Yeah," she said. "That's right. Uncle Roger. He died in Vietnam and I cried for what felt like a whole week. He wasn't really my uncle, though."

"That's what yo' mama said, but he was her brother usin' another name because he had killed a man in Alabama and then took on another man's identity. He died under a false name. He really was your uncle, but nobody said it so that he didn't get put on a Alabama chain gang."

"You remembah all that, Pitypapa?"

"Doctor cured me, baby," Ptolemy said as he rose to his feet.

Robyn stood behind him, her hand still in her purse, her eye on Hilliard.

"He opened my mind all the way back to the first day I could remembah as a child. I can think so clear that I could almost remembah what my father's father was thinkin' the day he conceived my old man. So you could say what you will but that boy there's a thief an' if you don't tell him sumpin' he gonna go the way that Roger would'a gone if anybody evah breathed his real name."

Robyn kept her eyes on Hilly while Niecie stared at her uncle, looking for the man she'd seen little more than a month before.

When she didn't speak, Ptolemy addressed her again: "I'ma give you that six hunnert dollahs for these kids here ev'ry month. As long as they with you I'ma give it to 'em, but I won't if you send 'em back to they mama."

Ptolemy gazed down at the children and they cowered. The boy scrunched up his dark face, trying to understand what the money had to do with him and his sister.

"They wit' me," Niecie said, and Ptolemy nodded.

He then turned to the brutish boy. "Hilly, you saved me from that crazy woman and so I forgive you. I'ma call on you sometime soon 'cause I need to know somethin'."

"What you wanna know from me?"

"Later."

Ptolemy touched Robyn's shoulder and they walked out the door and away from the house, moving slowly, like royalty surveying the plight of the poor.

"Why you wanna get Hilly all mad, Uncle?" Robyn said on the bus ride home.

She was wearing the yellow dress that he'd bought her at the women's clothes store. He knew it was wrong, that the dress reminded him of the day he met Sensia Howard, but he couldn't stop himself—he loved both women so.

"Yellow's my favorite color," he'd told her, "and you my favorite girl."

But on the bus he just nodded and said, "I need a inroad."

"What you mean, Uncle Grey?"

"The men just come to you, don't they, girl?" he asked instead of answering her question directly.

"Huh?"

"Men," he repeated. "They just come to you—on the street, in the bus, at the movies. They all wanna know you, want you to smile at 'em."

"Nobody I wanna know."

"Imagine if nobody evah looked at you twice," Ptolemy said.

His mind straddled two worlds. He no longer needed a translator to decipher what was going on around him, but he was still sitting by the Tickle River, talking to Coy and making plans for a future eighty years from then.

"What you mean?" Robyn asked.

"Some people got a magnet in 'em," Ptolemy said, pulling his mind away from the deep-blue past. "No one understands why, but there's people you just wanna know. You might be quiet and shy, but that someone walk by you and you climb right ovah your fear an' say, 'How you doin'?' just like you was old friends. That's you, Robyn. I know, 'cause my Sensie was like that. Men, and women too, would come up to her and ask her to be wit' them. She met this schoolteacher one time, Mrs. Gladys Pine. Gladys told Sensie she loved her and for a week or two they'd meet in the afternoons at a motel on Slauson."

"When she was married to you?" Robyn asked.

"Sensie told me she liked Gladys's mind and she didn't feel like she was cheatin' 'cause it was a woman and not a man."

"That's crazy."

"Anyway, Gladys finally told her husband that she was leavin', that she had fount her true love. The next day Sensie told her that they'd have to stop meetin' at the motel. The day aftah that, Paul Pine put a bullet in his head."

"Damn."

"That's how powerful you are, girl," Ptolemy said, taking Robyn's hand in his. "You pretty, but pretty alone's not what people see. You the kinda pretty, the kinda beauty, that's like a mirror. Men an' women see themselves in you, only now they so beautiful that they can't bear to see you go."

"Uncle Grey, was you always thinkin' all these things even when you couldn't talk so good?"

"When you get old," he said, and then he paused, thinking about Coy and Lupo, who were known in the colored community as the Dog Brothers. They ran together as young men, and when they got into their forties, old for men back then, they could sit together for hours, never saying a word and never getting tired of the company. "When you get old you begin to understand that no one talks unless someone listens, and no one knows nuthin' 'less somebody else can understand."

"And nobody was listenin' to you, Uncle?"

"And nobody understood until you, child."

"But what's that got to do with Gladys Pine?"

"She nevah touched anybody outside'a herself. She was like I was when you met me—alone in her mind. And then she seen Sensie and reached out and my girl took her hand and helt it to her breast. You know, I almost cry when I think about it. It was beautiful, even though it was a blues song too. Some people might say it was love on one hand and a fickle heart on the other, but what would have come from them if they didn't see and say and feel . . . and die?"

"You deep, Uncle," Robyn said.

"No, baby. I'm just like everybody else—everybody else."

That night Ptolemy woke from a dream about Coy's death. He had a fever but didn't wake Robyn. He thought that he might die if he stayed in the bed, so he got up and went to the bathroom, where he swallowed four aspirin and turned on a lukewarm shower.

The water soothed him.

After a while he hunkered down in the tub and let the cool

water cascade over his bony form. He wondered what was in the Devil's medicine that kept his knees from hurting too much.

In that position, in the tub, he was seventeen again, lugging the heavy bags of coin from out of Coy's secret cave. He borrowed his cousin's Terraplane car and drove to Memphis, where he secreted the stolen treasure for three years. Every time he touched those coins he felt the cold of that cave's water and the chill of death.

When he began to shiver, he rose up under the spray, turned off the water, and dried himself with a big thick towel that Robyn had bought. After he was dry he stared at his head and torso in the water-stained mirror. He probably weighed less than the sleeping child in the next room, but he'd put on weight. His face was not nearly so wrinkled as some old people he'd known, but he could see the ninety-one years in his eyes. He could see the old confusion hovering above his crown, waiting to settle back on him like a venomless smothering snake around its prey.

"Uncle?" Robyn said.

She was standing at the door.

Ptolemy took the towel from the sink and wrapped it around his skinny waist, using his hand as the clasp. He stared at the girl but did not speak.

"You okay, Uncle?"

He nodded.

"What's wrong?"

"I know how a man could lose his mind, but how do he find it again?" he said as she approached him.

"You're cold."

"I was burnin' up there in my bed. I was thinkin' about the river . . ."

"Where you and Coydog used to fish?"

"How much money we got in the bank now?" he asked.

"All of it. Forty-two thousand in the savings account an' the rest in that deposit box. Come on, Uncle, you should go back to bed."

"What's that boy's name? The one you seein'."

"Beckford?"

"Yeah . . . him. You like him?"

"He all right." Robyn looked away and Ptolemy knew for sure that she had made love to the handsome friend of Reggie.

"You said he live with three other young men?"

"Uh-huh."

"Now that the money's gone, you could bring him ovah if you want. You can sleep in the bedroom. I don't care."

"I don't wanna talk about this, Uncle."

"Why not?"

"I don't know. I mean, it makes me feel embarrassed."

Ptolemy hooked Robyn's chin with the index finger of his left hand and lifted her face to regard him. She was wearing just a T-shirt, and all that covered him was that towel. Ptolemy thought about that but he wasn't ashamed.

"I love you, Uncle Grey," Robyn said.

"'Course you do," he said. "I'm like family."

"Uh-uh," the woman inside the child said. "I got family. I know what that feels like. No, Uncle, I could sit an' listen to you for days. Even when yo' mind was confused an' you was scared, I still looked up to you. And you treat me with respect an' you still be lookin' at my legs an' stuff. I don't want Beckford in this house wit' us."

Both Ptolemys, past and present, heard the love in her voice; neither one had the words to answer back.

Where'd you put my toolbox?" he asked Robyn the next morning as he rummaged through the living room closet.

"I put it under yo' bed," Robyn said. She was lying on the couch that was also a bed, watching a show about strange fish in the deep ocean.

"Could you get down there and get it for me, please?"

When she jumped up from the couch, Ptolemy said, "You could finish your show, child. I don't need you to snap to."

Instead of sitting back down the girl came up to him and kissed his cheek and hugged him tight. Ptolemy would always get lost in a woman's hug. His mind still drifted under the spell a soft embrace.

"What's that for?"

"Would you marry me if I was twenty years older and you was fifty years younger?" she asked.

"You could do bettah than somebody like me."

"God couldn't do bettah than you, Uncle Grey."

It wasn't the words so much as the hunger in the child's tone that brought the pain into his chest. It was the same pain he felt when the giant roach flew up in his kitchen. He gripped her shoulders and she gazed at him.

"Are you," he asked, "are you goin' out with Beckford tonight?"

"Not if you don't want me to."

"No, it's all right. I actually wanted to sit quiet and read some."

"Are you tired'a me bein' here, Uncle?"

"No, baby. You put a fire in my mind and love at my doorstep."

He'd heard the words somewhere before, maybe in a song.

Robyn left at six o'clock and by six-ten Ptolemy was in the living room closet, working his crowbar on the back end floor. There was a slot there made specially by Ptolemy almost five decades before. His apartment was on the ground floor. Below the floor was three feet of concrete. There he had carved out a place for Coydog's treasure. It took him a while to jimmy the jury-rigged trapdoor but after some work he flipped it over. The ancient hinges screamed and parts of the wood floor splintered and popped.

Ptolemy wondered where all the dust came from. The box he hid from himself was covered with a quarter-inch of thick gray soot.

He used the iron key to open the chest but he didn't even touch the bag inside. He knew the gold was there, coins that went back all the way to the Civil War and before, some used, some like new. But it wasn't his treasure. He was just the guardian, obeying a long-ago command from Coy the thief, martyr, and partisan.

He didn't need to fondle the gold but he took out an oiled cloth that was wrapped around a blue-black .25 pistol—which still gleamed darkly.

The grin on Ptolemy's lips was not welcomed by him. He had never shot even a rabbit. But he smirked at the gun, turning it over and over in his hand.

Hello?" Hilly Brown said into the receiver.

"That you, boy?" Ptolemy asked.

"Papa Grey? Hey. Listen . . . I'm sorry for bein' rude the other day. Mama told me to call you up and apologize."

"Why haven't you called, then?"

"I'ont know," the brooding, bulbous, and brown man-child said. "I mean, I don't know why I didn't. I'ma pay you back, okay?"

"Why you take my money in the first place?"

"I didn't think you would realize. You acted like you was drunk or high or sumpin'. So I thought it would be all right."

"All right to steal?" Ptolemy asked while he opened and clenched his right hand slowly.

His knuckles hurt every time the fist got tight—but not that bad. His fiery mind was still in an old man's body. He was weak as a boy and old as a man can get, but not as bad as he was—not half as bad.

You know everything," Li'l Pea said to Coy one day when Coy had told him about George Washington Carver and the peanut.

"No, child," Coy said in a surprisingly gentle tone, "it's you know more'n me."

Li'l Pea giggled and said, "Me? I'ont hardly know nuthin'."

"That might be, but still you know more'n me."

"Like what?" the child asked, not realizing the impossibility of his question.

"You know how crickets smell and what pebbles sound like

when they fall on the ground around yo' feet. You see deep in the sky without havin' to look or think about it, and you love your mama an' yo' daddy so much that they would die if God took you from them."

"Don't you know all them things?" the boy asked, sobered by the seriousness of the older man's words.

"Like a suit'a clothes," Coydog said. "I got them things like a new suit just off the rack, but they fit you like skin."

"I don't get you, Coy," the boy said.

"The older you get the more you live in the past," Coy intoned like a minister introducing his sermon. "Old man like me don't have no first blue sky or thunderstorm or kiss. Old man like me don't laugh at the taste of a strawberry or smell his own stink and smile. You right there in the beginnin' when everything was new and true. My world is made outta ash and memories, broken bones and pain.

"Old man see the same things and walk the same roads he know so well that he don't even have to open his eyes to make his way. Right and wrong two sides'a the same coin for me, but for you there's only right. Somebody say sumpin' an' you hear 'em just like they say."

"But what do you hear, Uncle Coy?"

"I hear everybody I evah knew talkin' 'bout things nobody know no more. I hear preachers an' judges, white men and black. I hear 'em talkin' 'bout tomorrow when I know that was a long time ago."

Ptolemy the old man considered his uncle. Maybe that's when Coy made up his mind to rob Jersey Manheim. Maybe he was so tired of following the same path that he decided to jump off the road and make it through the wilderness one more time.

Papa Grey?" Hilly was saying through the line. "Papa Grey, you there?"

Ptolemy realized that he was drifting again; but not the way he had when he was feebleminded. Now he carried the past with him rather than being carried on the back of the brute that was his history.

"Was you an' Reggie friends?" Ptolemy asked Hilly.

"We cousins, man."

"But was you friends? Did you go out drinkin' together? Did you talk?"

"Sure, we talked. We lived in the same house until he moved out with Nina."

"But," Ptolemy asked, dimly reminded of his first phone conversation with the boneheaded boy, "did you share your secrets wit' him an' did he tell you what was what?"

"I ain't got no secrets, Papa Grey. I'ma man, not no child."

"Did you tell Niecie why I didn't wanna let you back in my house?"

After a long, angry silence, Hilly said, "No."

"We all got secrets, boy. An' the older we get the more secrets we got. Child tell ya anything, but a man just sip his drink an' keep his mouf shet. But he might have one friend he talk to. Was you that friend to Reggie?"

"No."

"Do you know who that friend was?"

The silence no longer shivered with anger. Ptolemy could almost hear his taciturn great-nephew thinking.

"Billy Strong," Hilly said at last.

"Who's he?"

"He run the gym on Slauson and Twenty-third."

"Him an' Reggie was close?"

"Yes, sir. They'd get together all the time. All the time."

"An' he work at the gym?" Ptolemy asked.

"Uh-huh."

"All day?"

"Every day, Saturday and Sunday too."

Ptolemy Grey hadn't really slept after he'd awakened from the coma. He'd close his eyes and enter into a world both new and old to him. There he'd talk to Coy along the Tickle River and carry boxes of medicine in France for soldiers, most of whom were destined to die. He delivered ice and swept streets, made love to Sensia Howard so hard sometimes that he'd limp for a day or two afterward.

One night, with his eyes closed and his mind imagining, he inhabited his old feebleminded self, sitting in front of the TV. The black woman, who looked like a white woman passing for black, was talking about the war.

"More than a hundred Iraqis died in a suicide blast in the city of Tuz Khormato today. The suicide bomber set off his truck bomb in a crowded marketplace at midday."

"Excuse me, lady," Ptolemy said.

For a moment it seemed that she'd continue her report, not hearing his interruption, but then she turned and looked at him, into his living room. It was the old living room filled with stacks of moldering and unread newspapers, furniture, and trash.

"Who are you?" the woman asked.

"I'm Mr. Grey," Ptolemy said formally.

The woman looked as if she wanted to turn away from him but found that she could not. She touched her ear as Ptolemy had often watched her do in the old days when he didn't understand hardly anything. She touched it, but her ear didn't help her change the subject or look away.

"My name is Ginger," the woman in the vision said.

"Tell me, Ginger, what are you talkin' about twenty-four hours a day?"

"The news, Mr. Grey. It's the news."

"What news?"

"There's a war going on. People are dying."

"Who's the enemy? Is it Hitler again?"

"We aren't quite sure who the enemy is. That's what makes this war so hard."

"If we don't know who we fightin', then how can we fight 'em?"

"We . . . ," she said, and paused. "We . . . we aim our weapons at them and when they become frightened and take out their guns we know who they are."

"I don't get it, Ginger."

"Me neither, Mr. Grey."

"How can a man have a enemy an' fight that enemy and still not know who he is?" Ptolemy asked, proud of his ability to string his words together like a necklace of great big black Hawaiian pearls.

"Haven't you ever heard of Zorro?" Ginger asked.

"The masked man?"

"Yes, he was a man who hid his face and struck against his enemies."

Ptolemy's stomach grumbled. It was a deep, hungry sound that surprised him. He opened his eyes in the bed, realizing that sleep was no different than wakefulness and that he hadn't eaten all day.

A groan and then a whimper scurried at the edge of his consciousness. He knew that it was this sound, and not his stomach, that had pulled him away from Ginger. He climbed out of the bed in the dark room and crept toward the door.

He peeked through the crack and saw that it was Robyn moaning. She was naked, on her back, and the boy was above her, his arms at the side of her head, his middle going up and down like the oil-well derricks in Baldwin Hills pumping the oil out of the ground.

"Oil is the earth's blood," Coy had told Li'l Pea one day. "Men cut deep into the world's skin an' suck out the blood like it belong to them. That's why they's earthquakes and tidal waves, because the earth is our mother, but she don't like our ways."

Robyn's feet went up straight and trembled and she said something that had no real words. The boy moved faster and grunted, and she took his face in her hands. They gazed at each other in the murky room; a candle set on top of the TV was the only light; then

Beckford fell on his side next to the girl and kissed her cheek. They whispered in the darkness, stroking each other's face and head.

Ptolemy watched them as if from a great distance, maybe even through time itself. After a while, when their hands came to rest and he knew that they were asleep he went back to his bed and closed his eyes, finding Ginger there waiting for him, ready to continue their conversation about the invisible, nameless enemy and the war waged against him.

When Ptolemy came out of the bedroom, at six in the morning, Beckford was already gone. Robyn was sprawled in her bed with her mouth agape and left breast exposed. Ptolemy pulled the blankets up to her chin and went into the kitchen to boil water in an old tin saucepan for instant coffee and to think about his last days.

He sat down at the small table, one of the pieces of furniture he wouldn't let Robyn throw out. It was at that table where he and Sensia Howard had their morning visit for so many years. If he looked down, he felt her presence, and then he'd look up, expecting to see her.

"I'll be back later," she'd always say. "Don't wait."

But he did wait for her . . . even after she died and had gone for good. That was the beginning of his descent into confusion. Many a morning he'd awaken, looking for her. Some days he didn't remember that she was dead until afternoon. He could see this all clearly now with the Devil's medicine running in his veins.

"All them years wasted," he said to himself, sipping the hot coffee and wishing he had a cigarette.

He walked out to his gated porch that opened onto a concrete backyard. It was a large space, a forty-foot-by-forty-foot square of bleached, synthetic stone. There was a wobbly redwood fence along the back, twelve-foot-high foot-wide slats that leaned and teetered in the slightest breeze. Three apartments opened onto the prison-like yard, but no one ever went there. Ugly red-brick buildings rose on every side. Looking up, he could see small patios jutting out from the upper floors, gated by iron bars and for the most part forgotten. These were used to house bicycles and crates, a place to dry hand-washed laundry and for rusted-out barbecue grills.

A middle-aged woman was sitting outside, six stories up. She was smoking and staring out.

Ptolemy watched her for many minutes, but she didn't look down. The years flashed across his mind's eye while he waited for the mature woman, who was young enough to be his daughter, to look down on him. In that time, women had loved him and men had cursed him. He'd been seduced by his friend Major's wife, LeAnne. It was a spur-of-the-moment thing, something LeAnne did all the time. Major never knew, or maybe he didn't care to know.

Sensia saw it the second Ptolemy walked through the door.

"Who is it?" she asked him. He hadn't taken off his coat yet.

"Who is what?"

"Her."

"I don't know what you talkin' 'bout, Sensie. I just been down at the bar with Ralph and them."

"It's LeAnne, ain't it?" Her rage was cold and fierce, not a human fury but that of an animal who knows no fear or reason.

"I don't know what you're talkin' 'bout, Sensia Howard. You the one might flit off with a man at the drop of a hat."

Her silence was worse than her questions or insights. Ptolemy, standing in that concrete yard, could still feel the wrath coming off of his first true love.

He didn't know what to say, so he left. He already felt bad about Major. LeAnne had just offered him a drink, and the next thing he knew they were on the checkered sofa of Major's house, rutting and laughing, stopping to drink wine from time to time.

And now that Sensia was mad, he left L.A. and went out to Riverside, where he took a room and got a job at the gas station. That was Tuesday. He knew Sensia would never love him again. He knew that he broke a pact by sleeping with his friend's wife. Between Tuesday afternoon and Saturday morning he downed a pint of sour-mash whiskey each night, sinking into a stupor rather than falling asleep.

Sensia was at his door that Saturday morning. She wouldn't say how she'd found him out. The only person he told was George Fixx, who lived in San Francisco, and George swore that he never told anyone.

"What the hell is wrong with you?" Sensia asked at his door.

The landlady was pacing downstairs because she had a strict rule that no women were allowed in her by-the-week rooms. But Sensia had pushed past Mrs. Tinman and gone right to Ptolemy's room, number six.

She looked bad. There were bags under her eyes and her skin was dry. Her hair wasn't even brushed, and she was wearing pants and a blouse that didn't match.

"You didn't want me no mo', Sensie."

"I might not want you here and there, Ptolemy Grey, but I need you. I need you to stay alive. You know that. You know that!"

She wasn't talking normally, like people do. She was preaching or speechifying, addressing an invisible host of dead souls whose job it was to attest to Truth.

"You need me?"

"I'll be dead in a week if you don't come home," she said. "God is my witness and pain is my choir." She broke down in tears and Ptolemy took her in his arms.

"No women in the rooms, Mr. Grey!" the landlady shouted.

"We leavin' now, Ms. Tinman," Ptolemy said.

"I ain't gonna refund none'a yo' money. The week up front is final."

"Okay, ma'am," Ptolemy said as he stroked his wife's hair. "You keep that money. It's worth every dime."

It was only then, in the empty concrete lot, that he remembered Sensie's cousin, who lived in Riverside at that time. She must've seen him and called Sensie and, in doing so, saved both their lives— for a time.

"God bless you, Minna Jones," Ptolemy whispered to himself.

"Uncle?"

Her voice was the constant refrain defining the form of his improvised last days. "Uncle?" Robyn would say, and all the words and thoughts that went before formed into sensible lines, became plain memories that no longer engulfed his mind.

"Yes, child?" he said without turning.

The woman on the bleak patio above looked down at the sound of their voices.

"Why you out here in your robe?" Robyn asked. "It's cold."

"Not in my skin," Ptolemy said. "Dr. Ruben's medicine lit a fire in me."

The back of Robyn's cold fingers pressed against his cheek.

"You *are* hot."

The woman's eyes from above met with Ptolemy's and locked.

"Come on inside, Uncle. Lemme get you some aspirin."

Ptolemy wanted to do as the girl said, but he was looking into the face of the smoking black woman. He wondered what she thought up there in her perch above the concrete yard.

The woman stood up, and Ptolemy wished that she would throw something down to him: a cigarette . . . a tattered length of rope. But she turned her back and went into her home.

"Come on," Robyn insisted.

Do you need me for anything today, Uncle Grey?"

They were sitting at the small table in the kitchen, drinking iced tea that Robyn made. She was right, the cold liquid cooled him.

"No," he said. "I wanna go see somebody, that's all."

"Miss Wring?"

Ptolemy hadn't thought about that. Robyn had given him the emerald ring and he hadn't gotten around to thanking her.

This forgetfulness wasn't like before, when his thoughts were faint and half forgotten. Now he forgot because he was thinking about the moment and how the present was an extension of things that transpired long, long ago.

The ring wasn't important. It was just a trinket. It was the woman, Shirley, who occupied his mind.

"Yeah," he said. "I'ma go see Shirley. She give me her address. Did you have a good time with Beckford last night?"

Robyn clasped her hands and then unclasped them, got to her feet, and went into the living room. Ptolemy smiled, realizing that he had meant to bother her. He rose, too, barely feeling the pain in his feet and knees, and followed her into the room, the living room that she had cleared out the way the Devil's medicine had cleared out his mind.

Robyn was sitting on the bed that was a couch at the moment. When Ptolemy came in she turned her back to him.

"You shouldn't be embarrassed by what I say," Ptolemy said to his keeper.

He sat beside her, placed his hand on her shoulder.

"I didn't want you to know, Uncle," she said.

"Why not?"

"'Cause I didn't."

"How can I adopt you as my daughter if you don't tell me all about you and your life?"

Robyn turned around and peered at him cautiously, suspiciously.

"I'm too old to be adopted," she said.

Ptolemy felt a humming in his veins like a trilling wire carrying a strong charge of electricity. Somewhere Coy was wanting to give him a lecture but he would not listen.

"No," Ptolemy said, partly to Coy but mostly to Robyn, "you not too old. You my girl, my child. I love you and I wanna make sure that you have a life, a good life. I know that a young woman like you got to have a man. That goes without sayin'. You want a good-lookin' man who's strong but don't treat you bad."

Robyn smiled and looked down. She took one of Ptolemy's hands in both of hers.

"I just want you to be careful, child. I don't want you to go too fast. Maybe Beckford okay an' maybe no. It's hard to tell when you young and hungry."

"Shut up, Uncle," Robyn said with a giggle and a grin.

"Young man, all he got to do is see them legs you so proud of an' he'll say anything, anything you wanna hear."

Robyn sucked a tooth and smiled again.

"I'ma die soon, girl," he said.

"Don't say that."

"It's true, though. I can feel the poison. It's good 'cause it makes me see, but I won't make it too many more weeks. And I got to know before I die that you'll take care'a Artie an' Letisha and that you ain't with no man gonna take what I pass along to you."

"Maybe we should take you to a new doctor," Robyn suggested.

"I would marry you if I was fifty years younger," Ptolemy said. "I would. But as powerful as you are, girl, as much as you done for my mind, you cain't give me no body like Beckford. You cain't make me no younger man. So will you be my li'l girl? Will you take me as your father and listen to my advice?"

"I'll be eighteen in a few weeks, Uncle. I could marry you then."

Ptolemy's response to Robyn's offer was to look up at the ceiling and around at the walls. He was smiling but didn't know it. He was thinking about the solitude of private rooms where people said things to each other that had no place in the outer world. He thought about LeAnne and how she leaned over on the couch before he suspected their lovemaking and whispered, "My pussy itch, Daddy," and he gasped and she touched his thigh.

He looked down at his hand in Robyn's grip and thought, *Yes, I could marry this child*. But he knew that that was just a moment in a closed room between two people who wanted to break down the walls around them but still be safe from the outside world.

Ptolemy meant to say, "No, child," but instead he asked, "What about Beckford?"

"I like him but he not there for me like you. An' I'm not there wit' him either. You bought me a bed, Uncle, an' turned all your money ovah into my hands. You the only one I evah know could put your finger on the feelin' I got."

"I need a daughter, not a wife. I need you to love me like I love you," Ptolemy said, tightening his fingers around hers.

"'Kay," she said. "But how do we do that?"

"The way everybody does what no one can understand," he said. "We go to a lawyer and let him put it into words."

After Robyn left, Ptolemy donned his suit and, with an ease he hadn't felt in many years, tied his new shoelaces. He went to the door, paused for a moment, went back to his kitchen, and pulled a foot-long steel pipe from under the sink.

Don't th'ow out that pipe," he had said to Robyn when his mind was still confused.

"Why not, Uncle? It don't fit nuthin'."

"It make me feel safe."

He locked his apartment and walked down the hallway and through the outer door. He was outside on his own for the first time in years.

The sun was dazzling and he was a barefoot child walking along a dirt road, a young man in a Memphis back alley, a soldier walking down a French road with the bodies of dead soldiers stacked along the sides according to their nationality, race, and rank. He was a groom in his forties walking up the aisle with a bride so beautiful that he thought of her like a movie star or a queen that a man like him could only ever see from afar or on the screen. He was an old man following her coffin to the grave, still amazed that he was even in her procession.

"Hold it right there, Pete!" Melinda Hogarth yelled.

He was walking down his own street not quite as old as he was now and a woman with the face of a demon was running him down. This vision was a dream of who he had hoped to be, a wish he'd prayed every night for, for years after Melinda Hogarth had mugged him the first time.

For a moment Ptolemy understood that the doctor's medicine had made him into many men from out of all the lives he had lived through the decades. It was certainly a Devil's potion, one that could give him the power to relive his mistakes and failures and change, if only slightly, the past events that hounded his dreams.

While thinking these things, Ptolemy's body was in motion. He was old and without great strength, but his mind was sharp as a razor and he could see Melinda coming up from behind in his visions. As she approached him he turned, raising his arm. As she reached for him he brought down the whole arm as if it had no joints. His wrist and elbow were fused and the steel pipe hit the knuckle of Melinda's index finger with a whoosh and a snick.

The big woman yelped and jumped backward. She cried out when Ptolemy raised his arm again. This was the dream he'd had for years. This was why he wouldn't let Robyn throw out his pipe, even though he couldn't have told her then.

Melinda Hogarth sidled away like a crab with a woman's voice, hollering for safety. Ptolemy brought down the pipe again through the now-empty space where she had stood. He wanted her to see what he could do even at this age, in this body.

The pain rose in his chest again. A man across the street was watching the incident, weighing the facts that his eyes and ears gave him. For a moment, even in his pain, Ptolemy wondered if he would have to explain to the man why he'd struck the wino drug addict. But this reverie was interrupted by the trilling in his veins and the smell of garlic. He looked around him as Melinda shouted and ran down the street. Nobody was cooking, as far as he could tell. And when he looked back, the man had continued his walk, no longer interested in the years-long drama of the old man and Melinda Hogarth.

Ptolemy took the Central bus up to Twenty-third Street. There he disembarked and looked at the four corners. There was a storefront on the northwest corner of the street that had a display window. Inside the window was a Spanish man jumping rope at a furious pace.

"Can I help you?" another man said to Ptolemy when he walked in the door of the long, sunlit room.

It was a poor gym. A few mats on the concrete floor and a punching bag, a bench for weight lifting, and a bar screwed into a doorway for chin-ups.

The man who asked the question was on the short side but he had extraordinarily broad shoulders and muscles that stretched his T-shirt in every direction. His face was light brown and his neck exhibited the strain of a man pulling a heavy weight up by a long rope.

"I'm lookin' for Billy Strong," Ptolemy said.

"You lookin' at him."

The men both smiled and Ptolemy understood why Reggie had called this man friend. He was powerful but there was no anger to him. This was the kind of man that you wanted to know, wanted to work shoulder to shoulder with.

"My name is Ptolemy Grey," the old man said, continually astonished at his renewed new ability to communicate.

The smile on Billy Strong's face diminished. It took on a sad aspect but did not disappear.

"You Reggie's great-granduncle."

So many children, Ptolemy thought, and children getting children and them doing the same. It seemed to him like some kind of crazy math problem worked out in streets and churches, dance floors and cemeteries. Reggie was his great-grandnephew, now dead. And Ptolemy was his survivor, like the small sum left over at the end of long division, like the few solitary and dumbfounded men who had survived the first wave on D-Day.

"Yes, I am," he said simply.

"Reggie told me that you was havin' some problems with your, um, thinkin'."

"Robyn Small took me to a doctor give me some medicine help me put my words and my thoughts together."

Strong smiled broadly, saying, "Robyn, huh? That little girl gotta backside on her that's a crime."

Ptolemy smiled in response. Even when he was in his confused state he had noted Robyn's hips.

"What can I do for you, Mr. Grey?"

"Lemme buy you a drink and ask you a couple'a questions is all."

"You wanna go to a bar?"

"Someplace quiet an' upscale, so we don't have to get in no fights."

"No place around here like that. We have to drive if you want to go to a nice bar."

"You drive and I'll buy," Ptolemy said with a sly grin.

"Julio," Billy exclaimed.

"Yeah, Bill?"

"I'ma be gone for a hour or so. Look after the place while I'm out."

"You got it."

You know my nephew long?" Ptolemy asked Billy Strong at the Aerie Bar, on top of the Fredda Kline Professional Building on

Grand Street in downtown L.A. If they had turned away from the bar they would have seen all the way to the ocean through a blue and amber sky.

"'Bout six years, I guess," Billy said. He had put on a pale-gray sweater and a pair of dark trousers as formal wear for the bar.

Billy ordered a beer. Ptolemy asked for a double shot of sour-mash whiskey. Billy had convinced the older man to leave his steel pipe in the car.

"Somebody kilt him," Ptolemy said. "They murdered my boy, shot him down like a dog."

"I know. I was at the funeral. I didn't see you there, Mr. Grey."

"Niecie sent Hilly to get me, but I don't like that boy, he's a thief."

"Yeah. He's not the kinda son I'd be proud of."

Ptolemy smiled.

"Why somebody wanna shoot a boy sittin' on a stoop mindin' his own business?" Ptolemy asked.

Billy took that opportunity to sip his drink.

"I mean," Ptolemy continued, "I don't know much about the streets today. When I was movin' around, there wasn't gangs or these drive-bys, but Reggie wasn't a part'a no gang, was he?"

"No, sir. Reggie stayed outta that."

"So you think that it was just some mistake, somebody thought he was somebody else?"

Billy finished his beer and Ptolemy raised his hand to catch the bartender's attention. When the slim, mustachioed white man looked their way, Ptolemy pointed at the empty glass. He was astounded by this simple gesture, aware that only weeks before it would have been beyond him.

"Did Reggie talk to you about moving away to San Diego?" Billy asked.

"Uh-uh. At least I don't think so. You know, the medicine I took cleared up my mind, but a lotta things I heard when I was, I was confused are still jumbled up. You sayin' Reggie was gonna move outta town?"

"Yeah."

The bartender brought Billy's second beer, along with an outrageous tab. Ptolemy put two twenty-dollar bills down on the bar.

"Why?" Ptolemy asked.

Billy sipped again.

"Why?" Ptolemy asked.

"You know Alfred Gulla?"

The image of the brutal man with the name not his own hanging from his chest sidled into Ptolemy's mind.

"Reggie's wife's boyfriend."

"Yeah," Billy said. "Reggie found out that Nina was still seein' Alfred and he decided that he was gonna move with her an' the kids down to San Diego. He asked me if I could find somebody to look after you, because he didn't trust Hilly either. But before we could make plans, he got shot."

Ptolemy tried to slow his mind down, to make himself believe that he didn't yet know enough to say who had killed his great-grandnephew. He tried to make his mind muddy again so that confusion would wash away the words that Billy was saying. But he could not turn his mind's eye away from the ugly man that had his arm around Reggie's woman.

"When did they shoot my boy?" Ptolemy asked.

"Eight weeks ago yesterday."

"What time?"

"It was four in the afternoon."

"Bright day?" Ptolemy asked.

"Yeah."

"Out in the open?"

"Car drove by and opened fire. Every damn bullet hit Reggie."

Billy looked up into Ptolemy's eyes. The truth was there between them, like a child's corpse after a terrible fire that no one
could have prevented.

Billy parked the car in front of Ptolemy's apartment building. After hearing about Melinda Hogarth, he offered to walk his
friend's great-uncle to his door. A man shouted at them from
across the street.

"Hold up!"

It was a big dark-skinned man with bright eyes and a nose that
had been broken more than once, a man who wouldn't be daunted
by a ninety-one-year-old man swinging a steel pipe. Behind him
was Melinda, her finger wrapped in thick white bandages and
gauze.

"You done attack my girlfriend," the man said to Ptolemy.

The old man wasn't afraid. His revelation about Reggie had
taken up all of his feelings and pain. The blustering man in army
surplus pants and purple T-shirt was nothing to him; death was
nothing to him. All he wanted to do was remember if Reggie had
talked about going to San Diego.

In his oversized gray sweater Billy didn't look powerful or strong. He was shorter than Melinda's brute, but he still moved into the space between Ptolemy and the big man, who, on closer inspection, was past fifty and paunchy.

Ptolemy expected Billy to say something, to warn off the thug boyfriend of the woman mugger. But instead Billy threw a straight punch, hitting the man in the throat. After that the bodybuilder kicked and bludgeoned the big man until he was on the ground, crawling away down the sidewalk. There was a streak of blood on the pavement behind the bully, and the only sound was the beaten man coughing, trying to catch a breath through his bruised windpipe.

"Go on in, Mr. Grey," Billy said in a mild, friendly voice. "I'll stay out here and watch these mothahfuckers until you inside."

Ptolemy saw that Melinda had retreated across the street. She wasn't complaining or even trying to help her *boyfriend*.

"Mr. Grey?"

"Yeah, Mr. Strong?"

"If you need it, I'll come by an' get you anytime, ya hear?"

"Yes sir, I sure do."

Inside the apartment Ptolemy thought about Robyn, who was so quick to fight, and now Billy, who didn't even utter a warning. He could see that the world outside his door had become more dangerous than it was when he was a younger man. Poor people had always fought and killed each other, but it wasn't so fast and unpredictable. People shot out like rattlesnakes on these modern streets. There was no warning anymore.

The phone rang at 7:27 that evening.

"Uncle Grey?"

"Yeah, Robyn."

"I'ma be home late, okay?"

"Sure it's okay. But be careful when you come back in. That Melinda got her some boyfriend threatened me."

"What you do?"

"I was wit' Billy Strong. He beat the bejesus out that man."

"Billy? He's nice."

"He said the same about you. What time you comin' home?"

"'Bout eleven."

"Okay. I'll prob'ly be up."

"You don't have to wait up for me, Uncle."

"No. I'm just thinkin' 'bout things."

"What things?"

"The modern world."

At 8:30 there came a knock at the door.

"Who is it?" Ptolemy asked.

"Dr. Ruben, Mr. Grey. Can I come in?"

Ptolemy opened the door and said, "Hello, Satan."

The doctor was wearing a herringbone jacket, black trousers, and a dark-red dress shirt that was open at the collar. He seemed to grimace under the bale of hair that passed for a mustache.

"How are you, Mr. Grey?" the beady- and green-eyed doctor asked, forcing his scowl into a smile.

"Burnin' up and singin' in my veins, rememberin' all the things that went to pass like they was just this mornin' and not fifty, sixty, seventy . . . eighty years ago."

The doctor's smile grew as Ptolemy watched him. This stand-off went on for a while, until the doctor asked, "Can I come in, Mr. Grey?"

Ptolemy spent maybe twenty seconds more trying to think if there was some rule against letting Satan in your door.

"Come on, then," he said when he couldn't think of any strictures pertaining to the Devil and simple civility.

Ptolemy sat on his lightweight stool and bade his guest sit on Robyn's couch.

"Your mind is working well?" Ruben asked. "You're remembering and able to get your words out?"

"Bettah then evah. I could tell you the kinda cake my mama made on my sixth birthday, and what the driver talked about when I took the bus up to Twenty-third and Central this afternoon."

"By yourself?"

"Excuse me?"

"Did you take the bus by yourself?" Ruben asked.

"Yeah. Yeah."

"Do you have any problem walking, handling things?"

"Naw. Mattah fact I seem a little more handy than I was." He was thinking about the pipe he had swung at Melinda. "I seem to be more—what you call it?—coordinated."

The doctor smiled and nodded.

"And you say you have fever?" he asked.

"I get so hot sometimes I can feel it comin' off my skin. I take aspirin an' a cold shower an' it go away."

"That's just right, Mr. Grey. A shower and aspirin will work for a while. Maybe a long while."

"Fevah gonna kill me?" Ptolemy asked with no self-pity or regret.

"Could be," Ruben said. "But you say you feel an electrical sensation inside?"

"In my veins," Ptolemy replied. "Like a trill played on a flute. It makes me feel like I got butterflies for blood."

"That's the medicine," Ruben said. "It's working on your chemistry and your body's electrical system, your wiring. But it should only be in your brain. That's what we're trying to work out . . . how to keep the brain alive and functioning well without affecting the other parts of your body. May I take your pulse?"

"The Devil playin' a healer," Ptolemy said as he extended his right hand.

After feeling various points on the old man's arm, Ruben said, "Your blood pressure is elevated." He reached into his pocket and came out with a small green bottle.

"These pills are very small but potent. There are a hundred of them. Take one when the fever and flute playing bothers you and it should subside for a while."

Ptolemy took the green bottle and shook it, listening to the beads of medicine tinkle against the glass.

"Tell me sumpin', Satan. Will I live to finish off this bottle?"

"To tell you the truth, Mr. Grey, I thought that you'd have died by now. I came by to make sure that Robyn was keeping your agreement."

The candor of the demon brought a smile to Ptolemy's lips.

"Coy told me about you."

"Who's that?"

"My uncle. Well, he wasn't really my blood but just a old man who taught me everything I know—almost. He told me that even though you called evil in the Good Book that I still had to give you respect. Yes he did."

Ruben leaned forward, clasped his hands, and placed his elbows on his knees. He was looking deeply into Ptolemy's eyes.

"I ain't crazy, Dr. Ruben, if that's what you want me to call ya. I ain't crazy at all. But I know the Devil when I see him. You don't need no college degree to see evil in front'a yo' nose. Man play with life have crossed ovah. That's a fact."

"But . . . Mr. Grey, I'm helping you, aren't I? Didn't you come to me and ask for my help?"

For a passing moment Ptolemy felt fear. Had he sold his soul and not quite realized it? Had he been tricked as so many before him on the long road to ruin?

"But we traded, right?" Ptolemy asked. "You wanted my body, not my soul."

Satan smiled on Ptolemy Grey. His whole face was alight with friendliness.

"That's right, Mr. Grey. I only want your body. I'm trading that light in your mind and that tickle in your veins for your body after you no longer need it."

"Will you shake on that?" Grey asked, and both men extended their hands and grasped each other, reaffirming an oath that they both wanted and needed.

After a moment or two of silent reverie, Ruben asked, "Where's your niece?"

"Out with her boyfriend."

"She leaves you alone and you can take care of yourself?"

"If I had a fifty-gallon drum I could barbecue a pig in the cement yard," Ptolemy said proudly.

"I bet you could, Mr. Grey. I bet you could."

For a long time after the Devil had left, Ptolemy considered their conversation. He remembered every word and intonation, every gesture and phrase.

Satan had called the feeling in his body a tickle, meaning that he knew about the Tickle River and Coy and the theft of the gold coins. He was telling him that Coy had sinned but that he would be forgiven if Ptolemy lived up to his side of the bargain over the disposition of the treasure.

It was a delicate transaction, dealing with the Devil, but in Ptolemy's mind that was his only hope. How else could he save Letisha and Artie, and Robyn too? How else could he make sure that Reggie's killer did not escape judgment?

Ptolemy was feeling giddy after such a close call with oblivion, because he knew meeting the Devil was always a threat to the immortal soul.

What's a soul, Coy?" Li'l Pea had asked his mentor and friend.

For a long time the old man sat and puffed on his cherrywood pipe. After a few minutes went by, Ptolemy thought that he wouldn't get an answer to his question. This wasn't unusual. Sometimes Coy didn't answer. Ptolemy knew that sometimes he had to find his own solutions.

"Do you look at your mama sometimes and feel love in your heart for her?" Coy asked.

"Yeah . . . I guess."

"It's either yes or no."

"Yeah. Sometimes when I come home and she's cookin' an' the house smell like chicken and dumplin's an' she see me and smile I get the jitters in my legs and start laughin' an' she smiles harder and calls me her li'l brown nut."

"That love in your heart is your soul," Coy said.

"But . . . but what if I said no?"

"Some people lose they souls along the way. They don't feel no love or pride or that there's somethin' in the world bettah than they lives."

"How do you lose your soul, Coy?"

"Because," he said, "it is a delicate thing, a special thing. You can live without it, but you might as well be dead. That's why heaven an' hell is always fightin' over the souls'a men. Our souls, when we got 'em, is so beautiful that angels always lookin' to take 'em. That's why when the Devil comes up on you you got to hold tight on the love in your heart."

P tolemy picked up the phone and dialed a number that he remembered thanks to the Devil's medicine.

"Hello?" Niecie Brown said.

"Hey, Niecie. How you doin'?"

"Pitypapa, is that you? You dialin' the phone by yourself? I don't believe it. I mean, I believe it, but it's still a shock."

"Hilly there, baby?"

"Uh-huh. He here watchin' the TV. I told him that he was gonna have to pay you back for what he took. But you know he ain't a bad boy. He just feel like he been cheated, losin' his daddy so young and all."

"Lemme talk to him, honey."

"Hello?" Hilly said, bringing to mind some big dense creature like a hog, or even a hippopotamus.

"I need some bullets for my pistol."

"Say what?"

"I need some bullets for my pistol, an' I don't want you tellin' your mama about it neither."

"What kinda pistol?"

"Twenty-five caliber. You get me that and we even. You won't owe me a dime."

"Okay. I'll bring 'em ovah tomorrow."

"Put 'em in a can of peanuts."

"I gotta buy them too?" the brooding boy complained.

"Yeah. You got to buy them too."

"All right. But we even then, right?"

"Right."

The evening after that went smoothly for Ptolemy. He found a music station that was playing Fats Waller recordings.

He'd once seen the great Moon Face playing in an after-hours big-city juke joint in Memphis. In those days the music halls only allowed whites, except on special days, and so after a performance in front of an all-white audience there were many famous musicians that went to the black part of town to jam with their people.

Listening to the song "Two Sleepy People," he was remembering a girl named Talla who turned to kiss him because the romantic lyrics made her. He remembered the smell of beer and the sawdust on the floor, Fats Waller himself winking at the momentary lovers, and a feeling that being Ptolemy Grey was the best thing in the whole world.

"Uncle?" she said, and the vision evaporated. "Uncle, you okay?"

Ptolemy turned his head, feeling pain between each vertebra, but he didn't wince or curse.

"Is it eleven already?"

"It's past midnight," Robyn said. "I thought you'd be asleep."

"Your boyfriend here?" Ptolemy asked, looking toward the bathroom.

"No. He walked me to the door, but then I heard the music an' told him to go on."

"You cain't give up your life for me, child."

"You my father-like, right?" she asked.

"Yeah. Yeah right."

"A girl got to respect her father, Uncle."

The old man noticed an intimacy and a knowledge in the girl's tone that he hadn't known since the days that he lived with Sensia. His heart clenched like a fist trying in vain to crush a solitary walnut.

"Are you okay, Uncle?"

"It's a shame, the feelin' I got for you, Robyn. If I wrote it down in a letter the police would come in here an' take me off to jail."

"We cain't help how we feel," she said in a modest tone that reminded Ptolemy of the way Sensia would sometimes shrug and her dress would fall to the floor.

"The Devil came to see me tonight," he said.

"Dr. Ruben? What he have to say? Did he leave you his numbah? Did you tell him about your fevah?"

"He the Devil, baby. He know all about fevah. Fevah's what keep him in business."

"He just a man, Uncle. A man playin' with your life."

"Tomorrow we gonna go up to Beverly Hills," Ptolemy said, changing the subject so effectively that Robyn didn't frown, much less complain.

"To do what?"

"To talk to a man named Mossa."

"Who's that?"

"You'll see."

That night the fever roused Ptolemy from a moment in his past when he saw Corporal Billy Knight, a Negro from South Carolina, kill a white man, Sergeant Preston Tooms, with his bare hands in a back alley in Paris. After four days Ptolemy was called to report to the commander of his and Knight's division, a white colonel named Riley.

"It has been reported to me that certain people feel that there was bad blood between Corporal Billy Knight and Sergeant Preston Tooms."

Ptolemy thought that Billy had probably bragged about the

crime amongst his black brothers. He was used to his neighborhood down in Alabama, where no Negro would ever turn in another. But the U.S. Army had black soldiers from Chicago, San Francisco, and even New York City. Some of them thought it was their responsibility to follow the white man's law.

Billy probably bragged, and everyone knew that Billy and Ptolemy were close.

"Well, soldier?" the colonel asked.

"I wouldn't know nuthin' about anything like that, sir."

"Are those tears in your eyes, Sergeant Grey?" Riley asked.

"Must be the smoke, sir."

"Does doing your duty hurt that much?"

Riley was a good man; tall and proud, he never insulted his soldiers because of their race. He respected every man according to one standard. And so when he asked Ptolemy that question, the soldier froze, unable to speak. But in the vision, not a dream but a trancelike memory, Ptolemy inhabited his former self and spoke up.

"Sir, that sergeant said a word to Billy that stung him in his heart. Aftah all we been through, Billy heard in that white man's one word that he would come back home to the same sorry situation that our mothers and grandmothers and great-great-great-grandmothers suffered under. Billy couldn't help himself, but still that don't wash away the blood."

Ptolemy opened his eyes because the fever was burning his face. He sat up, remembering that Colonel Riley "volunteered" Billy Knight for duty at the front lines when the casualty rate was over ninety percent. He didn't press charges, because that might have caused a riot among the soldiers.

Billy died a week later. His mother and father received his Purple Heart posthumously.

Ptolemy wondered if his memories were the cause of the fever. Was it hell calling for him?

Running his fingertips along the sheet, he felt a thrill of excitation. He had not experienced so much or so deeply since he was a child. The bottle given to him by Satan, or maybe one of Satan's agents, sat on the bureau across from his big bed.

His temperature was rising quickly and the strength was draining from his limbs.

He got to his feet and took two quick steps. He had to grab on to the bureau not to fall. He opened the bottle, spilling a dozen tiny pills across the top of the chest of drawers. He had to suck his tongue four times before drawing out enough spit to swallow even one small pill.

Slumping down to the floor, Ptolemy thought about Billy. He was betrayed but did not know it. He was sentenced to death but thought that he was being chosen to fight because of his valor and bravery. He had murdered a man but felt that he was vindicated by his people's suffering and shame. Ptolemy imagined Knight grinning while he was killing, about to die himself. The executioner's hand was disguised, and the battlefield substituted for justice.

Ptolemy smiled and opened his eyes. He was on his back on the floor in a room that was once teeming with insects and rodents. A frigid river flowed over his fevered skin and now he was strong and able.

He got to his feet without arthritic pain in his joints. He took a deep breath and went back to his bed, where he could recall history and change it slightly—an old man deified by the whim of evil.

W hat we doin' here, Uncle?" Robyn asked after they had gotten off the bus at Wilshire Boulevard and Rodeo Drive a few minutes after ten the next morning.

"Goin' t'see see Mr. Mossa. He a Jerusalemite, a Palestinian he calls it, but he was born in Jerusalem, same place that Christ our Lord was born."

"This place is full'a rich white people," Robyn argued. "We shouldn't be up around here."

The girl was looking about her, a severe frown etching her lovely dark features. Ptolemy smiled. There was a bench across the street, at the foot of a steep cobblestone road that didn't allow cars. An old white woman was sitting there. Ptolemy brought his adopted daughter across the street and sat her down at the opposite end.

"I been afraid'a white people my entire life," the old man said, holding the glowering girl's hands.

"I ain't afraid," she said. "It's just that we don't belong up here. My mama told me that."

"Your mother made you sleep on the floor behind a couch so that her boyfriends didn't see you," Ptolemy said.

"So?"

"She didn't think she was wrong doin' that, now, did she?"

"No."

"But she was wrong, wasn't she?"

"Papa Grey, I just don't like it up here. I ain't scared'a no*body*, but I'm scared I'll do sumpin' wrong."

"I know. That's why we here together. I'm helpin' you."

"If you helpin' me, then take me home."

"Did you like bein' a child?" Ptolemy asked.

Robyn wanted to look down, but she forced herself to gaze into her guardian's eyes.

"I was happy when my mama died, Papa Grey." A tear came down her left cheek. "I wanted to be sad an' lovin' but I knew that Mama had worked it out for me to go to Aunt Niecie if she died, and I hoped in my heart, even though I didn't want to, that my mama would pass and I could come out heah. I'm the one you should call the Devil."

Ptolemy noticed that even though the right eye filled with water it was only the girl's left eye that shed tears. He thought this must have been an important sign, but the meaning escaped him.

"Then I come to stay wit' Niecie an' she put me on a couch in the livin' room an' Hilly was always tryin' to fuck me—excuse my French."

"I got you on a couch in the livin' room," Ptolemy said gently.

"But that's *my* couch, an' it's a proper bed too. An' it have drawers like a dresser, an' you bought me some clothes. An' anyway you offered me your room an' all your money an' you trusted me to do right. An' you try an' protect me too. I love you, Papa Grey. I don't evah want anything to happen to you."

"Did some'a the men in yo' mama's house mess wit' you?" he asked.

"I don't wanna talk about that."

Ptolemy smiled and said, "Okay. But you gotta know that the money I offered you is only a small part'a what I got an' that we up here today so that you can know how to take care of what I'ma leave to you. So I won't aks you no questions hurt your heart, but you got to trust me with the rest."

Her left eye streaming, lips apout, Robyn nodded just barely and Ptolemy smiled. He pulled her up by her forearms until they were on their feet again, walking up to the top of the pedestrian roadway lined with fancy boutiques and stores.

There they came upon a gleaming white and gold store where, above the entrance, the name *Mossa* in red letters was inlaid across a band of sky-blue mosaic tiles.

"Mr. Grey!" an older man exclaimed.

At first Robyn assumed that he must be a Mexican.

"Mr. Mossa," Ptolemy replied with equal enthusiasm, "long time no see."

"How are you, my friend?" the old, ecru-skinned Middle Easterner asked. He took one of Ptolemy's big hands in both of his, smiling and nodding as he did so.

The shop was crowded with glass cases crammed full with jewelry, coins, and small objects that were from other times and other places. The rest of the room was overflowing with rows of statues, sculptures, paintings on wood, wall hangings, ancient carpets, and large items of gold and silver, marble and jade.

The white stone bust of a small child caught Robyn's attention. The face seemed so innocent and wise.

"Julius Caesar," Mossa said to the girl.

"Excuse me?"

"That is a bust of Caesar as a boy."

"How they know how he looked when he was a kid?"

"He sat for the sculptor, of course," Mossa said, and then he turned to Ptolemy again.

It slowly dawned upon Robyn what the aging Muslim had said.

"You mean, this thing was made when Caesar was just a little boy?" she asked his back.

"Yes," Mossa said, turning again. "Everything in my shop is very, very old. I have a room filled with treasures from ancient tombs of Kush and Egypt."

"This is Mr. Mossa, Robyn," Ptolemy said. "Mossa, this is my adopted daughter, Robyn Small."

"Pleased to meet you," Mossa said. "Your father is a great man with a long history. He understands beauty and the past. And of course his name has been legend for thousands of years."

"Thank you," Robyn said, not quite knowing why. "Your store is very beautiful."

The Palestinian was short, like Ptolemy, and a bit stooped over, round but not fat; his smile was both beneficent and inviting. He wore a large yellow diamond on the index finger of his right hand and a ruby embedded in onyx on the pinky of his left. Robyn had never met anyone like him, had never been in a place like his *shop*.

"It has been a long time, Ptolemy," the store owner said. "Fifteen years?"

"Maybe more," Ptolemy agreed.

"I've never seen you in a suit before."

"Bought it for a funeral," Ptolemy said lightly.

"Whose?"

"Mine," the old man said.

The men stood there for a moment, Ptolemy smiling and Mossa wondering about that smile.

"I think of you on the first day of every year," Mossa said to break the silence. "I send up a prayer for you and hope that you are alive and well."

"That must'a been what done it," Ptolemy replied. "'Cause you know there ain't a reason in the world a man's bones should get as old as mine is. I'm ninety-one, be ninety-two soon—maybe."

"There are trees that don't live so long."

Ptolemy took two dull gold coins from his pocket.

"I know you don't have much interest in things only a hundred or so year old, but I thought . . ."

The antiquarian took the coins from Ptolemy's hand and held them in his palm. With his other hand he took out a jeweler's lens and studied the metal disks.

"I belong to a coin guild now," he said, still staring at his palm. "We trade, back and forth. Sometimes an American dealer will come across ancient treasures that he cannot sell. Sometimes we trade."

Mossa looked up at Ptolemy and both old men smiled. To Robyn it seemed that they were talking without words, communing like monks being passed messages from God.

"Thirty-six hundred each," Mossa said.

"Cash," Ptolemy added.

The antiquarian put the CLOSED sign on the front door and brought Ptolemy and the girl into a yard that was filled with flowering plants that Robyn could not identify. There Mossa made tea and brought out strange-tasting pastries.

Mossa asked Robyn about her college aspirations, and even offered to give her a recommendation for school.

"I'm only goin' to junior college," she said.

"But you will transfer one day."

"Yeah," she said, surprise coming through in her voice, "I might."

"This is my daughter, Mossa," Ptolemy said at one point. "Give her your card and do business wit' her fair an' square like you always done wit' me."

Mossa did not speak. He smiled, took a business card from his vest pocket, and handed it to the girl. The white card was engraved with golden letters. She placed it in her bag next to the knife—her mother's only gift.

On the street again, waiting for a westbound bus, Robyn and Ptolemy sat side by side, holding hands.

"How you get to know Mr. Mossa, Uncle?"

"Every once in a blue moon I'd get a part-time job at a restaurant they used to have around here called Trudy's Steak House. If they had a big weekend and one'a their people got sick they'd call me 'cause I was a friend of a guy worked there called Mike Tinely.

"I always took the early bus because the boss wanted you there on the minute. One time I saw Mossa's place and I wondered if he could cash my coin. A week aftah my job was ovah I went in the store. It was him there, an' he walked up to me and said, 'Can I help you, Father?'

"That was twenty-four years ago. He was in his fifties and I was already retired. We talked for a while and then he put up the CLOSED sign and took me to his garden for some tea. I nevah met anybody like that. My skin didn't mean nuthin' to him. I knew what the coins were worth from books, but I didn't tell him that. He paid me top dollar and we been friends evah since."

"Where you get them coins?" Robyn asked.

"Later, child. Let's get out to Santa Monica first."

An hour later they were walking on a street in Santa Monica. They came to a slender brick building between a women's clothes store and a shop that sold leather goods in all forms and shapes. Robyn stopped at the window of the clothes store, gazing at a dress that was diaphanous and multicolored. Ptolemy stood back, watching her turn slightly as if she had tried on the frock and was checking her reflection in the glass.

Abromovitz and Son Legal Services was on the fourth floor of the slender building. There was an elevator but it was out of order, and so the young girl and the old man took the stairs, half a flight at a time. Ptolemy counted the steps, seven and then eight three times, with one-minute rests between each.

The door was open and Ptolemy led the way into the dimly lit room.

"May I help you?" a middle-aged black woman asked. She was sitting behind an oak desk that blocked the way to a bright-green door that was closed.

Ptolemy smiled at the woman, who was maybe forty-five.

Half my age, he thought, *and twice my weight.*

"Yes?" she asked.

"I'd like to speak with Abraham," he said, echoes of Coy's blasphemous Bible lessons resounding in his mind.

"He," the woman said, and then winced. "Mr. Abromovitz passed away five years ago."

"Oh," Ptolemy said, "I'm so sorry. He was a good man. I liked him very much."

The black woman, whose skin was quite dark and whose nameplate said Esther, nodded and smiled sadly.

"Yes," she said. "He always asked how I was in the morning, and he would listen too."

"Moishe still here?" Ptolemy asked.

The receptionist registered surprise at the question.

"Who are you?" she asked.

"Mr. Ptolemy Grey."

Mr. Grey," a middle-aged, paunchy white man was saying a few moments later, after Esther had made a call on the office line.

Robyn followed her adopted father into the small dark office. There was a window but it only looked out onto a shadowy airshaft. Bookcases lined every wall. Along with law books, there were novels, piles of magazines, and stacks of typing paper held together by old brittle rubber bands. The room reminded Robyn somewhat of Ptolemy's home before she had cleaned it out, and a little of Mossa's rooms filled with ancient treasures.

The only free space on the wall held a painting of a naked

white goddess standing in the foreground with a medieval village behind her. The people of the village seemed unaware of the voluptuous maiden passing before them.

"I haven't seen you since I was a young man," Moishe Abromovitz was saying. "I think I was still in school."

His face was young but his hair had gone gray and the backs of his hands were prematurely liver-spotted.

Ptolemy pressed Robyn toward one of the four visitors' chairs and then took one himself. Moishe remained standing next to a pine desk that was probably older than he was.

"What can I do for you, Mr. Grey?"

"I'm sorry to hear about your father," Ptolemy said. "I didn't know."

"I thought we sent you a notice," the fortyish man in the aged body said. "I hope we didn't forget you."

Ptolemy wondered if the letter had come in and Reggie had read it to him. Remembering himself as a feebleminded old fool was painful and frightening; next to that memory, Death didn't seem like such a bad fellow.

"You still got that file on me?" Ptolemy asked.

"My father had sixteen clients that he wanted me to take special care of after he was gone. You were one," Moishe Abromovitz said as he went to a wooden file cabinet behind the elder desk. He drew out an old manila folder, about three inches thick, and placed it on the pine desk. "He said that you were a gentle man with a good heart and that I should handle your estate when the time came."

"You mean when I died."

Moishe sat down behind the file and smiled.

Ptolemy put his left hand on Robyn's forearm. The girl seemed uncomfortable and he wanted to put her at ease.

"This child has saved me," Ptolemy said. "I was sick, very sick and she cleaned my house and brought me to a doctor that made me well, or at least as well as a man my age can be."

Moishe's smile evaporated.

"I want you to make her my heir," Ptolemy said. "Put her in that trust your daddy said he made for me, and take care'a her business like you did with mine."

Moishe nodded noncommittally and Ptolemy placed a stack of ten one-hundred-dollar bills on the table.

"This should cover the first part'a the work you got to do."

The legal adviser turned to Robyn and asked, "What is your name?"

"Robyn Small," Ptolemy said before she could answer. "That's Robyn like the bird only with a y instead of an i. An' she got all her information in her bag."

"Robyn, would you mind waiting outside for a moment while I talk to Mr. Grey alone?"

The girl nodded and stood right up. She walked from the room, closing the door behind her without a word or gesture of complaint.

After she was gone Moishe turned to Ptolemy.

"How well do you know this girl, Mr. Grey?"

"That's not the question you should be askin' me, young man."

Moishe frowned and said, "No?"

"Uh-uh. No. I know what you thinkin'. You thinkin' that I'm a old man and this young thing is after anything she can get outta me. But how good I know her ain't what will tell you what you need to know."

Moishe smiled as if he perceived something he recognized in the old man's words.

"What should I have asked, Mr. Grey?"

"What you wanna know is how well I know anybody. Not just Robyn but ev'rybody in my life. You know, a old man don't have much to go on. He don't have a big social life. He don't cut the rug no mo'."

"Cut the rug?" the lawyer asked.

"Dance."

"I never danced very much," Moishe said apologetically. "My father did. He was a wonderful dancer. But I have two left feet."

"There's a lady upstairs from me get my mail two times a week," Ptolemy continued. "Her name's Falona Dartman. I'd like to leave her a li'l sumpin' when I pass. And there's a woman dope addict across the street try to mug me every time I stick my nose out the door. I don't wanna give her nuthin'. My grandniece Niecie Brown don't know what's goin' on, and her son stoled money from me because he thought I was too old to notice. My other great-grand-nephew, Reggie, took care'a me for years. He had a good heart but he didn't know what he was doin' and now he's dead anyway—shot down in the street."

"Oh my God," the younger Abromovitz declared. "That's terrible."

"Robyn cleaned out my house and took me to a doctor. She beat up that dope fiend and cooks for me twice a day. I offered her all my money and she turned it down. But, you know, Reggie, my great-grandnephew, have left two babies behind him, and my grandniece needs looking after too. Robyn the only one will see my family is taken care of."

"But how long have you known her, Mr. Grey?" Moishe insisted.

"You see that paintin' on the wall, Moishe?" Ptolemy replied.

"Yes."

"It's called *A Study of Darkness in Light.*"

"That's right. How did you know?"

"Your father bought it from a painter friend of his named Max Kahn. I remember Maxie. Him an' me an' your daddy used to go to this bar down on the boardwalk and drink beers and talk nonsense."

"Max Kahn," Moishe whispered. "I remember him. My mother never liked Max."

"Your father told me that he bought the paintin' because of the naked woman, said he liked to have a nude to look at all day. Your mother didn't like the girlie magazines your father bought, but she couldn't argue with oil paintin's."

Moishe smiled and nodded. It was as if Ptolemy had become a doorway to his lost youth.

"But as the years went by, Abe found himself looking more at the background, at the people in the town who had a light shined on 'em by the deity but didn't know it. There's a old woman leading a young woman toward a doorway. One day your father noticed that the young woman was blind. There's a poor man leanin' down to pick up a wallet—"

"That a wealthy merchant had dropped on the street," Moishe said, remembering the words of his father for the first time in many years.

"There's a watchmaker with no hands explaining to his young assistant how to fix a clock, and a dog headed down a dark alleyway. At the end of that alley is a woman's face glowing and smilin' down on the cur."

"You remember all that, Mr. Grey?"

"Your father lost interest in the naked woman, but he saw somethin' new in that paintin' almost every week. He realized after Max died that he was a real artist whose work spoke out aftah death."

There was benign joy in the face of Moishe Abromovitz. He nodded and smiled at the old man.

"Okay," he said. He picked up the phone and pressed a button and said, "Esther, ask Miss Small to join us, will you?"

You sure it was all right, signin' all them papers, Uncle Grey?" Robyn asked on the bus ride back to South Central L.A.

"You mean because he's a white man and he might cheat us?"

Robyn nodded and the old man smiled.

"No, baby. Moishe ain't gonna cheat us. All you got to do is tell him money you get from Mossa and get him to make out what the taxes ought to be. He'll charge you maybe thirty dollahs an' send you the forms to send in your taxes once every three months. That's the deal me and his father made. I never did it, though. You the one. You the one gonna make Coy's dream into somethin' real."

"What happened to Coy?" Robyn asked.

The pain that invaded his chest was sharp and sudden, like a knife stab.

"What's wrong, Uncle Grey?"

"Pain," he uttered.

"From what?"

"I cain't talk about what happened, Robyn. I cain't."

The girl took his right hand and pressed the thick muscle in the webbing between his index finger and thumb.

The hurt, and then the release from the girl's massage, eased his memory of Coydog dancing on feet of fire, being strangled by a white man's noose.

"He died," Ptolemy whispered. "He's gone."

When they got to Ptolemy's block Robyn took out her knife and held it so that it was hidden by her wrist and forearm.

"He try an' mess wit' us an' I cut that mothahfuckah like a Christmas goose," she said to Ptolemy as they walked.

"You evah et goose?" the old man asked.

"No," she said.

This caused Ptolemy to laugh. He giggled and tittered, and then so did Robyn. They were like childhood friends remembering days long ago and carefree. In this way they made it to Ptolemy's door with no attacks or retaliations.

There was a small can on the floor in front of Ptolemy's door.

"What's this?" Robyn said to herself, kneeling down.

"Is it a peanut can?" Ptolemy asked.

"Yeah."

"That's a treat Miss Dartman bring down for me sometimes. Hand it here."

Ptolemy put out his hand and dutifully his newly adopted daughter complied. He could feel the heft of the ammunition Hilly had left him.

"It's heavy, Uncle," Robyn said. "What is it?"

"Nuthin'. Nuthin' at all."

The phone rang later that night as Ptolemy watched a comedy show on TV with Robyn. Watching television was the closest thing to revisiting his previous state of dementia. The people spoke too fast and the jokes weren't funny at all. People dressed like they were going to fancy parties but instead they were at work or walking down the street in broad daylight. Everybody was in love all the time, and in pain too. The stories never went anywhere, but Robyn laughed and giggled from the first moment to the last. He liked to see the young woman laughing. It was to him like a gift from God, and so he liked watching TV with her, when her hard life let up for a moment and she didn't need her anger or her knife.

Ptolemy was just getting ready to get up and say good night when the phone rang. Robyn bounced off the couch and answered.

"It's for you, Papa Grey."

"Hello?"

"Hello, Ptolemy," a woman's voice greeted.

"Hi. How are ya, Shirley?"

"Just fine. I was bakin' me some fudge here and I thought about you. Do you like chocolate?"

"I like you, and if you make chocolate, then I like that too."

"You must'a been a mess when you were a young man, Mr. Grey."

"No. Not me. When I was younger I couldn't take three steps

without trippin'. I was quiet and shy, couldn't put my words together for love or money."

"What happened to make you like you are today?"

I sold my body to the Devil, he thought.

But he said, "Some people just come into focus wit' age,
I guess."

"Would you like me to bring you over some fudge tomorrow?"

"Please do."

"Noon?"

"Sounds like a date to me."

In his room that night Ptolemy cleaned and loaded his pistol.
Hilly had put the bullets in with half a can of salted peanuts and
so he had to use a chamois cloth to wipe off each cartridge. He
enjoyed this process. It made him feel that he was getting ready
for some great event. He remembered how it felt on D-Day, when
the Allies stormed the Germans in their French strongholds. He
was an American that day. He stood side by side with tens of thousands of men, and even though he didn't die for his country, he
felt a part of something big.

And now, loading his pistol, he was a soldier again, at war again,
ready to lay down and die for an idea that was so powerful that it
didn't seem to matter that it was based on a lie.

That night Ptolemy fell asleep for the first time since the plain-
faced European nurse had given him his last shot of the Devil's

medicine. He dreamed about normal things, like the bus ride and Mossa's lovely flower garden. At one point in his dreaming he was standing in front of a mirror, watching as he grew older. At first he was a child in a light-blue suit that his mother had sewn. The sleeves and pant legs were too short because he had outgrown the dimensions before his mother could finish the job. Then he was a young man, a soldier, an ice deliveryman, and an orange-suited civil servant, cleaning anything from sewers to demolition sites, from municipal buildings to the downtown train station. He wore a black tuxedo for his first wedding, and a white jacket with black pants for his second. Both suits were still in his closet, cut for a bigger frame than the shrunken old man he finally saw in the glass.

He was withered and naked, with a small fire blazing in his chest. The fire had been loaned to him by Satan, an errant angel who coveted men's souls.

Gazing deeply into the fire, he could see his first childhood love, Maude Petit, running around in the blaze looking for succor, for Li'l Pea to save her. He reached out into the reflection and lifted the child from her torment. He placed her on a high shelf and blew on her to extinguish the flames and heal her cracked skin. Then with his hands he covered the fire raging in his breast and the heat began to rise.

Now that he knew that Maude was safe, Ptolemy reveled in the flames that Satan had given him. The fire grew in the small space of his chest. It went from yellow to red to white-hot intensity. Ptolemy felt the heat coming from Maude and knew that he had saved her somehow by reaching into Hell itself and rescuing her.

The flames were licking the back of his throat, leaping up behind his eyes, but he didn't awaken. Maude was safe at last, after eighty-six years of torment in Ptolemy's memory. He had saved her, put her out of harm's way. He had swallowed the flames that burned her, and that made him crazy with joy.

He opened his eyes to find himself writhing in his fevered bed. He was now in the burning house that consumed the Petit family. His body was that house, the attic of his mind aglow.

He went to the bureau and opened the green glass bottle. He'd placed a small juice glass filled with water by its side. He held the pill a moment before putting it in his mouth and drinking. He smiled as he swallowed, feeling as close to heaven as he ever had in life before. Somewhere the choir of his church was singing, cheering him on.

The medicine was fast acting. Ptolemy's fever began to lower in less than five minutes. As his skin cooled and the fire abated, Ptolemy the old man sat at the foot of the big bed that Sensia had made him buy so many years past.

We need a big bed, baby, she'd told him. *A bed big enough to hold all the love I'ma give ya.*

"I almost threw it all away, Sensie," Ptolemy told the memory. "I almost failed at my duty. A man only got to do one thing to set him apart. A man only got to do one thing right."

Ptolemy realized that the fever wasn't fully gone, that the medicine was losing the battle against the fire in his mind. He climbed up on the bed and slept on top of the covers. He was a child again and Maude and he were playing down by the Tickle River and nobody else, not even she, knew that she had ever died.

. . .

Robyn got up early and left. She'd put a note on the small table in the kitchen telling Ptolemy that she'd be out all day. At the bottom of the note was the number to a new cell phone that she'd purchased.

Ptolemy knew what cell phones were. Little radios that acted like phones. This knowledge burned in his mind, wavering, shining brightly. He knew that in some way this understanding in his ancient brain was some sort of abomination. He knew that the Devil would have his due. But that was further up along the trail. He picked up the house phone and dialed a number automatically without even having to recall it.

"Hello?" the heavy voice of Hilly answered.

"Hey, boy."

"You get my peanut can, Papa Grey?"

"Yeah, I got it. But tell me sumpin'."

"What's that?"

"Why you wanna leave live ammunition out in the open where any child or fool could pick it up?"

"I knocked but you wasn't there," Hilly complained.

"You could'a called. You could'a taken the peanut can back home and called me and come ovah when I told you to."

The young brute sighed through the line.

"That don't make sense to you, boy?" Ptolemy asked.

"I know what you sayin'," he countered.

"You do?"

"Yeah," Hilly said. "But I didn't wanna waste my time comin' all the way ovah there again. You wanted the bullets and now you got 'em. I don't see why you raggin' on me."

Ptolemy thought about what his great-grandnephew was saying. But it was as if they spoke different languages and came from different peoples far removed from each other by thousands and thousands of miles and many generations. Hilliard was a Catholic and Ptolemy a Hindu, or something else far removed from what his nephew believed in. He tried to think of how he could explain the great expanse of separation to the boy, but even the Devil's injections had not made him that smart.

"You got Nina's phone number somewhere around there?" Ptolemy asked after giving up on the young black man.

A familiar man's voice came across the line. "Hello."

"That you, Alfred?" Ptolemy asked.

"Who's this?"

"Ptolemy."

"Who?"

"The man Reggie used to look aftah. The one you met at Niecie's house when you took Reggie's wife away."

"What you sayin', man?" Alfred asked angrily.

"I'm sayin', is Nina there?"

A few seconds passed before the receiver banged down and Alfred called out, "You bettah tell that mothahfuckah to be respectful."

"Hello?" a feminine voice asked. "Who is this?"

"Ptolemy Grey . . . Reggie's great-uncle."

"Oh . . . Mr. Grey. Why you callin'?"

"I'm fine and how are you?"

"Oh, okay. Uh . . ."

"How was the funeral?" Ptolemy asked, trying to repair the broken conversation.

"Very sad, Mr. Grey. The children were so sad. Reggie's sistah come down from Oakland with her kids. What is it you wanted?"

"Did you bring Alfred to the funeral?"

"No . . . how can I help you, Mr. Grey?"

"I got everything I want," he replied. "I don't need a thing, thank you very much."

"But why are you callin' here?" she asked, beginning to lose patience.

"That Robyn is a miracle," he said. "You know that?"

"She okay."

"No . . . no, no, no. She's a honest-to-God miracle."

"I got to go, Mr. Grey."

"When she come here to my house," Ptolemy said, as if he had not heard Nina's complaint, "she saw the mess and the junk and cleaned it all up from one end to the other. Washed and cleaned and threw out and poisoned the bugs too. And then, when she looked at me and seen that I was a mess, she took me to the doctor and got me the kinda medicine you people got out there today. Strong stuff, the kinda penicillin open up your eyes."

"That's, that's wonderful," Nina said. "You go, Mr. Grey."

"Get off the phone with that old fool," Alfred said in the background.

"I got to be somewhere, Mr. Grey."

"So you know," the old man went on, "when Robyn brung me to that doctor, that handsome Devil with the thick mustaches, I started to remembah things."

"That's nice but I—"

"One thing I just remembered was somethin' Reggie wanted me to give you."

"I said get off that phone!" Alfred shouted.

"Just gimme a minute, Al. I'll be off in just a few minutes."

"I'ma go wit'out you, Nine," he threatened.

"Go on, then," she said. "Go on an' I'll meet you there."

Errant sounds came through the line for a time. This period was ended by a loud bang that Ptolemy thought was a door slamming.

"Mr. Grey? Are you still there?"

"Sure am. I hope I didn't cause any trouble with your man."

"Don't worry 'bout him. He just get mad sometimes."

Suddenly, and without apparent reason, Ptolemy had a startling memory. It was an afternoon that Reggie was visiting with him. It was back in the time when his mind wasn't working right, but still he had a clear image of the young man showing him a photograph.

"These my kids, Papa Grey," the old man remembered the young man saying. "Tish an' Artie. Aren't they beautiful?"

"Mr. Grey?" Nina was saying. "Are you there?"

"I don't want that man'a yours to know about this," he said.

"Okay. I won't tell him. What is it? What did Reggie have for me?"

"I wanted him to have it," Ptolemy said. "But he said that he wanted it for you and them beautiful chirren. Are the kids still stayin' wit' Niecie?"

"For a while longer," Nina said. "Until I get myself together."

"Uh-huh. You go and visit them?"

"On Tuesdays and Wednesdays, every week. Those are my days off from the department store."

"Hm. That's good. A mother should see her kids. They need to be seen by her. That way they know they okay. They know it by the look in her eye. You know, if your mother look at you an' smile, then you know you doin' all right."

"What was it that you had for Artie and Letisha?" Nina asked softly.

"I don't want that Alfred to know nuthin' about it," Ptolemy said again. "Reggie didn't like him."

"I won't tell."

"Okay, okay, then I'll tell you what. One day I'ma come by Niecie house when you there with the kids but Alfred ain't. That way I can talk to you without worryin' about him hearin' it."

"But what is it?"

"I'll tell you that when I see you."

"Why don't you tell me now?"

"I would if I could but I cain't 'cause I ain't."

"Why not?"

"You just make sure to go to Niecie's on Tuesdays and Wednesdays. What time you usually go there?"

"'Bout eleven in the mornin'."

"Keep that up and you will get Reggie's gift."

"But, Mr. Grey, I need to know what it is."

Ptolemy hung up the phone and grinned. He chuckled to himself and then laughed out loud.

· · ·

Sitting in the living room in the late morning, Ptolemy tried to remember the last time he laughed out loud. He could feel the laughter in his hands and knees. The happiness had replaced his arthritic pain. He never laughed like that when he was with Sensia. She laughed for him. He was already beyond elation and wonder by the time he was a man. It was way back in his childhood, when he would walk around the woods with Coydog and the old thief made crazy faces and sounds and told jokes about things that other adults didn't think were proper.

Ptolemy wondered how he could have lived for so long but still the most important moments of his life were back when he was a child with Coy McCann walking at his side. How could the most important moments of his life be Coy's last dance on fire and Maude's death in flames? Hadn't he lived through poverty, war, and old age? Didn't any of that mean anything?

The Devil's fire ignited in him and he was able to laugh again now that he was burning alive.

He thought about Robyn's legs, about how firm and brown and strong they were. Many a time, when she was walking around the house in only a T-shirt, he wanted to get on his knees and hug those powerful thighs to his cheek and chest. This desire made him happy. He was as old as Methuselah but a child's legs made him happy. He could no longer feel sex, but he remembered . . . maybe knowing it better in hindsight than he ever did when he was able.

"I love her," he said into the silence of the apartment.

As the moments passed, Ptolemy thought about stars wheeling through the night sky. They moved past, getting on with their business while men had their feet in clay.

We born dyin', Coydog used to say sometimes. *But you ask a man an' he talk like he gonna live forevah. Nevah take no chances. Nevah look up or down.*

"I love you, Robyn," Ptolemy said as a reply to words spoken so long ago. Death was coming, but Love was there too. Robyn was a far-off descendant, an adopted child, a woman he might have loved as a woman if he were fifty years younger and she twenty years older.

Pain tittered in his knucklebones and burbled in his knees. His joints were like music, like transistor radios calling out from under his skin. The knock at the door was a new strain, another musician deciding to jam with him. He waited for the knock to come again before getting up, going to the bedroom, pulling the bureau drawer open, and retrieving his .25-caliber pistol.

He walked to the door purposefully, like a soldier marching into battle.

"Who is it?" he asked in a mild voice.

"Shirley Wring," she answered sweetly.

Changing his mood as quickly as an infant child distracted by a sudden sound, Ptolemy stuffed the little gun into his pocket, threw the four locks, and opened the door.

She wore an orange dress and largish, bone-colored beads. Her half-blind eyes glistened behind glittering glasses. Her short hair was done recently, forming a cap that wrapped in arcs down under her ears and got curly over her forehead. Her tennis shoes were white and sensible. And instead of the red bag, she carried a pink paper box in her hands.

"Can I come in?" the small woman asked.

Ptolemy reached out to take the box and then backed away for her to enter. As she went past, he could see the red bag hanging from her left shoulder. For some reason this made him happy.

"Come on in an' sit," he said. "Can I get you somethin'? Water? Tea?"

Shirley Wring set her bag on the couch and took the box from Ptolemy.

"You sit down and rest and I'll put together some coffee an' fudge for us," she said.

"I'll be right with ya," he promised. "First I'ma get sumpin' in the bedroom."

He put the pistol back in the drawer and took out a smaller item, which he placed in his shirt pocket.

You okay, Ptolemy?" Shirley asked when he sat down heavily at the kitchen table.

"Ain't no way a man could be almost ninety-two an' okay at the same time," he answered. "But I'm as good as a man like that can get. That's for sure."

Shirley lit a match to start the burner under the kettle and then she came to sit across the table from him. Her eyes were watery and slightly out of focus, he could tell.

He must have frowned, because she asked, "What?"

"Oh . . . nuthin'. I was just thinkin' 'bout gettin' old."

"Once you get our age," she said, "I guess that's what we always be thinkin' 'bout."

"How old are you, Miss Wring?"

"Seventy-four last March."

"I was almost a man when you was born. I got old in these bones make you seem like a wildcat on the prowl."

"Old is old," she said, and smiled, enjoying a moment that she didn't see coming.

"No, baby," Ptolemy said, wondering at the words coming out from his mind. "No. That's what I was thinkin' about. You know, I got every tooth I was born with except for one canine that got knocked out when I fell off'a the ice truck one day when Peter Brock took a turn too fast. That was sumpin' else. I looked at that bloody tooth in my hand and I knew I was not nevah gonna work on that ice truck again. Not nevah. Damn.

"But you know, I nevah had a cavity, an' I nevah needed no glasses."

"And here I got nuthin' but dentures," Shirley said, "an' I got to squint just to see you across the table."

"Yeah, but just a few weeks ago I didn't even have half a mind. If you told me the apple was red an' then you right away asked me what you just said, I wouldn't remembah. I'd stutter and think about my wallet, or Reggie, or maybe I wouldn't even'a understood the question."

Shirley's smile slowly faded. Her eyes retained their blind fondness, though.

"Yeah," Ptolemy continued. "I sold my body to the Devil an' I can only hope that he don't care 'bout no old niggah's soul."

"Don't say that."

"What?"

"That word."

"That word begins with a *n*?"

"Yes. That word."

Ptolemy smiled at this genteel black woman. The kettle whistled and she got up to make filtered coffee and arrange her homemade fudge on a white plate.

When she was through preparing and serving she took her seat again, but now she wouldn't look her host in the eye.

"What's wrong, Miss Wring?"

"I didn't mean to snap at you," she said.

"Snap? Girl, all I got to say is that if you call that snappin', then you must think kissin' makes babies an' a argument makes a war."

Shirley smiled and looked up. Ptolemy could see the young girl in her features and for a moment Shirley and Robyn and Sensia came together in one.

"You're hot," she said.

It was only then that he realized that she'd reached across the table to take his hand.

"Devil's medicine," he explained.

"Why you keep talkin' 'bout the Devil, Mr. Grey?"

"When you met me, I was, was confused, right?"

"A l'il bit."

"A lot. But then I went to this doctor, and now it's like I'm a whiz kid on the radio. I know everything I ever known. I know things that I didn't know fifty years ago when they happened. Who else but the Devil gonna give you all that?"

"The medicine make you hot?"

"Yeah. It sure does. Tell me sumpin', Shirley." He squeezed her hand and she smiled at the tabletop.

"What's that?"

"Who are you?" It was a question he had never asked before. Naked and unadorned, it was like something Coy would have asked a young girl he was courting.

"I ain't nobody."

"Now, I know that ain't true 'cause I can see you right there in front'a me. I feel your fingers, see your pretty face."

"Mr. Grey," she complained.

"You know, Shirley, I wouldn't push you if I was a young man. Back a long time ago we would'a been up in a bed before I asked you 'bout your favorite color or what you do when they ain't nobody else around."

"Please, Mr. Grey, Ptolemy, don't say them kinda things to me. I'm a shy woman."

"Men like me like shy women. We see 'em an' wanna tickle 'em, you know?"

"I was born in Tulsa," Shirley Wring said. She brought out her other hand to hold his. "But there was a depression and so my daddy took us to California. We got to a rich man's estate outside'a Santa Barbara . . . lookin' for work. But instead he let us live in a big cabin by the ocean that was on his land."

"What your father do for that man?" Ptolemy brought out his other hand.

"Oh," Shirley said, "he didn't do nuthin'. That rich man was a Communist and he just wanted to do somethin' nice for his fellow man.

"We lived there for 'leven years. My first memories is the sound of waves and things that washed up from the sea. My first boyfriend was a little blond-headed boy named Leo who lived in the big house with his sister. They were the rich man's grandson and granddaughter. We'd swim in the ocean every day, almost."

Shirley smiled, her eyes gazing backward in time. Ptolemy knew that look. He'd spent many years watching his own youth. He had stared so hard that the vision blurred and the memories were shut away.

"That's wonderful," he said. "But how did you eat or get the other things you needed?"

"Mr. Halmont, that was the old white man, he gave us food and anything we asked for. My mother made our clothes and my father drove one of Mr. Halmont's old cars."

"Eleven years," Ptolemy marveled. "Eleven years livin' by the ocean an' you didn't even have to lift a finger. Did they make you go to school?"

"Leo and his sister had a tutor, and they let me sit with them. We studied in English and in French, but don't ask me to speak French. I lost that tongue a long time ago."

Ptolemy rubbed his fingertips across the back of Shirley's left hand. Their skins were wrinkled and brittle, two tones of deep, earthy brown. Ptolemy's heart stuttered, partly because of a feeling that he'd forgotten, and also because he sensed a tragedy.

"Why you leave that house on the beach?" he asked.

Shirley shook her head but said nothing.

Their hands moved together, tangled, Ptolemy thought, like seals playing in the surf of Shirley Wring's long-ago ocean yard.

"My father and Mr. Halmont used to talk about the world of communism. Every night Daddy would come home and tell us about how in Russia men was just men and there wasn't no difference in the races or anything."

"And your father believed that nonsense?"

"My mother was scared, but finally one day Daddy decided to move to L.A. and get a job in a defense factory and work with Mr. Halmont to organize the workers—black and white."

"Did they kill him?" Ptolemy asked.

Shirley put her forehead against his hand and nodded.

They left the sour taste of their talk and went into the living room. When they were seated on Robyn's couch, Ptolemy took Shirley's hands in his, pressing his fingers against her palm.

"What's this?" she said.

Looking into her hand, she saw the emerald ring she'd left with Robyn.

"Will you be my friend for the rest of our life, double-u ara eye en gee?"

She kissed his lips and threw her arms around his neck. It was the embrace he'd always run after. It was his only chance and his downfall. There was nothing like it in the world.

"You're hot, Ptolemy."

"Woman like you in my arms, it's a wonder I don't burn up."

"I like it, because I'm always so cold," she said.

They sat back, facing each other as well as their ancient bodies would allow. Their arms and hands were tangled up together, their shoes were touching.

"What about you?" Shirley asked.

"You mean you wanna know who I am?"

She nodded and smiled and caressed his cheek with her right hand, the hand that wore their ring.

"That there's a hard question," he said. He kissed her fingers, pretending in his mind that he was a younger man who had the right to do such a thing. "I mean, if you asked me any other time I'da had a answer. That answer might not'a been right or true, but I would'a believed it, and so would you have. But, but now it's all different."

"I don't understand."

"I nevah been the kinda person go out an' do sumpin' first," he said. "I usually look at somebody else and see what they was doin' and either I'd join in or walk away. My first wife wanted to get married and so that's what I did. I didn't really want it, and she knew it, but we had kids and stuck it out for a while. Kids hated me. My ex-wife did too—before she died. But that was okay.

"My second wife come to me before her first marriage was ovah. Come right up to my door. We loved each other, an' she died by my side, while I was sleep."

Shirley squeezed his wrist.

"But that's not what I'm talkin' 'bout," Ptolemy continued. "I know all that stuff. That's who I *was*, but I ain't like that no more."

"What are you like now, Mr. Grey?"

Ptolemy inhaled, feeling the breath come into him. It felt like a hot wind rushing through a valley of stone. His heart pulsed, which for some reason brought to mind the moon in its sky.

"First there was you, Shirley Wring," he said, or maybe Coy said through him.

"Me?"

"Yeah. I was like a blind man on a clear day. I lived in the dark of my eyes, and then you walked up and spelled your name and I remembered it. That was the first thing I remembered right off for the first time in years. You give me that treasure but what was even better was when I give it back. That was before I fount out that Reggie was dead, before I knew that Hilly stoled from me. That was before Robyn, and before I met the Devil behind his garden of roses and a green door.

"But it all started out with you. Reggie tried, but now that I look back on it I can see that he was a good boy but he couldn't see the man in me. I was a chore that he did every couple'a days. That's what old people turn into, chores for the young."

Shirley hummed her agreement and kissed Ptolemy's hand.

"And most of 'em don't even take on that responsibility," she said.

"If I coulda thought about it I woulda killed myself," Ptolemy said. "But instead I met Satan and he injected me with his fire. Here I been runnin' from fire ever since my childhood friend died in the blaze, and when I stopped runnin' they put a fire in my blood."

"And what you gonna do now?" Shirley asked.

"Robyn gonna be my heir," he replied. "I'm gonna ask her to take care'a my estranged children, my family and friends, and, and, and you."

"Me?"

"Yes, you. You and my great-great-grandnephew and niece and their aunt Niecie."

"All them?"

"That's what Coy McCann told me to do and I'ma do it."

Upon the last word uttered the door to the apartment came open. Robyn, loaded down with four shopping bags, stared at the old folks holding each other on the couch.

Ptolemy turned toward his heir and smiled but Shirley gasped and pulled away from him. She disentangled her arms from his and pulled her feet away too.

"What's goin' on?" Robyn asked.

"Me an' Shirley talkin' 'bout our past," the fevered old man said.

"I bet you were."

"I got to be goin', Mr. Grey, Ptolemy," Shirley said.

She got to her feet and looked around, finally seeing her red purse behind her on the couch. Robyn saw it too. She put down her shopping bags and picked up the cherry-red leather sack.

"Thank you," Shirley said.

Robyn grunted and frowned at her elder.

"Good-bye," Shirley said to both of them.

"You don't have to go, Shirley," Ptolemy said, getting to his feet.

"Oh, no, I mean, yes I do. But I will call you," she said. "I'll call."

She scuttled out the door, which Robyn had not closed because her hands were full. Shirley didn't close it either, and so Ptolemy walked to the front. Shirley stopped at the end of the hall and turned back. She smiled across the concrete expanse and Ptolemy waved at her, though he doubted if she could see.

When he turned away, after Shirley was gone, he met Robyn's stony stare.

"Why you got to be rude to my friend?" he asked, unintimidated by the anger in her face.

"Why you got to be makin' out with her on my bed?"

"Girl, I'm ninety-one."

"I know what I saw. You was just movin' back from a kiss when I come in here."

"Kiss?"

"You got your own bed," Robyn said. "You could take her up in there."

He had had this argument many times in his life. Sensia could tell when he was holding back from turning his head to see a fine woman's gait. Bertie, his first wife, once got mad because he left a fifteen-cent tip instead of a dime for a cute waitress.

"But, baby," he'd said to at least a dozen women, "I didn't mean nuthin'."

But he had meant it. He had.

Robyn's hands had become fists and her cheek wanted to quiver.

He turned away, walked into his bedroom, and closed the door on the rippling seas of love.

He went to the bureau and took out one of the Devil's tiny pills. His fever was raging. He could hear it boiling in his ears, feel it huffing like a bellows against his rib cage.

He swallowed the profane medicine and smiled.

Later on, sitting in Sensie's wicker chair by a window that looked out on the barren concrete yard, Ptolemy opened his mind.

. . .

A child had come to his door two years after he and Sensia were married. She was eleven years old and her face was his face on a girl-child's head. Her name was Pecora and she had been living in a foster home with five other girls.

"I don't wanna live there no more," Pecora, who was named for her mother, had said.

"Why not?"

"'Cause they nasty an' mean an' you my real father an' my mother have died."

"I cain't take you," Ptolemy said. He didn't question that she was his, one look at that face and he knew it must be true. He and Pecora Johnson had spent a weekend together a dozen years earlier, but she never said anything about a child.

Ptolemy and Sensia had discussed children, and Sensia said that she was no mother and so would have no child.

Ptolemy had girded himself against his own blood frowning at him and Pecora turned away. He watched the child walk down the hall. She got all the way to the door, and he would have let her go into the cold arms of the street except that Sensia came home just then. All she had to do was look into Pecora's eyes and she knew everything: that this was her husband's love child, that she had come seeking shelter, and that Ptolemy turned her away because he didn't want to lose Sensia's love.

"Come on in with me, child," Sensia said.

Pecora and Ptolemy had two things in common: their faces and their love of Sensia Howard.

"I started her out on the road," Ptolemy would say to Sensia, "but you brought her home."

Yes?" he said when she knocked.

"Can I come in?" Robyn asked through the door.

"Come on."

She had been wearing jeans and a red T-shirt when she'd come in from shopping, but now she wore a green dress that made her look younger.

"I'm sorry, Papa Grey," Robyn said from the doorway. "I didn't mean to get all mad. It wasn't my bed right then but just a couch in the livin' room and what you do ain't none'a my business anyway."

"Come on in an' sit down, baby," Ptolemy said to the girl.

Robyn slouched into the room and sat at the edge of the bed across from his wicker chair.

Robyn had her head down while Ptolemy looked at her, thinking that every heartbeat in his chest was like a grain of sand through an hourglass.

"Every minute I got wit' you is precious," he said at last. "I don't care if you get mad."

"You don't?"

"You bein' mad is just that you love me. At least I'm old enough to know that. But I want you to be nice to Shirley. I need you to take care of her after I'm gone."

"Why you got to talk about dyin' so much?"

"Because I'm dyin', baby. Dyin' just as sure as the sun go down."

"I'm sorry, Papa Grey."

"Sorry 'bout what?"

"Gettin' mad. Takin' you to that doctor."

"If I was fifty years younger and you aged twenty years . . ."

Robyn smiled, and then she giggled.

"And then would you only look at my legs?" she asked. "Or would I find you on the couch with Shirley Wring?"

"I might be lookin' but the couch would be all yours."

"One'a my mama's boyfriends used to make me take off my clothes an' lie up on top'a him," Robyn said, answering a question he'd asked days before.

Ptolemy did not reply right away.

Robyn squirmed, turning her left shoulder toward him and averting her face. Then she twisted the other way, shoving her right shoulder in his direction. Finally she got up from the bed, falling down on her knees at his feet. She put her head in his lap and he placed a hand on the side of her face.

"When I was a boy I had a friend named Maude. She was so black that even the darkest little children made fun of her."

"But you didn't?" Robyn asked into his fingers.

"No."

"Did you think she was beautiful?"

"I guess. But even if she wasn't lovely that wouldn'ta mattered because she was my friend. She was my friend and she died in a fire and nobody could save her."

Robyn raised her head to regard him.

"You are my girl, Robyn. Everything I have is yours. Everything. Do you understand me?"

She took his hand and squeezed it.

"How do you feel when I tell you about that man?" she asked.

"That I would kill him if ever I saw his face."

"I only ever told you about it."

While they were eating takeout Chinese for dinner a hard knock came on the door.

"Who is it?" Robyn asked while Ptolemy came up behind her, thinking about his pistol.

"Police."

Robyn opened the door.

Two Negro policemen stood there, wearing uniforms and stern frowns.

"Yes, Officer?" Robyn asked.

"Can we come in?" one of the policemen asked. He was shorter, maybe five ten, and lighter-skinned. A plastic rectangle on the left side of his chest said ARNOLD.

"What for?" asked Ptolemy. His throat was filled with phlegm and so he coughed twice.

When the old man spoke up, Robyn moved back, giving him the lead.

"There was a man attacked in front of your apartment building a few days ago," Officer Arnold said. "Darryl Pride. He was seriously hurt, hospitalized, and we're here investigating the assault."

That was the first time since his coma receded that Ptolemy felt his mind slip. He was confused for a moment, just a moment. He didn't understand the words, or where he was, or why people were complaining.

He tried to speak but the words were caught in his mind,

and then these words, his own thoughts, were incomprehensible to him.

"Sir?" the officer named Arnold said.

Ptolemy didn't answer, didn't know what to say.

"Papa Grey?" Robyn said, and the wheels started turning again.

"Darryl Pride?" he asked.

"Yes, sir."

"I don't know the name but do he have a girlfriend name of Melinda Hogarth?"

"That's him, sir."

"You are a very polite young man. It's nice when a policeman is civil."

Officer Arnold smiled.

"You young men come on in," Ptolemy said, once again master of his own mind.

The officers, Arnold and Thompkins, sat on the couch while Ptolemy took the folding stool and Robyn brought out a chair from the kitchen.

"Ms. Hogarth says that you were involved in Mr. Pride's beating," Arnold was saying.

"Did she tell ya that she been muggin' me on the street for three years? Did she tell ya that she pushed her way in this house an' stoled all the money outta my spendin' can an' slapped me to the ground an' here I'm ninety-one year old?"

"We're not here about that," Officer Thompkins said. He had a baby face and dark skin that was so smooth, it could have been called perfect.

"When my great-grandniece come to stay wit' me, she told that heifer that she bettah not be robbin' me no mo',"' Ptolemy said. "That's when she turned to this man Pride. Imagine that. A man named for self-respect tellin' me I got to pay up."

The officers looked at each other.

"He stole from you?"

"No, sir. No, he did not. He told me that I should pay, but I told him that I would call the cops."

"He says that you were involved in his beating," Arnold repeated.

"Look at me, Officer. Look at me. How'm I gonna beat up a man the size of a icebox? I might could shoot him if I owned a gun. I might'a would'a shot him if I did. But all I said was that I didn't have no money and that we was gonna go to the cops if they do anything else. He's afraid'a the cops. Him and Melinda both dope fiends. Both of 'em."

"So you deny that you had anything to do with Pride's beating?" Thompkins asked.

Ptolemy did not answer.

"Did you see him get beaten?" Thompkins pressed.

"No, sir."

"Did you, ma'am?" Thompkins asked, turning to Robyn.

"I don't even know who you talkin' 'bout," she said. "Papa Grey had some trouble with that bitch, but I gave her the news."

"We . . ." Arnold said. "We heard that there was another family member taking care of Mr. Grey."

"No. Just me."

"Ms. Hogarth said that there was a young man," Arnold said. "She claimed that he beat her and that another man, a heavyset guy, and a young woman had beaten her."

"Damn," Robyn said. "She been beat by just about everybody on the block accordin' to her."

Officer Arnold couldn't help but smile.

"Will you please answer the question?"

"You didn't ask no question. You just said that somebody said somethin'."

"Do you know of anyone else taking care of your uncle?"

"There's Reggie Brown."

Ptolemy's heart lurched in his chest when Robyn uttered that name.

"Where is this Reggie Brown?"

"Dead."

Again the policemen looked at each other.

"He was killed in a drive-by 'bout nine weeks ago. Killed him on Denker when he was sittin' out in front'a the house of a friend'a his."

Thompkins frowned and Arnold rubbed his fingertips together.

"Listen," Robyn said. "Melinda do dope. I'ont know her boyfriend but he prob'ly a dopehead too. My uncle's a old man. He ain't in no gang. He ain't runnin' down no dopehead, beatin' him on the street. That's just stupid."

"And what about you?" Officer Arnold asked.

"What about me?"

"She said that a young woman beat her with an electric fan."

"So? She tell you that she the Virgin Mary when she get enough dope in her blood."

"How old are you?" Thompkins asked.

"Eighteen."

"Are you in school?"

"Got my GED and I'm gonna start LACC in the fall."

Ptolemy could see Robyn's chest heaving.

The policemen stared a minute, but neither Ptolemy nor Robyn crumbled under the scrutiny.

Then the policemen looked at each other, nodded, and stood as one.

"We may have more questions later," Officer Arnold said.

"We always here, Your Honor," Ptolemy told him. "At ninety-one, with dope fiends all ovah the street, I don't get out too much."

You bettah call Billy Strong an' tell him not to come by here for a while," Robyn said after the cops were gone.

"I almost lost my mind when them bull was at that do'," Ptolemy said.

"What you mean?"

They were sitting at the kitchen table, drinking ice water from purple plastic tumblers.

"I saw them uniforms an' my mind went blank. It didn't mattah that the cops was both colored, not one bit. It was like, was like I was feebleminded again. If you aksed me my name I wouldn't been able to say."

"But you talked to them, Papa Grey. You talked good too."

"But I could feel it, honey. It's like black curtains comin' down on me. Like a shroud."

They reached across the table at the same time, entwining their fingers. Ptolemy smiled and Robyn understood him.

"Come on ovah to the closet, baby," he said. "It's time I gave you my treasure."

. . .

In the night Coy came to him.

"You finally done did sumpin', huh, boy? What took you so long?"

"I was scared," a full-grown Ptolemy Grey said to the man Coy McCann.

"Scared? What you got to be scared about? Here you got a nice apartment, wit' two girlfriends, money comin' in every week, an' a treasure too."

"There's blood on that gold, Coydog."

"My blood. You know, for every grain of gold dust that make up that treasure a black mother have cried and a black son done shed sweat or blood, maybe even life itself. That man was a slave master, only he didn't have to feed his slaves."

"You stole," Ptolemy said.

"An' they stoled an' they murdered. So who gonna be in front'a who on the line?"

Ptolemy smiled then. His fever was raging but he didn't know it. He was with Coydog again, having a brand-new conversation like they did in the old days before fire and blood flooded the chambers of the child's mind.

"You right, Coy," he said in his delirium. "You sure is. I showed Robyn the treasure an' told her what to do an' how to do it. She gonna be your heir. She gonna take that gold an' see my blood outta down here. They all gonna go to college or rest easy in they final days."

Coy stood there for a long time at the foot of the bed. The sun was rising behind him, and Africa, from two thousand years before, loomed in those first rays of light.

Ptolemy remembered the stories Coy told him about Africa; about a land before the gods of the North descended; about kings and crazy men; about wars waged and done with and not a drop of blood drawn or even a bruise suffered by a single warrior.

How you know all that, Coy?" the boy, Li'l Pea, had asked. "You said that the white man's history books lie about us all the time."

"They do."

"Then how you know about how it was before the white man? No niggah know all that."

"Oh yeah, boy," Coy McCann said. "We from there. Some of us remembah with our minds. But even more got them stories jammed up in they hearts an' spirits. They tell white men's stories but changes 'em. They talkin' about things they know an' don't remembah. I listens an' tease out the truth that lay underneath."

Coy stood at the foot of the bed with the sun rising and the secret memory of Africa emerging out of memories that were forgotten but not lost.

Ptolemy began to fret that maybe he'd done something wrong. Maybe Coy didn't want a woman to lay hold to his treasure. Maybe he had waited too long to take action. But after a long time, at least two days by Ptolemy's reckoning, Coydog smiled, and then, a few hours later, he nodded . . .

. . .

A pain lanced through Ptolemy's rib cage. It was like a spear that had entered by his left side and went out through the right. He sat up straight in his bed and yelled.

Robyn was sitting there, and next to her was a man who was holding a syringe, leaning over and frowning.

"Hello, Satan."

"Good to see you, Mr. Grey," Dr. Ruben said.

"Am I dead yet?"

"If it wasn't for your niece you would have been. I'm surprised you've made it so long. I'm glad too."

"You ain't taken no money or nuthin' from him, have you, girl?" Ptolemy asked.

"No, sir. Nuthin'."

Ptolemy thought he could make out things crawling and bristling in the doctor's great mustaches. Ruben's eyes seemed to be blazing: yellowy-green flames on a brown sea.

"Lemme talk to this man alone a minute, will you, Robyn?"

"Yes, sir," she said again, relief at his revival in her tone and her shoulders, and even in the way she stood.

She closed the door and the doctor pressed a thumb against Ptolemy's wrist.

"You have the constitution of a man half your age," he said.

"How long have I been in this bed?"

"Three days." Ruben took out a little notebook and started writing. While he did this he continued to talk. "That niece of yours is something else. She went to Antoine Church with two men and they threatened him until he found a way to get in touch with me. I came as soon as she called. I thought you would die, I told her so. But I gave you this concentrated injection and you came to immediately. I've never seen anything like it."

"How long?"

"If you were anybody else I'd say two days. But at the outside it's two weeks."

"And then you cut me up like a slaughtered calf."

"Science will benefit from your sacrifice, Mr. Grey. Your niece and her generation will not have to suffer as you have."

Ptolemy smiled at that.

"I'm leaving you a stronger pill," Dr. Ruben continued. "And Robyn has my phone number. Whenever you feel hot, take a pill immediately. She will call me if you begin to fail."

"I went to Africa in my sleep."

"You did?"

"I saw it. Not today, but two thousand years ago, a thousand years before the Great Degradation, by Coy McCann's reckoning."

Dr. Ruben didn't say anything to that. Ptolemy closed his eyes, then realized that he must have fallen asleep, because when he opened them again Robyn was sitting there next to him, holding his hands.

Satan was nowhere to be seen.

"Hi, baby," he said.

"You look like a baby when you sleepin', Papa Grey."

"I got two weeks."

She kissed his fingers.

"What day is it?" Ptolemy asked.

"Tuesday."

"I got to go to Niecie's house at noon . . . Alone."

"Okay."

"You been takin' that gold to the safe-deposit box?"

"Yeah. A little bit at a time, like you told me to do. Shirley Wring come by in the mornin' to sit wit' you and I went to the bank. And then I got Beckford and Billy Strong an' we went to talk to Antoine Church."

"How soon before all that gold in the box?" Ptolemy asked.

"Three days. It'a be done by Thursday."

"I'ma sleep now, baby."

"Can I lie down next to you?"

"Will you tell me sumpin'?"

"What?"

"Anything, child."

When I was a little girl my mama an' my daddy and me was happy," she whispered into the old man's ear. "We lived in a house that was blue and white and had flowers in the front yard and a vegetable garden in the back. Mama took in li'l black children for daycare, and Daddy worked on a farm outside'a town. He coulda had a bettah job but he liked to be outside and to take time off between the seasons.

"Mama had a baby boy, and Daddy was so happy that he went up and down the block tellin' everybody that he had a son named Alexander and that his son was gonna do what Alexander the Great did. But then, only a few weeks aftah Al was born, he got somethin' in his chest and he was sick for five months.

"I think if he had just died right off that it wouldn'ta been so hard on Daddy an' Mama. But he took off'a work and she went wit' him to the hospital ev'ry day. Ev'ry day. An' Al got sicker, and men would come to the house an' tell me to pay the rent or the gas bill, or for heatin' oil, an' I was only six and half and they left me home 'cause they was at the doctors all the time.

"And Mama and Daddy would fight at night. And then, when Al died, Daddy went out to get drunk and he nevah came back. An' Mama moved to Memphis and she started gettin' drunk all the time.

"That's when I met Mr. Roman. He was the man that lived next door an' gave me peaches. He would take me in as much as he could when Mama had her boyfriends ovah. An' we would talk an' play board games, and I would read to him from my storybooks and he would ask silly questions.

"And one day when he saw that I was scared'a my mama's boyfriend who would make me lay on top'a him, he came and got me and kept me for a whole day. He gave me hot dogs and sweet potato pie and root beer. And when it got late and my mama still wasn't home, he gave me hot chocolate and made me a bed on a cot in his den.

"An' when my mama died and I was supposed to come up here, Mr. Roman took me ovah to his house an' told me that he loved me. I told him that I loved him too an' that I was gonna miss him, but he said that it wasn't the same thing. He said that if I was a young woman, even though he was old, that he would make me his wife and buy me a house with a swimmin' pool in the backyard and a movie screen in the basement.

"And I wished that I was older and that Mr. Roman could make me his wife. I was even thinkin' that I'd go back down home when

I was eighteen and ask him if he still loved me. And then I met you, Papa Grey.

"Papa Grey, are you awake?"

The old man was breathing heavily, snoring lightly on and off.

"Anyway," Robyn continued, "when I met you I knew that you loved me like Mr. Roman did but that you wouldn't let nobody take me away and just hope that I'd come back someday. Even when you couldn't think so good, and then when you could, you wanted to look aftah me. I don't need nobody to take care'a me, not no more. I just need somebody to want to."

While Robyn spoke, Ptolemy could hear himself breathing like a man asleep. He was asleep, but still he heard every word. He imagined the young girl eating peaches and the old man falling in love with her. This seemed natural. Children were there to be loved and looked after and cared for; sometimes you even had to sacrifice your life in order that a child might live.

After a while the girl talked about moving to Los Angeles and about Niecie and Hilliard and Reggie, who was an orphan too. The sleeping man listened with part of his mind, but he was also thinking about Letisha and Arthur and how Reggie was like a son to him.

Now he was an old man and there were children to look after, and one child to avenge.

Ptolemy smiled in his sleep, thinking all the way back to that day the white minister had shaken his hand. He had given that arrogant old white man something, and he had taken something away from him too.

. . .

In the morning the sleeping but still-conscious man opened his eyes. Robyn slept next to him, her arm flung over his chest. He rose up on a painful elbow and kissed the child's forehead. She opened her eyes and hugged him.

"Do you love me, Papa Grey?" she asked.

"More than anything . . . ever."

Pitypapa!" Niecie exclaimed when he showed up on her doorstep at 12:14 on Tuesday afternoon.

Robyn had hired him a limousine and a driver, a brown man with a Spanish accent named Hernandez. She had wanted to come with Ptolemy, but he told her that she needed to put Coydog's treasure where nobody could get at it but her.

"But why you got to go see Niecie so bad?" she'd asked him.

"For Reggie."

"Reggie's dead, Papa Grey."

"Ain't nobody full dead until no one remembah they name. Don't forget that, girl—as long you remembah me, I'ma be alive in you."

Robyn crying, it seemed to Ptolemy, was a woman at war with herself. She couldn't let herself go completely, but the tears rolled down her left eye, and her beautiful lips trembled.

He tried to put his arms around her but she pulled away.

"Robyn."

"Your car prob'ly outside, Papa Grey. You bettah be goin'."

. . .

This your family we going to?" Hernandez the driver asked Ptolemy on the way to Niecie's house.

"Yes, sir. Real blood family too. The kind you can't shake off."

The driver, a broad-faced man, laughed.

"What's your name?" Ptolemy asked from the backseat.

"Hernandez."

"Well, Mr. Hernandez—"

"No, Mr. Grey, not Mr. Hernandez, just Hernandez. I like that name."

"You from around here, Hernandez?"

"Fifty years here," he said. "Forty-eight, really. When I was seven my parents came up from a farm in the south of Mexico."

"You still speak Spanish?"

"No. I just got this accent is all. I know some words."

"Remembah back in the old days when we all lived together?" Ptolemy asked. "Mexicans, Negroes, Koreans, Chinese, and Japanese on the one side—"

"And white people on the other," Hernandez said, finishing the litany.

Both men laughed.

"What happened to us?" Ptolemy asked.

"White man shined a light on us and we froze like deer in the road. After that we all went crazy and started tearin' each other apart."

Ptolemy frowned and sat back in his seat. Even the Devil's fire couldn't help him to understand why what both he and Hernandez knew was true.

Hernandez dropped him at Niecie's door with a business card so that he could call if it was time to go home and the driver was off somewhere. The black man and the brown shook hands over the seat.

"Nobody evah put us on the news, huh, Hernandez?"

"What you mean, Mr. Grey?"

"Us gettin' along ain't news."

Hernandez laughed and got out to open the door for his client.

Niecie cried happily and Ptolemy walked in the house. Nina was there with her children. Hilliard was on a couch in the corner, watching a small TV in a pink plastic case.

"Come ovah here and say hi to Pitypapa," Niecie said to her son.

"Hey," Hilly said, going so far as to turn his eyes away from the screen.

"Go on back to your TV, boy," Ptolemy said, waving dismissively.

Niecie and Nina sat with their elder and talked and drank lemonade. Niecie was nervous, not wanting to ask for the money she had already come to expect, had already planned on.

They talked for a while about relatives that Ptolemy had only recently remembered. Many members of his family and his extended family had died. They stopped bringing him to funerals because he seemed to get upset during the services.

"That's why I send Reggie ovah to your house in the first place, Pitypapa," Niecie said. "You'd get upset and mad and you didn't seem to know where you was at."

Ptolemy appraised his grandniece's attempt to convince him, and maybe convince herself, that he really owed her something, that she had been there to help him when he couldn't help himself. He resented her trying to make him feel indebted, but on the other hand he did owe her what she said. She had sent Reggie, and Reggie had tried his best. She had sent Robyn to him.

"You know, one time Reggie lost his job at the supermarket because he wouldn't come in because he had to take you to the doctor's," Niecie was saying. "I told him that blood was thicker than water and that we owed you somethin'. I told him that I'd put him up and feed him and the onlyest thing I expected was that he took care of you."

"Do you have a checking account at the bank, Niecie?" Ptolemy asked.

"Wha?"

"A bank account. Do you have a bank account?"

"No. I mean, I know I should have one but they need you to maintain a three-hundred-dollar minimum, an' some months here I cain't even find three dimes in my coin purse."

"I'ma get Robyn to go to the bank wit' you an' start a account with nine hunnert dollars," Ptolemy said.

Hilly turned his head away from the TV to look at the old man.

"Then I'ma set it up to put eight hunnert dollars in there ev'ry mont'."

"You only get two hunnert an' sumpin' a week from retirement," Hilly said.

"That ain't all I evah got, boy," Ptolemy replied. "Maybe if you didn't steal from me right off the bat, you'da learnt sumpin'."

"How come you let Robyn do your business, Uncle?" Niecie

asked. "You know that girl ain't nuthin' but trouble. I only took her in outta the goodness'a my heart. But she's bad news. You cain't trust her. An' you know I'm the one sent her ovah there in the first place."

Ptolemy saw trouble in Niecie's eyes, trouble he'd lived with all through his life. He saw lawyers and lawsuits, maybe even threats and drive-bys coming from his one slip.

Ptolemy got to his feet, steadying himself by placing a hand on the back of the chair.

"Where you goin', Pitypapa?"

"I'ma leave."

"Don't go."

"Oh yeah, honey. I'm gone. I can see from talkin' to you that there ain't nuthin' but trouble in the future. I'ma cut that off right here and now. I shoulda known that givin' you a little sumpin' would make you want everything."

"No. I was just warnin' you 'bout that girl."

"Not another word, Niecie. Not one more word or I will cut you off without a dime, without evah speakin' to you evah again."

Niecie Brown saw the iron and the clarity in her uncle's eyes. She saw the intelligence surging up in him, the certainty in his words, and even in the way he stood.

"I'm sorry, Uncle," she said.

"Nina," Ptolemy said.

"Yes, Mr. Grey."

"Come on out on the porch with me," he said. "Hilly."

"Huh?"

"Bring me an' Nina two chairs out there."

The boy frowned.

"Do what your uncle tells you to do, Hilliard," Niecie commanded.

Letisha and Artie could be heard from the inside of the house, jumping and shouting. The tinny speaker of the pink TV made unintelligible noises while adult footsteps sounded at unexpected intervals. Helicopters roved the skies over South Central L.A. as brown and black folks passed beneath the aerial scrutiny. Ptolemy saw Hernandez leaning against the hood of his car across the way, while little Mexican children played around him on a curbside patch of grass.

Ptolemy thought about the world he lived in. It seemed to him that he had died and was resurrected twenty years later in an old man's body, but with the sly mind of a fox or a coyote. He was an ancient predator among great-bodied herbivores, under a desert sky filled with metal creatures that had passed down from man.

"Why you smilin', Mr. Grey?" Nina asked.

"You know, Nina, you are probably the most beautiful woman I have evah seen in ninety years."

Reggie's lovely young widow smiled and looked away.

"Mr. Grey!"

"Oh yeah," he said. "I had a wife named Sensia."

"That's a pretty name."

"And she was a beautiful girl. But not as beautiful as you."

Nina turned back to the old man, wondering with her gaze where he wanted to go with this line of flattery. "Really?"

"Oh yeah. And Reggie loved you too. He loved you so much that when he found out that some other man had caught your eye he decided to take you down to San Diego so that he didn't have to share all that loveliness."

Nina's smile froze. Her head moved back an inch.

"What?" she asked.

"I got a trust in the bank," Ptolemy said. "It's set aside for my family. There's money for your chirren's education and their weddin' days."

Nina's expression changed again. Ptolemy wouldn't let her get a bead on his intentions.

"Yeah," he said. "And I made a gift for Reggie."

He took an old gold coin from his pocket. The date on the coin read 1821.

"This here twenty-dollar gold piece. It's worf five thousand dollars or more to a collector. I got twenty'a them for Reggie. He told me to hold them for you."

Nina brought both hands to her mouth.

Ptolemy put the coin back in his pocket.

"But before I hand them ovah I got to know how my boy died."

"I don't know," she said. "I, I don't know who shot him."

"What about Alfred?"

"No."

"Did you tell him that Reggie was takin' you and the kids away?"

Nina tried to speak but could not.

Sirens blared and suddenly four police cars raced past Niecie's house and on down the street.

"He couldn't, Mr. Grey. My Al couldn't do nuthin' like that."

"What was he in prison for?"

"No."

"Was he wit' you when Reggie was killed?"

"I'm a good woman, Mr. Grey . . . a mother."

"Was Alfred wichyou when they opened fire on Reggie on the front steps of his friend's house?"

"My baby couldn't do nuthin' like that," Nina said, her eyes begging him.

"How long aftah you told Alfred was Reggie killed?"

"A, a, a day and a, a, a day and a half."

"An' you didn't think nuthin' about that?"

Nina's hands were back at her mouth again. She shook her head and tears squeezed out from her eyes.

This is the mother of Reggie's children, Ptolemy thought, *the mother of my blood.*

"I'm a good woman, Mr. Grey."

"But did you tell Alfred that you was goin' away with Reggie?"

She nodded almost imperceptibly.

"Did he say he wanted you to stay?"

She nodded.

"An' what else did he say?"

"That I was his woman. That I belonged wit' him."

Ptolemy thought about his great-great-grandniece and -nephew again, this woman's children.

"Why you wanna run around wit' him, treatin' Reggie like that?"

Nina looked away.

"Did you know?" he asked.

"No," she said to the splintery wooden deck.

Ptolemy looked out across the street and saw Hernandez gazing back at him. His heart thudded against his rib cage like the kicks of an angry mule against a barn door. His mind felt as if it might explode. He took out one of the Devil's pills and swallowed it without water.

He felt the life-preserving, life-taking medicine work its way down his dry gullet. It was a painful journey. Ptolemy thanked Satan for the ache.

"Did you suspect?" he asked.

"Why you wanna bother me 'bout all this?" Nina cried. "Why you doin' this to me?"

Hilly came out on the porch to see what was wrong.

"Go away, Hilliard," Ptolemy said. "This ain't none'a your nevermind."

The boy snorted and went back in the house.

When Hilly was gone, Ptolemy said, "Reggie took care'a me an' you did him dirt. I got to ask. I got to find out who killed him."

Nina stopped crying. Ptolemy thought she finally understood that Reggie's death didn't give her a right to blubber and moan.

"I asked him," she said.

"Who?"

"Al."

"An' what he say?"

"He slapped me. He knocked me down. He told me that he wouldn't nevah have Reggie's kids in his home."

"An' that's the man you run to when Reggie wanna be wit' you an' have his family wit' you?"

"Al was my first man evah, Mr. Grey. I was wit' him when I was just thirteen an' thought I was grown. I just don't know how to say no to a man like that. I loved Reggie," she said. "I loved him, but I just couldn't help myself."

The pill began to work. The fire in Ptolemy's mind extinguished, leaving the cold he'd felt in Coydog's treasure cave. The old man shivered and closed his eyes.

"You murdered my boy," he said.

Nina shook her head, but it was a weak denial. It was more like she was saying, *I didn't mean to. I couldn't help my feelings.*

"So I will make sure that Robyn makes sure that you get enough to live on, to take care'a them babies."

"But Al won't take 'em," she cried.

"I ain't talkin' to Al."

That girl you was with sure was pretty, Mr. Grey," Hernandez was saying on the drive back to Ptolemy's home.

They were sitting side by side in the front seat. Ptolemy wore the bright-red seat belt across his chest. He felt that the wide band made him seem small, like a child.

"She told me that her boyfriend mighta murdered my great-grandnephew."

"Oh."

"What's all them tattoos on your arms, Hernandez?"

"Just memories."

"Back when you was young and wild?"

"Just back when," the driver said. "Things change, but they don't get better."

They drove for a while. When Hernandez came to a stop at a big intersection he said, "She could be lying to you, Mr. Grey."

"Yeah."

"You know some crazy kids who lived a few blocks away from

my house said that my cousin Hector had got their little sister drunk and pulled a train on her with his boys."

Ptolemy didn't know what a *train* was exactly, but he could guess.

"They come and killed Hector and his main man, Pepe," Hernandez continued. "I know that Hector didn't do it 'cause I was wit' those crazy kids' sister by myself. And we were gettin' high, but there wasn't nobody else there."

"Yeah," Ptolemy said again.

The light changed and Hernandez drove on.

"Aren't you gonna ask me what I did, Mr. Grey?" the driver asked ten blocks further on.

"Why would I?" he replied. "Either you killed them or her or you didn't do nuthin'. Any way you go, you left with a dead brother and a lie."

They didn't talk again until Ptolemy climbed out of the limo in front of his house. He offered Hernandez five dollars as a tip but the Mexican waved it away.

"You all right, Mr. Grey. Watch out, now."

He came home to an empty apartment. Everything was clean because Robyn cleaned every day. She swept and mopped and dusted and washed. She even ironed Ptolemy's clothes and hers.

When Robyn did come home he told her that they would have to go see Moishe Abromovitz again.

"All the way down there, Uncle? Why?"

"'Cause I made a mistake an' told Niecie that you was gonna

take care'a my money. You know the minute I drop dead she gonna get some kinda lawyer and try to take that money from you."

"Niecie wouldn't do that."

"Baby, I know that's what you think. You think Niecie love you and care about you. But all that's just in yo' head." As Ptolemy spoke he realized that Coy had been coming to life in his mind for the past weeks; that his murdered mentor was coming back to see him through this delicate negotiation at the end of his life. "Niecie love you as long as you sleep on the couch and do the things she don't wanna do. She love you when the old men come around to look at you and you get behind her skirts. But when she find out how much money you gonna get, she won't love you no more. She won't ever again. She gonna say you stole her rightful inheritance."

"You wrong, Uncle," Robyn said, "Aunt Niecie wouldn't evah hate me like that."

Ptolemy reached across the small kitchen table to take Robyn's strong hands in his big one.

"I know how you feel and I respect you," he said. "But do you believe in me?"

"Yes."

"An' do you respect me?"

"Yes."

"So go wit' me to see Moishe so that I can make sure that your money is yours. And if Niecie come aftah you aftah I'm gone, then I want you to light me a candle on this here table for seven days. Will you do all that for me, baby?"

"I won't have to light no candle, because Aunt Niecie ain't nevah gonna think I'd steal from her."

. . .

I have three red apples, two oranges, and a sausage I bought from the market," Nora Chin said.

They were sitting across from each other at a large conference table of the Terrence P. Laughton Mental Services Center of Santa Monica. Moishe Abromovitz, the old man in the middle-aged man's body, and Robyn sat at the far end of the table. There was a large tape recorder sitting between Ptolemy and the psychiatrist. The spool of recording tape rolled steady and slow.

A big black fly buzzed past Nora Chin's face, but she didn't move or flinch.

"Today's Robyn's birthday, Dr. Chin," Ptolemy said. "She's eighteen today."

"How many apples do I have, Mr. Grey?" she responded.

"Two," he said. "Two apples, three oranges, and a sausage. You know pork sausage an' applesauce would make my whole day back when I was a boy."

Chin smiled. She was pretty, though somewhat severe looking. She looked at least twenty years younger than Moishe, but they were almost the same age.

Chin held up an eight-by-ten photograph of a highway scene. There were only four cars evident: three were coming toward the viewer; of these, two were white and one yellow. A blue station wagon, its red brake lights ablaze, was on the other side of the road. After a few seconds Nora Chin put the photograph face down on the table.

"What was the color of the car driving away from you, Mr. Grey?"

"Which way is Toledo from here?" he asked.

"What?" The stern-faced and lovely doctor of the mind was thrown off.

"The road sign said Toledo. I figure you must be askin' me where am I between that blue car an' Toledo."

"I think we've done enough testing," Chin said, her surprise turning into a friendly smile. "Do you know why you're here today, sir?"

In an instant a dozen thoughts flitted through Ptolemy's mind: his friends Maude and Coy on fire in the Deep South; Melinda Hogarth, Reggie, the lady newscaster; Sensia, who taught him about love past the age of forty; Robyn, who was sitting there, frowning because the presence of a Chinese woman and a Jewish man made her nervous.

"Because I'm old and for a long time I was confused in my mind," he said.

"You know that there's a video camera in the wall behind me, recording our conversation?"

"Yes, ma'am."

"And that there's also a tape recorder running." She tapped the big box with a slender finger.

"Yes, ma'am."

"And is that all right with you?"

"I want to make it clear that I'm of sound mind so that nobody can argue about my last will and testament."

Suddenly Nora Chin's face drew in on itself. It was as if she had heard a sound somewhere and was trying to identify it. Ptolemy decided this was how she looked when she was serious. He also thought that this was the face she put on before a kiss.

Women deadly serious when it come to kissin', Coy used to say. *They laugh all the way there, but when it come down to kissin' they like a cat when she see sumpin' shakin' in the tall grass.*

The black fly landed on the big knuckle of Ptolemy's left hand. He couldn't help but think that this was Coy coming to visit.

"Why would anyone question your will, Mr. Grey?"

"Because I'ma leave everything to Robyn Small."

"And why would anyone contest that decision?"

"Because she's young and not my blood. Because my real family think they deserve my savin's and property."

"And you feel that they don't deserve it?"

"Not exactly that. It's just that I don't have no trust in 'em," Ptolemy said. "Not even a little bit. They good people and I done asted Robyn to take care of 'em. I set up with Mr. Abromovitz to give 'em a little money every month. But Robyn need to be the one in charge."

"And why is that, Mr. Grey?"

"Because when she had the chance to take my money and use it for herself she didn't. Because she don't think that my family will evah be mad with her. Because she the one took me to the doctor an' got me the vitamins I needed to make me able to be of sound mind."

Ptolemy gazed at his young friend at the far end of the table. She was smiling and crying.

"But most of all, it's because when she see a mess she have to clean it up," he said.

"I don't understand," Nora Chin said.

"Robyn is more worried about where she is than where she

goin' to. She want her bed made and the dishes washed. She want to know that ev'ryone's all right before she go to sleep. She's a child, but chirren is our future. An' she have received charity, an' so she unnerstan how to give it out."

The black fly had wandered down to Ptolemy's index finger-tip by then. It buzzed its wings, sending a thrill through the old man's hand.

Nora's visage had softened. She seemed to have something to say but held it back.

Ptolemy wanted to go and have dinner with her and ask her all kinds of questions about how she saw the minds of white men who came to her for excuses and reasons why they didn't do right. Did she forgive them like so many brown people had and black people had? Or did she sneak in like Coy would have done and sabotage their wills?

"I think we have enough, Mr. Grey," she said.

"So is the camera off now?" he asked.

"Yes, sir."

"You like this kinda work, Miss Chin?"

"I do today," she said slowly and deliberately.

They gazed at each other for a long moment.

"It's all up in the head for you, isn't it, Miss Chin," Ptolemy said at last.

"Not always, sir. Sometimes we find a heart."

"Yeah. That's what Robyn know. For the rest'a my family it's the stomach or the privates or clothes ain't worf a dime. They don't know the difference."

"The difference between what?"

"Between raisin' a child and lovin' one."

263

. . .

Nine days later, Ptolemy woke up in his bed. He felt odd, older. His first thought was of the black fly in the Chinese psychiatrist's office. He felt the buzz against his finger and giggled.

"Uncle Grey?" Robyn said.

"Hey, baby. What day is it?"

"Thursday."

"How long I been in this bed?"

"Do you know my name?"

"Robyn."

The child got from the chair and sat next to him on the bed.

"You know me?"

"'Course I know you. You're my heir."

The beautiful child leaned over and kissed the old, old man on the lips. He closed his eyes to enjoy that unexpected blessing and then opened them again.

"What happened?" he asked.

"Aftah we got back from the head doctor you started talkin' like you used to when I first came here . . . only you didn't recognize nobody an' you was kinda like outta your head. I didn't understand most'a the things you said, and you'd be sleepin' almost all day and all night. I turned on the radio but you said that it hurt your ears, and you would get mad at the TV.

"Aftah two days I called Dr. Ruben. He come an' told me that you was dyin' but he'd give you a shot anyways. He said he'd give you a shot an' either you'd come back to the way you was, stay the way you was, or die."

"Devil said that?"

Robyn nodded, a serious look on her face, giving her the aspect of a young child.

"How long?" Ptolemy asked.

"Nine days since we come home from Dr. Chin, and one week since the doctor give you the shot."

"Damn. What kinda world is it we livin' in where you got to thank the Devil for makin' house calls?"

"He told me to call him if you passed, Uncle, but, you know, I wanna give you a proper burial."

"When I die," he said, "you call Moishe. He and me done made the proper plans for the funeral. He gonna give my body to Ruben, but aftah he finished with it you get it back for cemetery. And I wanna be cremated."

"No coffin or nuthin'?"

"No."

"Why not?"

"I lived a life afraid'a fire," he said. "In the last I wanna give in to it."

"How you feel now, Papa Grey?"

"You evah been to the circus?"

"Uh-huh. Mr. Roman used to take me when I was a li'l girl. He take me down early so we could go out back an' see the lions in the cages and the elephants in their stalls."

"Did you see the tightrope walker?"

"Yeah. But I'd look away sometimes 'cause I was so afraid that she would fall."

Ptolemy nodded and smiled.

"What's so funny?"

"It's like you an' me was the same," he said, "like we was born on the same day at the start of everything. We learned to talk from the same teacher, went to the same circus. We ain't related, but you my twin, and I'm smilin' 'cause I know that."

Robyn bit her lower lip and crossed her breasts with her arms. A fly whizzed past, over her head.

"But why you asked me about the tightrope walker?"

"Because that's how I feel right now," Ptolemy said. "Like there's a rope where there used to be a wide road home. It's a thousand feet above the ground and it's so long that you can't see the beginnin' or the end. I know I'ma fall off it sooner or later, but I keep on walkin' because where you fall matters. Do you know what I mean, Robyn?"

She shook her head and took hold of his hand.

"I told you how Coy took them coins and they hung him and burned him, right?"

Robyn nodded.

"In that way he chose the time that he fell. He didn't plan on it. He wanted to go north and start a new life. But he knew that he could fall right then and that didn't matter because he had done his important thing in life."

"Why didn't he take that gold with him, Uncle?"

"Country boy don't need no gold," Coy and Ptolemy said as one. "Sun and soil, whiskey and women all a black farmer need. I'd give away everything I had for the sun on my face and you there next to me, girl."

Ptolemy hoped the girl would kiss his lips again, but she didn't. He smiled, though, as if she had.

"Can you go stay with Beckford for two days?" he asked.

"You might need me."

"Call me every evenin' at six. If I don't answer, come on ovah and check on me."

"Why?"

"'Cause I need to be alone for just two days. I need it."

"Okay. If you say so. When should I leave?"

"In the mornin', baby. Tonight I wanna go out with you and Shirley Wring. I want Chinese at a big red restaurant."

When Ptolemy woke up in the morning, his mind was filled with the sound of dissonant flutes that played over and over at Len Wah's Mandarin Palace. Shirley wore her emerald ring, and Robyn had on a tight black dress that was short, with spaghetti straps over her shoulders. They laughed and talked and drank cheap red wine with their meal.

For Ptolemy each story they told was a piece in a stone puzzle that made up the ground below his rope. His head was burning but he didn't take the pill. His mind was soaring but he didn't worry about a fall.

At their small table he felt that there was seated a multitude. Coy and Sensia flirting at the far end, Reggie and Nina arguing at each other. As he looked around he saw a hundred faces. It was like when he was in the bank with Hilly, only now he felt that he knew every name, every face . . .

Robyn was at the kitchen table, waiting for him in the morning.

"I wanted to say good-bye," she said, apologizing.

"Me too."

"I love you, Papa Grey."

"If I was fifty years younger and you was twenty years older . . ."

"I'd marry you and make your children and we'd move to Mississippi and grow peaches and corn."

They kissed and embraced and kissed again . . . embraced again.

Ptolemy watched as she went down the hall toward the door. The sun was bright through the cracks, and when Robyn pushed it open her shadow threw all the way back to the old man's toes.

"Bye," she said.

He tried to reply, choked, and waved. He smiled but doubted that she saw it.

Hilly?" he said into the phone.

"Uh-huh."

"You know Alfred's phone number?"

"Yeah," he said defensively.

"Call him up. Tell him that I got Reggie's gold here at my house."

"What gold?"

"Just tell him what I said. An' if he don't know what you talkin' 'bout, tell him to ask Nina. Tell him to tell her that I said it was okay."

Forty-seven minutes passed. Ptolemy sat on Robyn's couch-bed, looking at the clock and remembering his life.

At some time it come to you that you only thinkin' 'bout the past, Coy had once said to him. *When you young you think about tomorrow, but when you old you turn your eyes and ears to yesterday.*

Ptolemy sat at the edge of the couch, aching in his joints and remembering. His life loomed before him like ten thousand TV screens. All he had to do was look at one of them and he'd remember driving the ice truck, moving to Memphis. He saw his father in a coffin, wearing a new suit that Ptolemy bought for the burial. He saw Sensia kissing a man down the street from their apartment. It was a long soul kiss that repeated itself again and again. He hated her when she got home but he didn't say anything because he couldn't stand the idea of her leaving.

He took out a yellow No. 2 pencil and a single sheet of paper that was so old that it had turned brown at the edges and was somewhat brittle. On this paper he wrote a note to Robyn, telling her, as best he could, about what he was doing and why.

Ptolemy was finally done with the Devil and his alchemy. He'd lived that life and now he was through.

There was a knock at the door.

"It's open," the old, old man said.

Alfred pushed his way in and stormed at Ptolemy.

Ptolemy's only response was to smile.

Alfred had on black pants and a fuchsia-colored shirt. Across his chest was the medallion that said *Georgie*. Alfred's strawberry skin was redder than it had been, and his freckles seemed darker. His pretty face was as brutal as ever and his breath was coming hard.

"Sit down, Alfred," Ptolemy said, pointing to the straight-back chair across from him.

There was a gold coin on the table between the couch and the chair; a twenty-dollar gold piece from before the Civil War. After sitting down, Alfred picked up the coin and caressed it with his thumb.

Ptolemy's smile broadened.

"Where the rest of 'em, old man?"

"Before I met Robyn, Reggie was the light of my life," Ptolemy said. "I couldn't think worf a damn, but you don't have to think straight to love somebody."

"You want me to go through your pockets?"

"It nearly killed me when I saw him in his coffin."

"I will tear this house up."

"Robyn brought me up to his grave 'bout a month ago."

"I ain't foolin'," Alfred said. "I will hurt you, old man."

"It was beautiful up there," Ptolemy remembered. "Big green trees and a breeze. He had a small stone, but it was respectful. You evah been up there?"

This question derailed the younger man's rage for a moment.

"I took Nina and her kids up but I waited in the car."

"That coin you put in your pocket was for him."

"He's dead."

"Then it's for his wife and his chirren."

"I'm lookin' aftah Nina."

"But you ain't givin' a care for them kids. Niecie got the kids."

Alfred's eyes bulged and he jumped to his feet, gesturing violently. Ptolemy looked up at him, wondering what the Devil could have put in that injection to make him so unafraid of impending death.

"What would you do with them coins if you had 'em?" Ptolemy asked.

"I already got one."

"Okay," Ptolemy said. "What you gonna do with that?"

"Take it to the pawn shop on Eighty-sixth Street. Gold is expensive."

"So he gonna give ya fi'e hunnert dollahs on a coin worf at least twelve thousand."

Alfred's rage was extinguished. His eyes took on a crafty slant.

"Maybe three times that," Ptolemy added.

Alfred sat back down.

"How?" Alfred asked.

"Did you kill Reggie, Al?"

"He was killed in a drive-by."

"Was it you with the gun in your hand?"

"Reggie's dead."

"An' you got his woman."

Alfred smiled then. He didn't mean to, Ptolemy could tell.

"Streets is hard, old man," Alfred said, still unable to repress the grin. "People die all the time. All the time."

"Oh, I know that. I prob'ly know it even bettah than you. I'm dyin' right now while you lookin' at me. My head is on fire. My bones feel like dust."

"You *will* be dead you don't hand ovah Nina's property. She told me what you said. She told me what you thought."

"And what did you say to that?" Ptolemy leaned forward, remembering leaning into a kiss with Natasha Kline seventy years before. The young white woman couldn't pay for the ice and so she kissed him instead. He'd never told anybody about that kiss. Back then, in 1936, a Negro kissing a white woman could get him killed anywhere in the country.

"Never you mind what I said," Alfred uttered through clenched teeth. "Just hand ovah Nina's gold an' tell me how to sell it for her."

"Did you kill him, Al? Did you kill my Reggie?"

Alfred reached across the table and slapped Ptolemy's face. The old man realized with the shock of the blow that his mind was beginning to slip. His mind had begun to wander. But when Alfred hit him everything snapped back into place.

"It's a easy question, man," Ptolemy said. "I got to know what happened to my boy. I got to know. I'm a old man, Al. I cain't hurt you. I cain't say I was there."

"What about the gold?" Alfred asked after clenching and unclenching his fist.

"If you tell me what I want to know I will go to Nina with you and hand her the gold."

Ptolemy could hear his own blood pumping. Alfred's lips twisted as if he had just bit into a bitter fruit.

"He was gonna take her away, you know," Alfred said. "He was gonna leave you with no one to look aftah you. He was gonna take Nina, but Nina's mine. She belong to me. I don't care if she married to him, but when I want that pussy it gotta come to me. I ain't gonna let no fool take away what's mine."

Don't evah mess with a man," Coydog McCann was whispering to Li'l Pea deep in the memory of Ptolemy the man. "Don't nevah give him a chance."

"But what if," the child asked, "what if you ain't sure that he mean you harm?"

"It's you that mean to harm him," Coy said, pointing his thumb and forefinger like a pistol. "Life ain't fair. Life ain't right. Life ain't no good or bad. What it is is you, boy. You makin' up your mind and takin' your own path. Don't worry 'bout that cop with the truncheon. Don't worry 'bout that white man in a suit. Don't worry 'bout a cracker with his teefs missin' and a torch in his hand. Ain't none'a that any of your nevermind. All you got to do is make sure he ain't got a chance."

Did you hear me?" Alfred was saying.

"No. I missed it. What did you say?"

"I said hand ovah the coins."

"But you just said what Reggie done. You didn't say if you killed him."

"Don't play with me, old man."

"Did you kill Reggie?"

"Y-yes," Alfred said, the confession snagging on his lip. "I kilt the mothahfuckah. All right? Now, where is the gold?"

"I ain't gonna give you no gold, fool. You killed my family, my blood. I ain't gonna pay you for that. You, you must be crazy."

Alfred reached for Ptolemy as the old man slipped his hand under the cushion beside him. Alfred lifted him into the air with ease, the younger man's muscles bulging under sweaty brown and strawberry-colored skin.

Ptolemy saw the rage in the killer's eyes turn to amazement as the pistol jerked twice in his hand.

When Ptolemy fell, he was certain that Alfred would use his last bit of strength to kill him. But the killer was more interested in the blood on his hands than he was in revenge. His breath was loud and fast, intertwined with a crying moan.

"Oh no. Oh no," Alfred said.

And Ptolemy felt pity for the fact that all men come to that moment in time: Coy, and his own grandfather, and Reggie on a friend's front porch.

Alfred backed away from Ptolemy, turning and lurching toward the door. He grabbed the green-glass knob but had trouble turning it because of the slick blood on his hands. He finally got the door open and staggered into the hall.

Ptolemy climbed to his feet and followed the murderer. He dropped the gun inside his own door and stayed a few steps behind the hulking man. Blood fell in dollops on the concrete floor but Alfred kept moving. They made it outside. Alfred missed the first step on the stoop and tumbled to the sidewalk. Ptolemy was sure that the big man would die there but Alfred rose up and reeled drunkenly into the street. When he got to the dividing line, he followed that. Ptolemy was a few feet behind him and to the left.

Melinda Hogarth screamed.

Ptolemy stopped and stared at her, perched on the stoop of an old brick apartment building. There was terror in her face and this surprised Ptolemy. He saw Melinda as an evil woman unable to feel for another's pain. But he was wrong. Her angry fists were in her mouth now. Her eyes were fearful.

When Ptolemy turned he saw that Alfred had made it as far as the intersection. There he fell onto his knees, his chest on his thighs, his forehead on the asphalt. Cars were braking and swerving around the penitent.

Melinda was also on her knees, crying hysterically.

On his way back to his apartment, Ptolemy forgot where he was going.

When he opened his eyes, all that had gone before was behind that locked door again. He was in a yellow room on a high bed. There was classical music playing and a TV tuned to a twenty-four-hour news station.

A white man with a huge mustache was seated there next to him.

"Mr. Grey?"

"Who?"

"You."

"That's me. I'm the one you talkin' to."

"I'm Dr. Ruben."

"Do I know you?"

The man smiled and a fear nudged at the back of Ptolemy's mind. It was an old fear, faded and flaccid like a balloon that had lost most of its air.

"I'm a friend of your niece," the man, whose name Ptolemy had already forgotten, said.

"Uncle Grey?"

Turning his eyes to the other side of the bed took all of his concentration. He saw and registered and forgot many things on his way. The empty room and the green door and the feeling that he had accomplished an ancient task that had been behind a door and under a floor. There was blood somewhere out in the world, through the window, and then came the girl: eyes like sharp ovals and chocolate skin, she was beautiful but what Ptolemy saw was that she was one of a kind, like the woman who had come to his door and yanked him out of his sad and lonely life.

"Rob, Rob, Robyn?"

Her smile was filled with gratitude. Ptolemy's heart surged like the, like the soil under his father's spade at the beginning of the season. There was pain in his chest.

"Are you okay, Uncle?"

"What's my name?"

"Ptolemy Usher Grey."

"That's a king's name."

"Yes it is."

"And why am I here?"

"You been sick, Uncle. Dr. Ruben come to see if you was still alive, but I told him that you'd outlive the Devil himself."

Ptolemy knew that the child was making a joke but he forgot what it meant. Still, he smiled for her, pretending he understood.

"Alfred died at the hospital, and the police wanted take you to jail but Moishe Abromovitz got a paper on 'em an' they said that they'd wait till you got better."

"Did I kill?"

The girl nodded. When Ptolemy tried to remember her name he was brought back to the yard in front of his childhood home where birds flocked around him, eating stale breadcrumbs and wailing out their songs.

"You was right about Niecie," she was saying.

"I was?"

"Yeah."

The man with the mustache rose and departed the hospital room. Ptolemy gave this movement his full attention until the green door had closed.

"What did you say?" he asked the girl-child.

"I said that you was right about Niecie?"

"What, what did I say?"

There was a piano playing on the radio.

"You said that she'd try and get the law on me. I had to move out yo' apartment. I had to get a place on my own. Beckford tried to stay there wit' me but he kept gettin' mad about the money an' finally he just had to go."

"Slow down," Ptolemy said.

"It's okay now."

"It is?"

"Yeah," she said, but he could tell that there was more to the story.

He held out his hand and the girl who reminded him of birds singing took it into hers just like he thought she would. He sighed and maybe she asked a question. The music became a sky and the words the man on the television was saying turned into the ground under his feet. One was blue and the other brown, but he was not sure which was which. Everything glittered and now and again, when he looked around, things were different. Another room. A new taste. The girl always returned. And the door that was shut against his forgotten life was itself forgotten and there were feelings but they were far away.

A coyote that talked like a man whispered in his ear, and then licked his face, and then . . .